THE NAYL

A NOVEL

by

J. I. M. STEWART

LONDON
VICTOR GOLLANCZ LTD
1985

First published in Great Britain 1985
by Victor Gollancz Ltd,
14 Henrietta Street, London WC2E 8QJ

British Library Cataloguing in Publication Data
Stewart, J. I. M.
The Naylors.
I. Title
823'.912[F]   PR6037.T466
ISBN 0-575-03538-2

Photoset and printed in Great Britain by
Photobooks (Bristol) Ltd

THE NAYLORS

I

'HAVE YOU HEARD the news?'

It was clear from Charles Naylor's tone that he was sure they hadn't. His hasty tumbling into the drawing-room might have been accounted for by his being late for whatever offered on the tea-table. But his question was obviously designed to startle. It had come with a mingling of gloom and glee.

'Uncle George has lost his faith again.' Grabbing the last scone, Charles directed this announcement chiefly at his father, Edward Naylor, who was George Naylor's elder brother and the head of the family. 'But not, of course, as with Clementine. Not lost and gone for ever. The article may be better described as simply mislaid.'

'Ah!' Edward Naylor said.

'Perhaps it was to be expected,' Mrs Naylor said. 'But will it be with the same result as before?'

'Definitely.' The glee now frankly predominated in Charles, who was proving slow to reach a responsible age. 'I've just taken a telephone call from Uncle George. He'll turn up on Monday or Tuesday. And I'll bet with a minder hotfoot in pursuit of him. So two more mouths to feed, mummy.'

The Naylors didn't really have to consider mouths in quite that fashion. In a wider context Edward Naylor made it understood that he necessarily nursed financial anxieties, but nobody knew whether or not these were justified, since in business matters he kept his cards hard up against his chest. Hovering penury had therefore become a routine family joke.

'Minder' was a joke of Charles's own. With a liveliness of fancy not particularly characteristic of him, he had come to posit the existence of a kind of corps of theological therapists maintained by the episcopate to cope with such spiritual crises as his uncle's now. It was certain that a chap detailed from this Special Duties squad would arrive at Plumley in no time, settle in unobtrusively as a family friend, and get to work during walks in the garden or through the park. Just what pressure a minder applied, Charles didn't profess to know. Presumably he didn't simply take Uncle George behind a tree and twist his arm until he screamed that he was recanting his errors. It would be murmured stuff about the momentousness of the thing, and what after all *is* faith, and let us define our terms with clarity. That was probably how a minder started in. And being a skilled man at his job he pretty regularly came out on top.

'We must do our best to support your uncle,' Edward Naylor said with gravity. He had managed without much difficulty to be thus tolerant when the problem turned up on a previous occasion, perhaps because there was something reassuringly old-world about clergymen losing their faith. It had been a painful but perfectly respectable phenomenon in the Victorian period, and Edward, although vigorously operative in an up-to-the-minute industrial environment, was—at least when at home—a man of conservative mind.

'Of course we must.' Hilda Naylor gave her father instant approval. Hilda was the eldest child and only daughter. 'I like Uncle George best when he gets in a fix. There's something endearing in it. He improves with tribulation in the most orthodox and edifying way.'

'So he does,' Henry Naylor said. Henry was three years younger than his brother Charles, and in his final year at Rugby. 'Uncle George is *much* improved . . .'

'Quiet, Henry!' Charles interrupted commandingly. He knew that Henry had enunciated the first line of a ribald quatrain in which 'improved' rhymed with 'removed' and Uncle George ended up singing soprano in the choir. Charles would have been perfectly ready to bawl out Fescennine songs on an appropriate occasion—a boat-club binge, say—but anything of the sort became smut when offered in the presence of women. You could make fun of Uncle George's difficulties over his Saviour only so long as you kept it clean. And, of course, only behind his back. Charles would have considered it bad form to

6

'cheek' an older man, whether a relation or not. 'Do you know,' he asked, 'that our dreary vicar has never registered the old boy's previous wrestling with the demon Doubt? As soon as he hears of his turning up at Plumley he'll invite him to preach to us. A difficult moment for Uncle George.'

'But Mr Prowse is a comparative newcomer to the living,' Mrs Naylor said. 'It's natural that your uncle's problems should not be known to him. Perhaps your father should say a quiet word.'

'I'd leave quiet words to the minder,' Charles advised. 'They're his thing.'

If quiet words were not the Naylors' thing, neither were loud and assertive ones. Naylors weren't aggressive; they didn't 'create'; but on the other hand they seldom suggested diffidence. According to Hilda, who had an unprofitable disposition to reflect on such matters, diffidence, or an air of it, was an upper-crust thing and didn't come, whether by nature or breeding, to people who were middle all the way through. And Naylors were just that: upper-middle, since it was a long time ago that they had hammered nails, and through several generations they had been *marchands en gros* rather than grocers. They ran a line in oddities occasionally: Uncle George, for instance, and, lurkingly, perhaps Hilda herself. But tribal solidarity was one constituent in their predominant self-confidence and sense of security. They could afford that joke about impending penury. They had plenty of property, and at Plumley they still had a servant or two. In the penultimate decade of the twentieth century this latter condition was a witness to tenacity as well as mere money in the bank.

They don't sound very interesting, the Naylors of Plumley. It has to be confessed that they fail to look promising. Anybody disposed to make a book out of them (among their own number Hilda, as it happened) would have to scratch around for that sensitive awareness one of another, whether in family or social life, which so many books nowadays set out to exhibit. So what about each—as the poet says—confirming a prison, much absorbed at least in himself or herself, anxious about the individual destiny which one wakes up with in the morning and then companions until falling asleep at 10.30 p.m? Sustained

7

introspection is something that Naylors find little time for. Their days are taken up with routine activities neither disinterested and altruistic on the one hand nor of a naked rat-race order on the other, but which are pursued simply because they are what come along. They have a decent regard for one another's physical well-being and undisturbed nervous tone; they converse, if sparely, upon indifferent topics; the younger among them even contrive to give some edge of gaiety to their talk. But the lid is kept down as a matter of good form. Needlessly, perhaps. Even if raised an inch or two it is probable that nothing very arresting would be glimpsed in the bucket.

But now a few days have gone by, and George Naylor is leaving London on a crowded train.

When George became a clergyman the family had felt it as no more than slightly out of the way. With people only a little grander than themselves it had once been the regular thing for a younger son to take orders. That had been because there awaited the devout youth, almost immediately after his adopting those minimal changes in attire which the nineteenth century deemed adequate to distinguish its Anglican priesthood, something like the clerical equivalent of a pocket borough. Even a century later the Naylors themselves could probably have made a certain amount of interest in the way of pushing George ahead. He had been at a promising Oxford college: one so endowed—indeed burdened—with ecclesiastical patronage that its dons had frequently to scratch around for a suitable man to shove into a benefice. Moreover, George was a strong candidate in his own right. He had taken an excellent degree, and while hanging on for a time at the university had shown marked talent as a theologian. He had dined with the Canons of Christ Church—a great thing, if Dr Johnson is to be believed—and when he did take orders had been hurried into that sort of 'testing' curacy—a species of trial by ordeal in a slummy city parish—which archbishops and bishops (who had been in their time fags in Arnoldian public schools) regarded as the right prelude to substantial preferment. There was no need for the Naylors to put a discreet hand in a pocket.

Unfortunately George Naylor liked his slum. He liked it very much. Unable initially to resist being railroaded from it into a tiptop rural living, he had scandalously thrown this up after a couple of years to join an anomalous, even heterodox, 'mission' in the East End of London. As far as the family could make out, he had become a kind of curate again. There was no money in the thing, and a large part of its traffic appeared to be with street arabs whether pubescent or adult. When this latter fact transpired male Naylors, men of the world, shook misdoubting heads. In fact George was only mildly attracted by young men. Having decided on celibacy, he had to learn at first hand a good deal about tormenting abstinence. Girls—alluringly honey-coloured rather than pinko-grey—habitually bobbed up on him in wet dreams. For a time he decided on a special devotion to the Blessed Virgin. Later he found that keeping up his theological scholarship was a better distraction from all that importunity of the flesh. His chosen field wasn't exciting, since it had nothing to do with the cut-and-thrust of contemporary theology and even kept well on the far side of the tenth century. There was, indeed, plenty of acrimony among the comparatively small band of professional persons who studied the doctrinal polemics of the early church. But if sparks sometimes flew, any resulting conflagrations were not of a devouring order. In a sense, it had all been rather dull. But George's ecclesiastical superiors, the remote ones right at the top, eventually judged that the quality of his labours upon the often rather odd pronouncements of the Fathers of the Church had to be acknowledged, and so George was dubbed a Doctor of Divinity. The street arabs and other juvenile persons at the mission, cottoning on to this, took to cheekily calling him Doctor or just Doc. It hurt George a little. Teasing aims to annoy and annoyance can shade into anger, and George believed anger to be a signpost towards sin far more often than not. So at the mission the joke became uncomfortable and was dropped. Back at Plumley, Edward Naylor would occasionally speak to acquaintances of 'my brother Dr Naylor' since it sounded a respectable sort of connection. George would have been touched had he heard of this.

Happening to get to Paddington early, he had secured a corner seat. But then the compartment filled up. A business man (or businessm'n, as the BBC now said) installed himself opposite

George, produced from a brief-case a sheaf of typewritten invoices, estimates, delivery schedules or whatever, and was poring over them even as the train pulled out past one of London's innumerable ugly behinds. Then he got out a pocket calculator and fell to tapping its little keys with a kind of vicious satisfaction. George decided that the man was in a bad temper. Perhaps—for George sometimes engaged in idle speculation—it was because his employers, in trouble with their cash flow, were insisting that their wandering representatives and even 'executives' should travel second class, like professors and impoverished peers and Fellows of the Royal Society. George was pleased with this thought, or at least with the alliteration in 'professors and impoverished peers', and then equally he was dismayed that he should indulge such trivial ideas when in his present serious situation.

Next to the businessm'n were two women who had plainly been on a whirlwind shopping expedition. Above their heads and on their laps and at their feet were bulging plastic bags bearing the names of popular Oxford Street shops. These women were still perspiring freely from their exertions, and when they conversed together, which they did only inter-mittently, exhausted wheezings and contented sighs made a prominent part of the exchange. Disillusionment perhaps lay ahead of them when they unpacked, but meanwhile they were as triumphant as Alexander furnished with the spoils of Darius. One of them was enormously fat—she might herself have been an over-stuffed and unaccountably porous plastic bag—and, although the other was not of exceptional girth, between them they left little room for the fourth person in the row, whom George was in consequence only fleetingly aware of as a small and drab male. Beside George sat a third woman, this one being of professional appearance. Beyond her were two young workmen with the tools of their trade in the rack above them; their bare arms were folded over open shirts and bronzed chests; they sat immobile and blankly staring as if in a state of brute insentience; George had to remind himself that this appearance conceivably masked profound meditation on man's nature, his destiny and his home.

George Naylor fell to meditation on his own account. It was

naturally of a painful order. Just as once before, his loss of faith had crept up on him disguised as a grotesque loss of memory. He had awakened from a normal night's sleep wondering about monophysites. What on earth were monophysites? Weren't they something it was rather useful to have in the blood-stream? But no—that was phagocytes. What *were* monophysites? George had panicked before the blankness in his mind, obscurely knowing it to be portentous. He had pulled himself together and thought of other things, which is the correct technique when one has forgotten somebody's name. And, sure enough, accurate knowledge almost at once bobbed up in his head. A monophysite believes that there is only one nature in the person of Jesus Christ. And George, in a happier time, had contributed to a theological journal a paper on Jacobus Baradaeus of Edessa, who had revived this pernicious Eutychian heresy in the sixth century. Perhaps in a sense the heresy might be said to have long harboured in the blood-stream of the Jacobite Church. Perhaps that was why he had thought of phagocytes. It had been a bad slip-up, all the same.

Then he had taken to forgetting all sorts of entirely commonplace things, and this morbid behaviour had persisted even after he had acknowledged what he was really up against. A couple of days ago he had been unable to recall whether or not he had prepared and eaten his breakfast. He knew that such amnesias often afflict the aged. But he wasn't aged. He was forty-three. And although he had become aware that his nephew, Charles, referred to him as 'the old boy', he was in fact a *well-preserved* forty-three. So his mind oughtn't so to misbehave. Even the petty awkwardnesses were discouraging. Only a few minutes ago he had been trying to remember whether he had or had not bought himself a railway ticket for the journey he was engaged upon.

George got to his feet. Rather, he found himself on his feet—somewhat insecurely, since the inter-city train was swaying on its axis. He found that he had brought his suitcase down from above his head, and was trying to open it with a minimum of inconvenience to the professional lady next to him. He didn't manage this very well; the lid behaved awkwardly; the lady received a dig in the ribs.

'I'm so sorry!' George exclaimed. 'I do apologize. I'm just making sure that I packed my . . .'

George was about to say, 'shaving kit'. But he hesitated. About 'shaving kit' there was surely something just a shade indelicate, even a hint of what the young people called (quite inaccurately) 'machismo'. So George said 'comb' instead. Realizing that his behaviour was entirely idiotic, he shut down the suitcase in a fumbling fashion, and managed to return it to the rack. The cord of his pyjama trousers was now inelegantly depending from it.

'I can lend you a comb, love,' the fat woman said, and by manipulating several of her larger packages she managed to free her hand-bag. 'And here it is!' she said triumphantly. She was under the natural impression that her fellow-traveller wanted to attend to his hair there and then.

'Thank you very much, indeed,' George said, and tried to purge his acceptance of the comb of any tinge of distaste. It had a few hairs stuck in it; it might even have been a little scruffy. Being (or having lately been) a Christian as well as a gentleman, George passed the undesirable object firmly through his hair, and then returned it. 'Thank you very much,' he said again. He did manage not to sound falsely effusive. But unfortunately he happened to glance across at the businessm'n, and judged the fellow's gaze to be singularly lacking in charity. 'Sir,' he said, 'may I ask whether you are a believing Christian?'

Nobody in the compartment was more astounded by this question than George Naylor himself. It was, of course, a good question to put. Any of the Apostles might have asked it of the first stranger met in the street, and for George himself it held its private urgency. Only the urgency had resulted in his no longer being approximated to an Apostle by exhibiting clerical dress. That morning—like John Henry Newman, he had recalled, in a related condition of doubt—he had put on a pair of grey flannel trousers. He had even—as is not recorded of Newman—adopted a turned-down collar and a quiet but incontestably secular tie. At the best he could only be regarded as one of those vexatiously evangelical laymen who pester with tracts and similar importunities entire strangers encountered on public conveyances.

George's interlocutor reacted badly. Not, indeed, that he

12

consented to be an interlocutor at all, since he simply remained silent and stared at George stonily as at a lunatic in no particular need of help. George, again conscious of *outré* behaviour but not feeling that this time he had anything for which to apologize, was silent too. And now the professional lady came briskly and surprisingly to his rescue.

'Well, I am,' she said. 'I'm a member of the Catholic Church, and I go to mass fairly regularly.'

This information wasn't offered aggressively. It was uttered without particular emphasis, and as if merely in continuation of normal chit-chat between casually encountering persons.

'Well, now!' the fat woman said comfortably.

'A catholic, are you?' the woman of average proportions said in quite a different tone. 'The trouble with you catholics is that you're catholics first and Christians afterwards. Or that's how it seems to me and I don't mind saying so.'

George quite liked this. It was a preposterous remark, but at least the woman had 'fired up' in a context of serious religious discussion. She had convictions, and it was wonderful to have that. So George, whose experience in his mission had accustomed him to debate with unsophisticated people, suddenly felt almost at home in the railway carriage, and he began on a cordial note what might be called an enveloping movement against the stark protestantism confronting him in the fat woman's friend. But he didn't get far with it. He was conscious of his thoroughly false personal position. The man opposite had resumed operations on his calculator: a defiant money-changer in this rocking and impromptu temple of the Word. Happening to glance aside, George detected the young workman in the corner, his own head correspondingly rotated, offering his companion a slow and appreciative wink. As for the fourth and imperfectly glimpsed man, he had produced a copy of *The Times* and retired unostentatiously but firmly behind it. George found himself simply conducting an untimely dialogue of a quasi-theological character with the woman who went to mass fairly regularly. She was clearly a normal and untroubled cradle Cat. George wished her well, but felt no real occasion to be talking to her. And then the train ran into Reading.

The cradle Cat got out with a goodbye to the company in

general, but not without a special glance at George which made him feel she had been wondering about him. His sense of discomfort grew. He wished he was in the other sort of railway carriage, now more common at least in the second class, in which one's near-anonymity is assured by dozens or scores of other passengers, instead of undergoing this boxed-up effect with four or five. The train was moving again and nobody else had got on. He cursed (or at least deplored) the impulsive start of pastoral curiosity by which he had set the whole embarrassing episode in motion. But now with any luck there would be silence at least as far as to Didcot or even Oxford. The man behind *The Times* seemed reliable; he had contrived to turn a page of the paper without lowering it from in front of his nose: technically a difficult feat which spoke of practice. About the two young workmen there was also something reassuring. A strain of feeling in George responded to them as wholesome and agreeable physical presences, and by this time the odd little flurry of talk would have passed out of their heads, even supposing it ever to have lodged there. The female shoppers had gone back to the proper area of their concern, the fat one having opened one of her shopping bags and produced a nondescript garment over a detected flaw in which they were tut-tutting in a kind of gratified indignation. The man opposite George was still occupied with his pocket calculator. It appeared to be occasioning him increasing displeasure. He was even emitting the sounds, or at least rendering the impression, of one grinding his teeth in fury. Then suddenly this emotional instability, although presumably generated by commercial considerations, found vent in a different and distinctly startling direction.

'Bloody Nosy Parker!' the businessm'n said to George. 'What the hell did you mean by it?'

This unmannerly harking back to an exchange (if it could be called that) which had taken place 30 miles away caught George Naylor unawares. The ferocity of its expression seemed almost an invitation to fisticuffs. George, who belonged to a period in which the sport of boxing still obtained in schools for the sons of upper-class people, might have been willing to oblige but for the conjoined influences of the presence of ladies and the still automatically operative tenets of his late religion. As it was, he

14

didn't even find anything to say, and it was one of the young artisans who spoke.

'Cool it, mate,' he said easily to the businessm'n. 'The gent only asked a civil question, didn't he? A bit barmy, you may have thought it, but there'll be things on which you're a bit barmy yourself, likely enough. It's just that we're not all cracked down the same side of our heads. A civil answer would have been in order, chum, believe you me.'

George felt himself agreeing with much of this, and he was pleased—as at his mission he had always been—that an individual who had presumably been denied much education other than of the banausic sort should prove capable of speaking out in a forthright and cogent manner. But George was bothered as well. That impulsive and unseasonable question of his (prompted he couldn't tell by what) was still heading him towards trouble. Its next instalment came from the fat woman.

'It was religious,' she said. Her tone could again have been described as comfortable, but now it held a hint of censure as well. 'It was religious, and I'm as religious as anybody, although Mrs Archer wouldn't maybe agree.' She had given a brief indicative nod towards her companion. 'But I wouldn't say it's a thing to be talked about in a common way.'

'It's not everybody that's called on to testify, Mrs Bowman.' Mrs Archer said this in a tight-lipped fashion which she had not exhibited when discussing Debenhams and John Lewis with her companion.

'That sort of thing should be left to the clergymen, to my mind,' Mrs Bowman retorted. 'I go to church as often as anybody else. Nowadays, that is. But as for talking about sin and repentance and the like, they should be let alone with it. They've had the training.'

'What about your prayers, ma? Do you say them as often as anybody else too—always remembering that nowadays, of course? Down on your knees by your little bed? *Those* knees? You must be joking.'

This speech came from the second of the young workmen. It was the more disobliging in that a certain cogency attended upon its mention of Mrs Bowman's anatomy. Her knees were on view only in the sense that they would have been visible had they assuredly existed. But so massive and columnar were her nether limbs that there was no evidence that they did. She reminded George of some mediaeval bestiary in which the elephant is described as 'stondand' because unprovided with joints admitting of any other posture. Here was a frivolous flight of fancy on George's part. It was Mrs Archer who recalled him to the sobriety required in face of this bizarre conversation.

'At the name of Jesus,' Mrs Archer said, 'every knee shall bow.'

'Not nowadays, ducky. You have to face it, not nowadays. That right, Len?'

Len was, of course, the young electrician or plumber or whatever who had advised the businessm'n to cool it. He now, and with entire good humour, offered his mate similar counsel.

'Belt up, Ron,' he said. 'What's kaput with you may be kicking still with the lady. You've no call to make a monkey of her. And Jesus Christ may be as good a stand-by as the pub when it looks like you're going to be short with the rent.'

'Just that,' Ron said. 'The opium of the people, every time.'

George pricked up his ears at this. In Ron's tone he had detected a hint of sardonic self-mockery which he was accustomed to take as evidence of a promisingly open mind. So with at least momentarily recovered confidence he chipped in.

'Would you agree,' he asked Ron, 'that it's natural to believe in *something*?'

'The international solidarity of the working class,' Len interjected. 'That's what our Ron believes in. Armed wage-slaves. And probably Noah in his ark as well. No harm in it in its place.'

The two young men were not, as George had casually assumed, much of a muchness. Even physically it wasn't so. Len was fair and of a robust but relaxed musculature; Ron was dark, adrenaline-commanded, ready to spring but not knowing quite where to. George (who had for a space quite forgotten his lapsed condition) had another go—and with a swiftly assumed familiarity he had with some difficulty taught himself to get away with.

'Come on, Ron,' he said. 'Nobody can get around without believing in one thing or another, if it's only tomorrow's breakfast. But what about when you take a larger look at the world? Do you really put your money on proletarian revolution imported from Russia?'

'I don't say all that hasn't taken a bit of a clobbering.' Ron was now giving George a keen but seemingly amiable once-over. If the young men did have something in common it appeared to be good humour. 'But yes, in a general way. I wouldn't mind a bash at manning a barricade or two.'

This was like old times, and the talk appeared to be drifting blessedly away from theological matters and into the field of politics. Ron was presumably a Trot, and George was quite prepared to discuss with him the pros and cons of world-wide socialist revolution. But this was not to be. It was blocked by Mrs Archer.

'What do you mean?' Mrs Archer demanded of Len. 'About in its place?'

This was so baffling that even the man with the pocket calculator stared at Mrs Archer in perplexity. But its unaccountability was rapidly resolved by Ron.

'Noah's ark,' Ron said. 'The old trout means Noah's ark.' He appeared to apply this term to Mrs Archer without any derogatory intention.

'Of course I do.' Mrs Archer pointed accusingly at Len. 'Didn't that young man speak some profane nonsense about its place? Ararat was its place. It's in the Bible.'

This weird inconsequence brought silence for several seconds. George found himself afflicted with one of his vexatious amnesiac episodes. *Was* Mount Ararat specifically mentioned in Genesis as the spot on which Noah's vessel finally grounded? It was odd not to remember the answer to that one. George ought not, of course, to have been particularly perturbed. Unlike Mrs Archer, he knew that there are all sorts of errors and inconsistencies in the curious little Hebrew library collectively named the Old Testament. And as the yarn about Noah and the Deluge was to be received (if at all) only in a mysterious sense, it didn't matter twopence whether the old gentleman found himself on Ararat or Mount Everest. Nevertheless George was worried—or rather he was even more worried than before. What if this simple woman herself fell into doubt about the

17

biblical status of Ararat, and appealed to him? Would it not be improper in him not to be able to afford her instruction at once? Confronting this question, George again forgot that he had opted out of the entire business, and that if one has ceased to believe that in Zero AD God uniquely entered History one may be perfectly light-hearted in washing one's hands of the patriarchs and all their kidney. Of course George knew that this didn't really end the matter. Not nowadays, it didn't. You could cease to believe almost anything so long as you continued to believe in something else. There had always been people who told you that religion could get along without Christianity, but recently it had apparently become fashionable to maintain that Christianity could get along without religion. It was a perplexing field. George hadn't properly been keeping up with it.

'What about the fish?'

'They stopped in the sea, of course. Why shouldn't they?'

'The Bible tells you the size of the thing—in cubits or whatever they were? Or was that about the Temple, later on?'

'You needn't talk to me about cubits, young man. Who knows what a cubit was?'

'But we're talking about the ark, ma. All the beasts and birds could be got into it?'

'Of course they could. Two by two. We're told so.'

'What about their feed, ma? Quite a lot would be needed. Think of the two elephants. They'd need a good deal more than the two humming birds. Even think of Mrs Noah having to make a shopping-list of everything required.'

George realized that he was listening to a species of disputation he'd heard often enough before. Such absurd questions could appear momentous in the minds of the folk. (They had also, of course, seemed momentous to Bishop Colenso in his day.) But at least Ron now advanced something George hadn't ever heard at the mission.

'Germs, ma,' Ron said. 'Do you know how many kinds of germs there are in the world? "Kills all known germs", the bottle says. Probably true enough. But for every known germ on the books, believe you me, there are thousands waiting to get in. Micro-organisms and amoebas and filterable virus and all. Heard of species, ma?'

18

'I take no account of species, young impudence, you. Species aren't in holy writ.'

'Of course they are. Adam named the animals, didn't he? Probably even let Eve chip in now and then. Well, there are more whole species in the world, mark you, than there are individual human beings. Just think of that.'

This was news to George. He suspected it of being a wild travesty of some known scientific fact. But he didn't interrupt. There was a horrid fascination in this demotic parody of grave debate.

'And how could old Uncle Noah check them in?' Ron demanded, pressing home his point. 'How could he *see* them, see? He didn't have a microscope, you know. That was invented no time ago, by Galileo or some chum of his.'

Microscope or telescope, George thought, Ron did have a point. If, that is, you believed with Mrs Archer that the sole authorship of the Bible lay with the Holy Ghost.

'That about germs,' Mrs Bowman said. 'Just fancy, now!'

This was Mrs Bowman's only contribution to the argument. She seemed unaware that it was generating a certain heat. But this was only in her friend. Ron was merely amusing himself with Mrs Archer, although George suspected that he could rise to genuine passion on topics of a political or social sort. Len had resumed his appearance of mindless repose, and was looking rather handsome as a result; he had probably heard Ron on this ploy before, and found it a bit boring. The businessm'n wasn't bored. In fact he was increasingly outraged, and even showed signs of gathering his possessions together preparatory to that definitive act of displeasure that consists in rising up and seeking another compartment. If George was calculating correctly, the man behind *The Times* had now been reading its Court page for ten minutes, and as this was something out of nature it had to be concluded that he too was an interested, if detached, listener. But now for some moments George's own attention wavered—if only because he was anxiously asking himself whether he had a duty to intervene. Only a week before, it would certainly have been so. Ought he, from his new position, to offer some reflections of an elevating, although agnostic, character? He was in sore perplexity of mind and spirit.

19

It was at this point that Ron went too far.

'So if that's your Bible,' Ron said, 'forget it.'

George had failed to pick up just what occasioned the giving of this advice, but he had sufficient acquaintance with current demotic speech to know that it belonged to the tolerant-dismissive rather than the contemptuous order. Unfortunately Mrs Archer didn't receive it that way. Only Satan, or at least one satanically possessed, could bid you forget your Bible. Mrs Archer knew instantly that it was her duty to 'testify'. Even in his present lapsed state, George was bound to regard that as an honourable activity, and he was therefore the more appalled by the way in which this lurkingly loony woman (entrenched behind the bastions of her shopping-bags) went about it. Mrs Archer raved.

There were particularly desperate nonconformist sects, George knew, meeting in conventicles furnished not with pulpits but with platforms or podia, in which vehement outpourings of Bible-based jargon were held to be uplifting and indeed regenerative. Mrs Archer—here in this small railway compartment, where one was squashed up with one's fellow-travellers hip to hip—was proving herself a mistress of this sort of thing. George found himself wondering whether she was of Scottish extraction and descended from those fanatic Covenanting windbags made well-bred fun of by Walter Scott. But they at least had whole extents of moorland and bog to absorb their outpourings, whereas here there was only this reverberating and insistently, if faintly, jolting box. So Mrs Archer's behaviour was not merely embarrassing, but unseemly as well. And George had the mortification of knowing that he had himself precipitated the whole thing.

'And large-limbed Og He did subdue!' Mrs Archer shouted. 'Is He going to have much difficulty with *you*?'

This recourse to the 136th psalm as mangled by John Milton was scarcely apposite as directed against Ron. It was Mrs Bowman, the stondand elephant, who might have been better likened to Og. But who *was* Og? George seemed to remember that Milton rhymed 'subdue' with 'crew'. Og had a crew. He had an over-something crew. Could it be an over-*hearty* crew? That seemed hardly possible. George realized that this trivial lapse-of-memory business was coming to worry him in a pathological way. Instead of badgering himself about Og he ought, in common charity, to be doing something to calm down this phrenetic woman. What was required was firm but courteous speech.

'Madam,' George said, 'pray compose yourself.'

'Please' might have been better than 'pray'. Prayer being one of Mrs Archer's things, she went off on it at once. But Ron had decided that enough was enough.

'Can't you see,' he demanded, 'that the reverend gent wants you to shut your gob?'

This was *not* courteous. In fact it was extremely rude. But the horror George now felt was occasioned by something else. Laterally across the compartment, Ron had thrust out a confident and indicative finger at him. Preternaturally, this disputatious young plebeian (whom it had been so pleasant to distinguish as intelligent beyond his station) had pierced through (if it may be so put) the grey flannel trousers, had stripped away the lay collar and tie, and acclaimed George Naylor in his true clerical character. And now Mrs Bowman, who had maintained a placid silence during the theological debate, addressed George in a tone of surprised respect.

'Fancy, now!' Mrs Bowman said. 'And are you really a clergyman, sir?'

The nub of this question—although Mrs Bowman wasn't aware of the fact—decidedly lay in that 'really'. George just didn't know, so for a moment he couldn't think what to say. In law he was undoubtedly a clergyman still. But morally regarded, even philosophically regarded, he had surely forfeited his claim to any such status. So what *could* he say?

'No,' George said. 'I am not.'

There was a rather prolonged silence, conceivably produced by a general perception that the gent, whether reverend or common-or-garden, was mysteriously in distress. George himself almost expected to hear a cock crow. What actually happened was that the train produced its newfangled whistle, de-accelerated with virtuoso precision, and within seconds was at a halt at Didcot junction. Then, quite suddenly, nobody was interested in George Naylor and his condition any more. Len and Ron with their tool-kits, the businessm'n with his documents and pocket calculator, Mrs Archer and Mrs Bowman with their innumerable packages draped around them: they all bundled into the corridor and vanished like a dream. It was an unspeakable relief, and it was not within George's power to refrain from an audible pious ejaculation.

'Thank God!' George said, and sank down in relaxation in his corner. The train was moving again; its next stop would be Oxford; only the harmless and silent man with *The Times* remained in the compartment.

But the harmless man now lowered his paper and spoke.

'It is interesting to speculate,' he said, 'what our young friend Ron would be like had he gone up to, say, Balliol.'

'Is it? I mean, yes, certainly.' George stared at his remaining fellow-traveller with an obscure premonition of yet further discomfort about to accrue on this disastrous journey.

'But I think it is Dr Naylor, is it not? Allow me to introduce myself. I am Adrian Hooker.'

'How do you do?' This conventional enquiry George managed to utter in a commonplace way. But he was conscious of now gazing at Father Hooker (for he knew him instantly to be that) much as if here were the Devil himself suddenly sprung up before him. Father Hooker was of course nothing of the sort. He was the high-powered pro sent to cope with the apostasy of his totally unimportant self.

'Your brother was kind enough to ring me up immediately he received the Bishop's letter.' Father Hooker said this pleasantly enough, but accompanied the words with a faintly disconcerting small bow. 'Although it must have been a surprise to him.'

'Well, no.' George spoke out. He was conscious he mustn't mumble. 'It has happened before.'

'Ah, yes. I am sure Plumley will be a delightful setting for our talks. There is something very bracing in the sanctity of the family and the home.'

'Perhaps that's so.' George found himself having to repel the thought that this had been a disagreeably canting kind of remark. 'I am glad to be going back to Plumley. But I'm not sure that it's in order to be braced.'

'It was in my mind'—Father Hooker continued, ignoring this—'to suggest a meeting in Oxford, where so many would be willing to receive us. And there came into my head—inconsequently enough, I suppose—the last meeting there of poor Newman and Mark Pattison. You will recall it.'

'No,' George said. Newman having been recently in his head—although in what context he couldn't remember—this had startled him.

'It was many years after Newman had left us, and he had never been in Oxford again. But now he heard that his old friend Pattison, who had been for a number of years Rector of Lincoln, was on his death-bed in the college, and much troubled in mind. Newman visited him. He travelled from Birmingham to Oxford virtually incognito. Attended, it is said, by only two chaplains.' Father Hooker did something with his eyebrows that perhaps signalled an ironical view of this provision. 'It was almost what we now call an ecumenical gesture. He was a cardinal, after all, by that time. They had tagged him, I seem to recollect, Cardinal of St George in Velabro.'

'He was certainly that,' George said a shade stiffly.

'Even two chaplains were a little awkward for the Pattison household as it then was. Miss Pattison had to scratch round for a couple of fowls for them. Or such is the story.'

'Two men wouldn't eat two fowls.'

'Dr Newman himself was extremely ascetic—although indeed it is said that at an earlier time he had introduced the Oriel Common Room to the pleasures of claret. His chaplains may well have been kept on short commons at the Oratory. That is as it may be. The sad part of the story is that there proved to be no possible meeting of those two minds: the Rector's and the Cardinal's.'

'Yes,' George said. He had realized that he was listening to an anecdote in fact familiar to him, and variously recounted in various places. Only his own extreme disarray had caused him to forget this.

'Newman supposed that it must be some obscure point of doctrine—some patristic quiddity, my dear Naylor, of the sort you know far more about than I do—by which Pattison was perturbed as his last hours approached. That it could be anything worse than that was beyond Newman's comprehension, and he braced himself, competent theologian as he was, to clear the matter up for his old friend in a jiffy.' Father Hooker paused on this, as if to let his command of the more colloquial uses of language sink in. 'But the truth was that Pattison's loss of faith had become absolute. So sunk was he in hardened agnosticism that he had even continued to celebrate Holy Communion in the college chapel long after concluding it to be mumbo-jumbo. To cease doing so, he felt, would create needless fuss. And I suppose he was anxious to guard his position as a scholar. He had spent a good deal of time in Germany and brought back notions of severe *Gelehrsamkeit*.'

'It was a very desirable import at that time, so far as the English universities were concerned.' George said this with a sharpness he at once regretted. 'And so,' he added in a more responsive tone, 'Newman returned to Birmingham sadly conscious of the failure of a mission.'

'Just so. He had been suddenly confronted with dereliction and apostasy, and it had not been granted to him to counter it.'

'Dereliction?' George repeated misdoubtingly—and realized that he was in danger of being lured (like Mrs Archer) into debate. But his query was met only with an impressive (if slightly uncivil) silence. This gave him leisure to tell himself that he had *not* taken a hasty dislike to Father Hooker.

But now Father Hooker, having sufficiently if obliquely expressed his sense of the gravity of his fellow-priest's lapsed condition, turned to general conversation. George supposed that he judged this to be the urbane thing. He also *led* the conversation, as a North Oxford lady might do with an awkward undergraduate at a tea-party. As he was younger than George, this didn't seem quite right. But George didn't resent it. The situation was as difficult for Father Hooker as for himself, and as the chap was a specialist in running down and rounding up lost sheep, he was entitled to his own techniques. Yet George, as he managed adequate chat on the weather and politics and cricket-matches and 'light' reading and other insignificant topics, did find himself wondering what had prompted the Bishop to choose this personally unappealing professional apologist in the present instance, and to set him on the hunt with such indecent expedition. The discreet spiritual counsellor provided on a previous occasion, old Dr Hunter, had been a quietly humorous Scot, and also one of the Hunters of Drumdrummie. There certainly wasn't a spark of humour in Hooker. And as for Drumdrummie—although this was, of course, totally beside the point—Hooker wouldn't recognize the place if he saw it.

George was properly perturbed by the snobbish slant in his thought here. Nevertheless it was perhaps still active in the back of his mind when he now went on to reflect that the Bishop might have acted with an eye to wholesome and deterrent penance. George had done it once too often, so let Hooker be loosed on him. Perhaps the Bishop had first thought of old Father Fisher in Cambridge, whose exquisitely adroit handling of such conditions as George's within the Anglican communion scarcely fell short of that achieved by his uncle, Father Fisher of Oxford, who had turned to Rome long after the John Henry Newman of this Hooker's so evidently standard anecdote, but with scarcely less éclat. George felt that, as a kind of recidivist or at least as an obstinate case, he had in a sense *earned* the top treatment of Father Fisher of Cambridge. But now there had come this horrid thought. It was almost a picture, indeed. There was the Bishop at his desk in his archaically denominated palace; in front of him was a memorandum; he wrote in its margin the single word 'Hooker', leaned back in his chair, and murmured to himself, '*That* will teach him.'

All this was unfair to Father Hooker, about whom George still knew little, and whose only fault so far revealed was a certain heavy-handedness incompatible with the customary amenities of polite intercourse. But now George's thoughts took a more relevant and sensible turn. Why should the Bishop of Tower Hamlets be much bothering about George Naylor (a totally obscure labourer in his thronged diocese) at all? There were two possible explanations. Either the Bishop felt that the loss of faith suffered by even a single Christian soul was a matter of infinite moment, to be striven against with the united might of Christians everywhere, etc., or he had acted merely in aid of the swift obviating or damping down of a very minor ecclesiastical scandal. Could these two motives be rationally linked or combined, or did each belong to a scheme of things incompatible with the other? George realized that here was a difficult question. He was going to plunge into a bog of difficult questions with Father Hooker.

And this was to begin almost at once. In fact it had begun already. George had a considerable regard for the Bishop of Tower Hamlets. He was a man admirably equipped for his sacred office: courteous, tactful but tenacious, a clear-headed and expeditious administrator. But George wished he had been a little less expeditious on the present occasion. George always took pleasure in a return to Plumley, whatever might be the circumstances of his visit. There was a good deal of creature comfort, for one thing: plenty of hot water and warm dry towels, excellent food of an uncomplicated sort, the space and privacy of the park with its not disagreeable suggestion of consequence in the county. As a break from life at the mission, all this had its charm. But what George chiefly liked was his family. His elder brother, Edward, although possessed of less sense of religion or even of the numinous than a Hottentot or probably a Neanderthal man, always treated him with a kind of puzzled respect, even deference, which was pleasing because entirely genuine; his sister-in-law was a reliable woman who seldom gushed or fussed; his nephews, although probably regarding his persuasions (or late persuasions) as chimerical, were friendly enough; his niece, Hilda, was attentive to his conversation and had indeed an air of considering him worth a good deal of thought. George liked everything about the lot of them, down to those no-nonsense Christian names, a taste for which had resulted in his own 'George' when he might have been Mervyn or Evelyn or Tarquin or something of the sort.

And now his present arrival was going to be wrecked by Hooker. It did have to be put as strongly as that. One Hooker or another was, of course, inevitable. He was part of a debriefing process (as the laity might call it) not properly to be declined or escaped. Last time, and under the guidance of old Dr Hunter, George had, as it were, debriefed his debriefing and rejoined the fold. George believed that nothing of the sort would happen this time. And he recalled that Dr Hunter had turned up at Plumley at a seemly interval after his own arrival. There had been correspondence, a written invitation from George's sister-in-law to his clerical colleague and friend: that sort of thing. But this time it all seemed to be hustle and huddle and hugger-mugger. (George repeated these uneuphonious words to himself almost resentfully.) He was going to return home under a species of wardenship—or wardership, if there were such a word—exercised by Father Hooker. Not even, so to speak, on parole! George remembered that his nephew Charles had some comical word for anybody exercising Father Hooker's office, although he couldn't for the moment recall what it was.

With only a short warning from reflections of this sort, it came to George that he very much didn't want to arrive at Plumley in the custody of Father Hooker. It would be indecorous—as if he had taken to something like compulsively pinching young women's bottoms in the street and had to be kept an eye on round the clock if there weren't to be little paragraphs in the papers with the word 'clergyman' in a headline. It would be just like that. Successive trains, perhaps yes. But the same train, decidedly no.

No sooner had this resolution been formed than their present joint train slowed down again. On a number of small placards in succession appeared the word, 'Oxford'. Wasting no time, yet without flurry, George Naylor stood up and reached down his suitcase. He took a moment to relish Father Hooker's surprise and displeasure, and then explained himself without recourse even to a shade of equivocation.

'I think I'll get off here,' he said. 'Please tell Mary'—Mary was the name of Edward's wife—'that I'll be on the early-evening train and get a cab out to Plumley. You'll find one of my nephews, I think, waiting for you at the station with the car.'

And thus George found himself in his old university town. Like Cardinal Newman on that abortive visit to Mark Pattison, he hadn't been there for quite some time.

It was the middle of the Long Vacation, and Oxford would therefore be 'empty' in the sense that London used to be described as 'empty' when people had gone off to watch yachts at Cowes or to shoot small birds in Scotland. But as much here as in London the 'empty' concept was purely notional, industry and tourism between them having swamped anything of academic appearance or disappearance on the streets. Only the large number of moderately ancient and for the most part architecturally unimaginative buildings distinguished the place from any other English city of equivalent size.

George parked his suitcase in one of a nest of metal lock-up boxes, not without a thought (for such is the era of our narrative) that a time-bomb might be ticking next door, or even ingeniously programmed to explode as he operated on his own box. He then headed for the dreaming spires. The first spire was presumably dreaming of Lord Nuffield, who late in the day had insisted upon its incongruous superimposition upon the tower of the college he had donated to the university and later come grimly to refer to as the Kremlin. Presumably, George thought, Nuffield's first batch of dons had turned out to show a faint tinge of pink.

Knowing that he ought not thus to have thought frivolously of a major benefactor who had once been a bicycle boy, George took off his hat to Nuffield College as he walked past its little gateway on New Road. He was feeling almost light-hearted. Here in Oxford, after all, were men of his own sort. Even now, at the waning of the twentieth century, the place was still thronged with theologians, some of whom had thought up and fortified behind impregnable bastions of polemical subtlety positions more coherently agnostic than George himself had yet got round to. It would be fun, he told himself irresponsibly, if a super Father Hooker, a Hooker of larger than King Kong dimensions, could be let loose on them. He began to chant aloud as he walked that tremendous passage in *Paradise Lost* descriptive of the backside of the world over which in windy vanity are blown embryos and idiots, eremites and friars, black, white and grey, and all their company. But this, of course, was near-delirium, and George was surprised at himself. Besides which, people were turning and staring at him as they went past. So George quietened down, and arrived at Carfax in a more sober manner. But he was still in high spirits, and he wondered whether this was entirely the result of his at least temporary release from Father Hooker. It seemed a bit mean to rejoice at being quit of the man when he was only endeavouring to do his job. And the railway

28

journey, although certainly trying in one aspect, had been full of interest. He had liked Len and Ron, and would have enjoyed an undisturbed chat with them.

He decided to start this unpremeditated Oxford jaunt with a visit to Blackwell's bookshop, so he turned north at Carfax and fought his way up Cornmarket Street. It was like that because the Corn was jam-packed with tourists who bumped into you as they anxiously consulted guidebooks, and also with skimpily-clad and husky young people of both sexes, bearing on their backs huge burdens suggestive of wayfaring life in the Middle Ages. Many of these latter were no doubt students, and could be regarded as wandering scholars of a sort. But they were wandering scholars who had come not to study but merely to stare.

Opposite Balliol an attractive young woman—her attractiveness only enhanced by unisex garments which somehow emphasized the charms of a far from unisex figure—offered George a leaflet which he accepted with a murmur of thanks. Out of her sight, he was about to crumple it up, when it occurred to him that it might be not a notice of some theatrical venture or the like but a summons to holy living to which in his present condition he ought to accord a fair hearing. So he glanced at it, and the words 'Forget it', printed in bold type, caught his eye. That was what Ron had said to Mrs Archer, so George took another look. He read:

CIVIL DEFENCE?—FORGET IT
There's no defence against nuclear weapons,
and no escape. Anybody left alive in the total
mess will die soon—or wish they had.

George thrust this—and along with it apparently other disturbing thoughts as well—into a pocket. He then found himself quickening his pace towards Blackwell's.

The entrance to this booky house (as a deceased Poet Laureate had styled it) was reassuringly unchanged, and George reflected that it was perhaps the most effectively symbolic structure in Oxford. Strait is the gate that leads to knowledge as well as to salvation, and the celebrated Blackwell doorway is surely by some inches narrower than any other in Oxford. Edging through it—which involved jostling with an American lady clutching a book called *English Farmhouse Fare*—George did, however, find that there had been alterations here and there. The odd little domestic fireplace near the entrance, which perhaps symbolized in its turn the undoubted fact that the best companion by one's hearth is a book, was still in evidence. But had it not, he thought, slewed itself round a little, as if disposed to cast the warmth of learning in a fresh direction? And where were the two commanding ladies who had sat hard by and taken your money as you went out? They had departed, and in their stead rather young women in the body of the shop now combined the sale of books with a mysterious gazing upon flickering electronic screens. Further on, you went down a small staircase—and there suddenly beneath you was a vast subterraneous chamber exhibiting terrace below terrace of books in divine but intimidating abundance. Not only is the gate to knowledge strait. Knowledge itself is as a deep well.

Boldly, George sought out Theology. It didn't, presumably, bear as high a proportion to the rest of Blackwell's stock as it would have done in any similar repository a hundred years ago. But there was still a lot of it—the presented spectacle, indeed, suggesting itself as most readily computable not in thousands of volumes but in hundreds of yards. And there was nothing second-hand about the exhibition. These were all *new* books— although many of them looked as if they had been that for a good many years. Hadn't he as an undergraduate mugged up Elliott-Binns on *The Development of English Theology in the Later Nineteenth Century*? And what about Schaefer's *Die katholische Wiedergeburt der englischen Kirche*: surely that had been on his own shelves for quite a long time now? There was rank upon rank of the heavy stuff, stiffly upstanding behind their gilded spines: armies of unalterable law. But fronting these, on a line of tables so long as positively to lend the impression of softening into distance, were exhibited, flat and face-upward after the fashion of a bookshop's most readily vendible wares, innumerable sprightly-seeming paperbacks of popular devotion. Fifty years ago—George reflected—these would have been known as 'religious tracts', and they would have been got up to look as forbidding as was inexpensively possible. Every need was catered for. There was a book called *What to Tell your Children about Jesus*. There was another called *Prayers for Busy People*.

George paused here before the evangelizing labours of the late C.S. Lewis, who in point of proliferation appeared to be neck and neck with a former Bishop of Woolwich. Overcoming the professional's unworthy predisposition to hold the work of amateurs in poor esteem, George examined some of Lewis's books, and decided to buy one called *The Pilgrim's Regress*. It appeared to be distinctly acerbic in tone, and might serve to attune him to Father Hooker. George then went upstairs again, found the current fiction, and chose the two longest novels on offer. He might be at Plumley, he was reflecting, for quite some time. He then wandered round the shop at random, wondering whether to pick up another book or two as he went. That was what you did. You accumulated as many books as you felt you needed, and then took them up to the electronic ladies.

Thus meandering through the booky house, George was happy for the first time in weeks.

'Ah, Naylor! A good afternoon to you.'

George turned round and saw that he was being addressed by an old man who, like himself, had a pile of books under his arm. A *very* old man. Realizing this, George offered his own 'good afternoon' with a deference that turned out to be entirely proper. For it was the Gumpher. It was the Gumpher, without a doubt.

'Gumphy,' the Gumpher said informatively, and with a hint of rebuke softened by a chuckle so high-pitched as to attract the attention of several of Blackwell's browsing customers. Even mute, the Gumpher appeared unlikely to pass without remark. He moved with the aid of two sticks of awkward length, as if somebody was neglecting to chop the requisite centimetres from them every now and then to accommodate a general shrinkage of his person. Second childhood had befallen at least the Gumpher's earthly tenement. His eyelids, distressingly everted, suggested a baby that ought to have been put to bed long ago. And he must literally have required bedtime attention, since it was impossible to imagine him successfully extricating his limbs from the stiff and snuff-bespattered carapace in which he tottered around. But he did so totter, and even managed to bear that burden of books along with him. 'It's some time since we met, my dear Naylor,' this abraded patriarch said. 'I don't forget a pupil. I don't forget a pupil, I say. I don't forget a pupil.'

Warden Gumphy (for George knew him to have become that) was (like George himself?) a clergyman. He had never been George's tutor of the ordinary workaday sort, having already become too senior a fellow of the college for such labour. But he had been George's *moral* tutor. He had seen George, that is, for a few minutes at the beginning of each term and inquired about his vacation reading. Not what he had been reading specifically for Schools, but his *general* reading. 'In a general sense. In a general sense, I say,' the Gumpher would insist, as he removed his spectacles, polished them vigorously, and returned them to his nose. It was less the Gumpher's self-evident nonagenarian standing than his retention of that particular idiom or trope that rolled back the years for George now. George found himself trying to secrete his two bulky novels beneath the inadequate cover of C.S. Lewis's belligerent fable. Then it struck him that the Gumpher would probably hold a poorer opinion of Lewis than even of Salman Rushdie or David Storey, so he abandoned this attempted concealment and sought for the proper thing to say.

'It's delightful, Mr Warden, to see you looking so well.' George felt that this, if conveyed without too much under-current of surprise, couldn't be far wrong.

'The daily constitutional, Naylor. The daily constitutional, I say. And how is the business, Naylor? Is it looking up? Is it looking up, I say?'

This was perplexing. The Warden was presumably referring to the business of pastoral care. Was George attracting good congregations when he preached at matins on Sundays? Was he attracting anybody at all to weekday affairs? These were natural and proper questions for a concerned priest to ask. But here again the Gumpher's idiom had been, like his person, a shade odd.

'I've had a small flutter on that stable myself,' the Warden said. 'Yes, a flutter, I say. Since people are to have more and more free time for it all, more and more free time.'

The Gumpher believed himself to be talking to George's father! As George realized this, his head swam a little. His father had been in on the first major expansion of those leisure industries which were now understood to be the main concern of George's brother, Edward. And George could recall that his moral tutor's having formerly been his father's tutor for some Honour School had been a point of minor college curiosity. Such linkings and continuities were not uncommon. And the Gumpher (who would surely be a centenarian quite soon) might very readily slip a generation when recalling his dealings with Naylors. They had neither of them, George or his father, been particularly memorable undergraduates. But this didn't make the present situation, here in Blackwell's shop, other than a bit dodgy. To say baldly, 'I'm not John Naylor; I'm his younger son George', might be disconcerting and almost, indeed, discourteous.

'And I warned you, I say,' the Gumpher was saying.

'I beg your pardon, Mr Warden?' It was evident that George in his bewilderment had let his attention wander.

'But I was wrong,' the Gumpher said, with that ready confession of error that marks (or ought to mark) the true scholar. 'At a Gaudy, it was. You remember it, Naylor? The first Gaudy we held after the Armistice, it must have been. Not ill fare, considering the times. And still plenty of sound wine.'

'The Armistice?' George repeated stupidly. He now felt that inside his head something was going awkwardly numb. 'In 1918?'

'Young and confident, Naylor. I was young and confident. You must remember that. I had only just got my fellowship. And I did approve of your buying land with that bit of family money. Nothing like it. Nothing like it, I say. But proposing to cover it with golf-courses was another matter. I was justified in urging caution upon you there. However, it all turned out well. Well, I say, well. Though to my mind still, Naylor, not quite a game for gentlemen. Cads and caddies, we used to say. Cads and caddies.'

A caddie had once been a cadet, George recalled. The semantic change showed what happens to younger sons. But this thought was only fleetingly in his mind. For now the full truth had come to him. He was being mistaken by this awful old man not for his father but for his *grandfather*. His grandfather had been at the college too—and had been the first founder of those family fortunes depending on golf-courses and bowling-greens and 'public' tennis courts. George's head was still swimming, but he managed a little chronology. The thing was feasible. The Gumpher had seen not two generations of Naylors through the college but three. *Three*. Somebody would probably rout out the fact and refer to it as edifying when the place held Warden Gumphy's memorial service.

George, as he got away from this weird colloquy, felt that he ought (inwardly of course) to be laughing. In fact he was rather frightened. The Gumpher had by no means been a clown all his days. In early old age he had been notable in the streets of Oxford as a person of grave consequence. In perambulating infancy he had been patted on the head by Matthew Arnold, probably with a little extra unction because the Gumphys were understood to have owned the greater part of Cumberland. Having become Head of a college, he had no doubt at some time served his term as Vice-Chancellor of the university. He would have been perfectly up to hob-nobbing with visiting Royalty and Ministers of the Crown. And now this: an old creature with generation upon generation squashed up and muddled in his disintegrating grey matter. 'Distressing' was the decorous word for the unexpected encounter.

This was certainly an unbalanced view of the episode. Warden Gumphy wasn't really comprehensively gaga. His memories, if they had reassorted themselves oddly, could hardly be called straitened. Leaving Blackwell's, he would return home to the villa of his retirement somewhere in North Oxford; read, and it might be pungently annotate, the books he had bought; and probably consume a satisfactory dinner. No, one needn't be upset about the Gumpher.

But of course George Naylor was revisiting Oxford in a vulnerable frame of mind, and this was still his condition when he took his purchases up to the pay-desk. Handed a bill by the young woman coping with him, he put a hand in a pocket and (since he was habitually inclined to be vague about such things) supposed that it had conveniently come in contact with a bank-note. This he presented to the young woman. She glanced at it without apparent surprise, and then turned it round so that George could inspect it too. So he read:

IN THE EVENT
OF A
NUCLEAR
WAR
there will be no chances,
there will be no survivors—
all will be obliterated—
nuclear devastation is not science fiction—
it is a matter of fact.

This was embarrassing. George offered apologies, mumbled explanations, and produced a pocket-book. The young woman smiled at him kindly, and even provided a free plastic bag—a kind of academic first cousin to the receptacles so abundantly carried by the Mesdames Bowman and Archer—for the labours of Lewis, Rushdie and Storey. George, having manoeuvred this through the narrow door, found himself back in Broad Street.

It now came into his head that it would be pleasant to drop into the Bodleian Library, a place in which random conversations weren't allowed. Readers did occasionally utter to one another —but almost furtively, and only upon matters of immediate learned concern. There wouldn't be time in which to order any books, but George knew of catalogues and check-lists and bibliographies which would at once afford him a view of the present state of Jacobite studies. 'Jacobite', of course, had nothing to do with Bonnie Prince Charlie and people of that sort; its reference was to that area of ecclesiastical history and doctrinal controversy in the sixth century upon which George had made himself an authority as a young man. That had been a long time ago, and he felt that he was not well up in whatever work had been done in the interval. Indeed, he was culpably rusty all round. It didn't much worry him that he hadn't much kept up with contemporary Christian apologetics. He could cope with logical positivism—so dire-seeming a threat in his youth—and demonstrate, at least to his own satisfaction, that it contradicted itself. But what about the larger implications of existentialism? He had already been losing interest as these hove up, and was undeniably hazy over such issues. But about all this he didn't really bother, although he had a foreboding that his negligence was going to place him at an awkward disadvantage with Father Hooker. But his own stretch of early ecclesiastical history was another matter.

Surely he should retain, although not a devout, at least a scholarly interest in recent contributions to research in the field? He recalled the names of several investigators quite as promising as himself. There had been Dom. Potter of Minnesota; and there had been Prebendary Delver of Durham; there had been a German at Göttingen whose name he forgot, but who had tentatively been putting forth disturbing views on political and economic conditions as having been factors in the Eutychian revival. George couldn't hope to muck in again. Indeed, he didn't want to. But he could take a peep at what was going on.

Having formed this resolution, George first visited the nearest Gents (whimsically described as *Schola Linguarum Hebraicae et Graecae*) and then made his way into the Bodleian.

Or rather he tried to do so. The entrance had been changed. It was no longer through the little door (almost as narrow as Blackwell's) saying *Schola Naturalis Philosophiae*. It was through the wider archway of what used to be called the Pig Market, and the Pig Market itself (which had formerly harboured not pigs but notice-boards) had turned into a shop selling picture postcards and colour slides and do-it-yourself cut-out cardboard models of university buildings. Straight ahead, the Divinity School (in which he had once been required to make a speech in indifferent Latin) was still on public view beneath its incredible roof; and to George's left, at the south end of the Pig Market, there was a kind of token barrier or horizontal wooden flap—the academic equivalent, one might say, of a turnstile as it exists in the turbulent outer world—and beyond this George could visualize the familiar long but shallow flights of steps to the reading-rooms. So he walked over to the flap, pushed it, and went through.

'Ticket, please.'

George turned round in astonishment, and saw that he had been addressed by a respectable male person standing in a species of lidless wooden box. He looked as if he had been standing there all day—despite which trying fact he had uttered those two words firmly indeed, but entirely politely.

'Ticket?' George repeated in astonishment. 'But I'm a reader. I'm a reader, I say.'

That this weird linguistic infection should have seized upon George's speech so confused him that there can be little doubt of his having instantly taken on the appearance of a frustrated arsonist.

'Readers can't go in without a ticket, sir.'

'But I've been in hundreds of times!' George said. He was now aware that he was behaving foolishly, but irrational indignation nevertheless overcame him. Being denied entrance to the Bodleian! Him (or He)! George Naylor M.A.; Clerk in Holy Orders; for some eighteen months (he had just remembered) a junior research fellow (supernumerary and non-stipendiary) of one of the most distinguished colleges in the university! It was wholly monstrous.

'When would you have been here last, sir?'

This was a type of question which often got George confused. He was no good at dates. So he ducked this issue.

'I only want . . .' he began.

'You can apply at Admissions, sir.' Sir Thomas Bodley's Janus spoke a shade impatiently this time. There was a small queue of readers, authenticating tickets in hand, formed up behind George. 'First doorway beyond the passage to Radcliffe Square, sir.'

So George, not being sure that he had comported himself quite courteously, produced one of his apologies and withdrew into open air. Halting by the little railing that surrounds the statue of Lord Herbert, runner-up as the putative lovely boy of Shakespeare's Sonnets, he considered his position. In a small way, he had made a fool of himself. He remembered that when as a young man he had worked for a time in the British Museum, and even though the nature of his researches had entitled him to do his reading in the privileged area known as the North

Library, he had been issued with a ticket which he had shown up every day on entering, at least until the door-keepers had got to know him. And at Cambridge, he had recently read, they now charged wandering scholars a fee for admission to the University Library. He decided that the man in the lidless box represented a praiseworthy precaution on the part of the Oxford authorities against evilly disposed persons. Most irrationally, he felt rebuffed, all the same.

The remedy against this improper emotion was at once to go through the drill required to regularize his position as a reader in the Bodleian. Somehow he no longer much wanted to inquire into the present state of affairs within that wide sphere of reference constituted by Jacobus Baradaeus of Edessa and his carryings-on 1,300 years ago. But he ought to seek out Admissions, nevertheless.

And, just beyond the tunnel-like approach to Radcliffe Square, there was a bright new board beside a doorway, *saying* 'Admissions' in letters so large that there was no overlooking them. (The doorway also said, in rather bogus-faded hues, *Schola Musicae*.)

George entered. There was a notice with a pointing arrow. It said, 'Applicants for admission to the library are earnestly requested to take a seat behind the screen, and there attend upon the ringing of a bell.' George did as he was bid. He took a seat and attended upon.

Nothing happened. On the other side of the screen there must be a business area with a brisk traffic going forward. But no sound indicative of this came from the *arcanum* or *adytum* from which he was now sundered by a full six feet. George began to think of his train, although he knew that its departure was still a couple of hours off. Then he did a very scandalous thing. Unsummoned by any bell, he stood up and peered round the screen. He saw the remainder of the small room in which this important admissions transaction was conducted. An elderly lady in an M.A. gown was seated at a table upon which stood several miniature filing-cabinets. She appeared to be asleep.

George was confounded. He couldn't possibly disturb this learned person's repose. Behind her were no doubt several hours of exhausting labour during which she had been struggling with clouds of exigent postulants for readership, any one of whom might have been secreting incendiary devices (backed up by fragmentation bombs) in his or her pockets. George could only stand and wait.

'Do please sit down,' the lady said, in tones every phoneme of which suggested Somerville or Lady Margaret Hall. She had presumably merely been resting her eyes even from the crepuscular light which alone penetrated to this Bodleian semi-dungeon. 'Shall you be in Oxford for long?'

This question, which might perhaps have been better phrased, seemed to admit only of the answer, 'Until about half-past five', and this answer George accordingly gave. A certain perplexity not unnaturally resulted on the lady's part, but she listened with well-bred patience to her visitor's further explaining himself. Then she fell to work on one of her filing cabinets. Having found what was clearly a relevant card, she glanced at it quickly, and then more at leisure and with perfect courtesy at George himself. 'Can you tell me, Dr Naylor,' she asked—but it was clearly information she no longer needed to seek—'in what year you were first admitted as a reader?'

For George this was a bad sort of question. Despite the severe scholarship to which he had been for so long habituated he was really, it must be repeated, a poor hand at dates.

'Would it,' he asked hopefully, 'have been about 1940?'

The lady didn't even elevate her eyebrows at this extra-ordinary suggestion, which of course implied a quite astounding precocity in her visitor. Indeed, she closed her eyes again—and for so long that George had to suppose that she really had dropped off this time. But she had merely been casting round for some tactful manner in which to proceed.

'We work under the most vexatious necessities here,' she presently said. 'We have occasionally to appear quite absurd. I wonder, Dr Naylor, whether you would deprecate being asked to identify yourself?'

'Not at all, madam! Of course not!' George made this reply with inappropriate and disconcerting vehemence, since it was his only means of masking what he knew to be indefensible indignation. The idea of it! It was scarcely to be believed. He rummaged in pockets: several of the wrong pockets before a more hopeful one. 'Here's a visiting card,' he mumbled. 'Grubby, I'm afraid. One doesn't much use such things nowadays, and they take on a shop-soiled look. Or one of these affairs?' Hopefully, he held out a small plastic object. 'A bank card, I think it's called. It's got my name on it. Oh! I see it has my signature too. George Naylor.'

Like the lady in Blackwell's shop, this lady managed a kindly smile. She had unmistakably decided that she was in the presence of a harmless Fool of God. Then she produced an object of her own. It was like a ping-pong bat, and it had some rigmarole pasted on it. George remembered having seen such things in the several rooms of up-to-date stately homes and picture galleries, telling you what you were looking at on the walls. The lady handed this to George—considerately, handle first.

'Can you solemnly assure me,' she asked with sudden sternness, 'that you clearly remember subscribing to this declaration when first admitted as a reader in the Bodleian?'

George stared at the ping-pong bat in a more or less mesmerized way.

'Well, yes,' he said. 'That is, I rather think so. I don't know about the clarity. But I do seem dimly to remember that bit about not making fire in the place.'

'I fear I must ask you to read it aloud to me.'

'Solemnly?' George repeated this word by way of attempting to suggest abundant and willing co-operation. Unfortunately it came out with the effect of a frivolous quip. He then managed, however, to read the thing aloud with a decent sobriety. He even got in what might have been called a hint of pulpit eloquence. And it appeared to satisfy the terms of this guardian spirit's mystery. She produced a little card of her own, wrote on it, had George sign it, passed it through a copying machine, and handed it back to him with a blessed air of accomplishment and finality.

'Thank you very much,' George said. 'Do I have to show it if I go into the Camera too? The Radcliffe Camera, one of Oxford's scattering of really splendid buildings, is a kind of free-standing annexe of the Bodleian Library.

'Certainly,' the lady said. 'They won't let you into the

40

Camera without it. It would be a serious breach of security.' She stood up, shook hands with George, sat down again, and immediately—and surely to a certainty this time—fell asleep. George left her like that, and went out round the screen. There was nobody, he noticed, attending upon the ringing of a bell.

He returned to the Pig Market—more properly the Proscholium —and showed his newly acquired passport. After that, everything was reassuringly familiar. Or at least it was so for a time. Soon, however, he realized that—at least in the common or garden working parts of the Bodleian—almost nothing was *quite* the same. There were fine displacements virtually wherever he turned, and these progressively confused him. Every day there must be numerous scholars from the ends of the earth who had to find what they wanted through a process of trial and error. Nevertheless, he felt that his own uncertainties must be attracting attention. Nothing was quite where it had been. Suddenly he felt something almost symbolical in this. His life was now going to be like that. Nothing quite where it had been.

'Over-*hardy*,' he heard his own voice saying to himself. 'Over-*hardy*.' He came to a halt before some irrelevant catalogue. Why ever should such words bob up in his mind? For a moment he knew only that his memory was again behaving badly. Then he recalled Mrs Archer and her citation of Milton's large-limbed Og, and he was so amused that he laughed aloud. This was not at all the thing in the Bodleian. Moreover, since it was the middle of the vacation, there were very few young people around, and the place seemed exclusively frequented by aged and desiccated persons, all deep scholars without a doubt, who looked as if they hadn't heard a laugh for years; had in fact forgotten about laughter altogether; and were now in some alarm, occasioned by the fallacious impression that George must have been taken ill.

This was unnerving, and George somehow wasn't helped by the fact that he was quite a deep scholar himself. It was almost certain that nobody in the Bodleian at this moment knew half as much about Jacobus Baradaeus of Edessa as he did. Nor, it soon seemed to him, did anybody anywhere else. Eutychian studies— his rummagings in bibliographies and check-lists soon revealed

—were in almost total desuetude. Dom. Potter of Minnesota had switched to Ebionitism. Prebendary Delver had ratted too, and had produced three volumes on Patripassianism, that fond persuasion that the Logos is to be identified with the Father. The man at Göttingen was still at it, but had switched from Marx to Freud as the best illuminant on theological disputation in the sixth century. The Göttingen man was called Gottschalk— which oddly enough had been the name, George recalled, of a particularly desperate heretic in the age of Johannes Scotus Erigena. Various ecclesiastical synods had attempted to wallop his errors out of the original Gottschalk, but rods had no better success than argument, and the wretched man had died still proclaiming whatever his particular nonsense had been. George wondered whether the current Gottschalk would have the guts for that.

Tantum religio potuit suadere malorum. Lucretius' hackneyed but inexpugnable line, George reminded himself, told only half the story. There was a great deal to be said for religion, and it was a pity that he himself had got in such a mess about it. But he wouldn't get out of the mess by nostalgic potterings in the driest dust of the thing. Surely among all these millions of books there must be a work that spoke to his condition more effectively than Gottschalk II? As he asked himself this question, something rather absurd came into his head. He had never read *Robert Elsmere*! Mr Gladstone had—and, following Mr Gladstone, pretty well all England in the year 1888 or thereabout. Mrs Humphry Ward's *Robert Elsmere* was a novel said to present with extraordinary skill the plight of an intelligent Anglican clergyman upon being confronted with the dire findings of what was then called the 'higher criticism'. Elsmere might be just George's man. He couldn't, of course, now read the book—and nobody may borrow a book from the Bodleian—but at least he could take a peep at it and estimate whether it might help. He remembered that undergraduates reading English Literature spent a lot of time in the Radcliffe Camera. Mrs Ward's illuminating masterpiece (for he thus thought of it for the nonce) would probably be over there, and on an open shelf from which he could take it down at once.

Strong in this persuasion, George hurried down the staircase of the Bodleian, intent of gaining the Camera, not a hundred yards away. He hurried so much that he found something bumping against his legs. It was Blackwell's gratuitous plastic bag, and it was knobbly because it quite plainly contained books. So might he be suspected of theft? Ought he to open the bag and display its contents—Lewis, Rushdie and Storey—to the man in the lidless box? Or would this be behaviour so *outré* in character that they would lock him up forthwith? The complete irrationality of this last apprehension so alarmed George (who occasionally went in for lurking fears of madness) that at the critical moment he actually took to his heels—bolting past the guardian presence as if the whole Bodleian were in conflagration, and he himself responsible as having 'made fire' in it. The guardian presence reacted only with mild curiosity. Eccentric characters abound in Oxford.

Although thus confused, George as he mounted the steps of the Camera didn't forget to fish his new admission ticket from his pocket. The woman who had bestowed it on him had insisted that it was essential here too. Inside the portal there was another flight of steps, curving down to a gloomy but deceptively non-subterraneous region the nature of which eluded his recollection. Was it a reading-room, or just an enormous book-stack? It was a reading-room, and at its entrance there was a notice saying *English and Theology*. This bobbing up again of the Queen of the Sciences disconcerted George, but then he reflected that the *mélange* was just right for Mrs Humphry Ward's fictional dealing with the Higher Criticism. Moreover, there was a thoughtfully provided line of coat-pegs, and on one of these he gratefully hung up Blackwell's bag. Thus disburdened, he found calm and confidence restored to him. He entered the great rotunda.

It was deserted. It was utterly empty. Such at least was his first impression—although he was equally conscious of its being thronged with books: thousands and thousands of books in a deep vacation slumber. Of course the Camera was predominantly an undergraduates' reading-room, although learned persons did occasionally frequent it as well. So it was unsurprising that on this fine summer afternoon there seemed to be nobody in evidence. But there must, of course, be a man to whom to show his ticket. No lidless box was on view, but there was a desk near the entrance which suggested itself as being for a member of the library staff rather than for a reader. But nobody sat behind it. Still clutching his ticket, George began anxiously to hunt around. The chap must also have the duty of returning stray books to their shelves: something like that. And the place had so many alcoves, radiating like the spokes of a wheel, that he might well elude notice for a time. Increasingly conscious of the high impropriety of being loose in the Camera without accrediting himself, George scurried from alcove to alcove, unconsciously holding his ticket head-high. And at length he came upon somebody: a somewhat unimpressive somebody, dusty and elderly, who was kneeling on the floor with his nose close to a row of books.

'Oh, there you are!' George said with perhaps an involuntary hint of reproach. 'I've got to show you this.'

Thus accosted, the elderly man got to his feet, turned round, and looked at George with detectable surprise.

'Good afternoon,' he said politely.

'My ticket, you know. Here it is. I understand . . .' George's voice suddenly trailed away. He had never seen this dusty old man before, but he had several times seen his photograph. Was he the Principal of Brasenose? Was he the Warden of Wadham? It didn't much matter which. He was a scholar of enormous eminence, and quite certainly at the moment President of the British Academy.

'Did you say your ticket?' the Principal (or Warden) asked. If he was perplexed he didn't show it. His was clearly an effortless alpha so far as academic courtesy was concerned.

'I'm terribly sorry,' George said. George wasn't exactly abashed. They were, after all, simply two scholars in an absurd situation. But he wasn't quite at ease either. In fact he was still holding out his ticket, so that the Warden (or Principal) was more or less constrained to take it from him and examine it.

'A reader's ticket,' George said helpfully. 'To admit one to Bodley. Or to the Camera. Essential security.'

'How very interesting.' The President of the British Academy handed George back his ticket. It was evident he had never seen one of the things before—or perhaps been aware that such objects existed. 'Can I help you in any way?' it occurred to him to ask.

'Thank you very much. But, no. I'm just looking for *Robert Elsmere*.'

This time, George's dusty but august interlocutor did permit himself to betray perplexity.

'But I *am* Robert Elsmere,' he said. 'How do you do?'

George recalled at once that this was *true*. There was some Head of a House—Warden or Principal or Rector or whatever —whose name was Robert Elsmere. It wasn't in itself all that remarkable. But two Elsmeres coming on top of two Gottschalks was just too much for George. All amenity deserted him.

'But now I have to catch a train,' he said. And he bolted from the Radcliffe Camera as quickly as he had bolted from the Bodleian itself.

Robert Elsmere must, of course, know about *Robert Elsmere*. Perhaps his parents—possibly of humble station?—had not been aware of the book. In decent society one doesn't exploit any humorous potentialities lurking in a man's name, but from time to time the real Robert Elsmere must encounter a little friendly badinage nevertheless. And the incident in the Radcliffe Camera had been so bizarre that the man would almost certainly add it with enjoyment to his stock of after-dinner anecdotes. So it was only something perfectly harmless that had happened.

George managed to tell himself all this before he reached the High Street. He was in renewed nervous discomfort all the same. He glanced at his watch and saw that if he went straight to the railway station he would still have a fairly long wait for his train. He could get a cup of tea in the refreshment place. He did badly need a cup of tea, but wasn't sure that he wanted it at the station. And now a bold idea came to him. He was within almost a stone's throw of his old college. He would go *there*.

George enjoyed certain rights at the college. Having as a young graduate hung on at Oxford for a time and tutored the college's handful of theology students, he had been made an honorary member of its senior common room: an exiguous distinction, but one tacitly understood to be for life. He knew

45

just what he could do—having once done it some ten years before. He would simply walk into the common room and push a bell. The common-room butler and under-butler would not be in attendance: they were probably touring the vineyards of Burgundy in pursuit of professional knowledge. But there would be some respectable elderly woman on duty; she would bring him tea (and even muffins); he would scribble his signature on a scrap of paper, and a term or two later receive a bill through the post. It was an alluringly arcane privilege—a tenuous but precious link, indeed, with an almost forgotten paradise.

So George Naylor walked hopefully up to the wide portal of his Alma Mater. It was flanked, as not in the past, with notices recording in some detail the terms upon which visitors were welcome to enter. 'Visitors', clearly, was the dons' civil near-synonym for 'tourists'. And planted in the middle of the carriage-way was an elderly but muscular man wearing a bowler hat. George saw at once that in a non-academic context this person would be called a bouncer—or, in a slightly older terminology, a chucker-out. He was thus—if with an additional hint of aggressive proclivities—first-cousin to Sir Thomas Bodley's man in the lidless box. But George stood his ground, or rather continued to cover it. And this intrepidity was at once rewarded. The bouncer raised the bowler hat and held it almost at arm's length above his head.

'Mr Naylor—sir!' the bouncer said in a military (or perhaps naval) manner. 'A long time since we've seen you, sir. But we had Mr Trelawny only last week—and Lord Tunsted and Mr Purnell (the younger one, that is: him they called Poodle) not long before that. All in your own year, Mr Naylor.'

'That's capital,' George said, and if the words were chosen at random they came from a joyous heart. He hadn't recognized Smithers, the college Head Porter. But Smithers had recognized him! Smithers, already a man of much consequence 20 years ago, was now not above taking on this bouncing job in place of a lesser servant now and then. 'Visitors' arriving by the coach-load he would firmly and with perfect aplomb direct to some more appropriate entrance. And he knew about a proper welcome and didn't let it linger on in gossip. The bowler was in place again. George entered the Great Quadrangle.

There it all-majestically was: the uncertain proportions, the misguided crenellations, the cloisters that had never been built, Bernini's fountain with its Neptune and Triton and dolphins stolen from he'd forgotten where. Nothing in the world could move George more, unless it was modest Plumley (acquired by his great-grandfather) screened by its grove of oaks. He skirted two sides of the quad (only the dons were allowed to walk on the grass, so of course they never did) and gained the typical Oxford tunnel in which the door of the senior common room stood.

Only it didn't. The tunnel harboured a permanent half-darkness, since there were a couple of obtuse angles to it as if it had been designed to promote optical experiment; it also possessed, presumably built in for fun, three or four stone steps, slant-wise set, which had for some centuries taken their toll of fractured limbs as bibulous Fellows toddled from their port-decanters to bed. So one moved cautiously. George had done so, and found no door. There seemed to be nothing but a blank wall. But this impression proved to be delusive, after all. There was a door of sorts, but it wasn't the old and familiar door. It was a newfangled and unobtrusive door such as one notices on well-designed delivery vans—not swinging on a hinge but gliding on a rail beneath itself. And it was locked. All it presented to the world was a sunken handle and an aperture for a Yale key set in a metal disk about the size of a tenpenny piece.

The common room was locked up! It took George's breath away. The thing was beyond his experience. He could remember how, in his final and most Elysian year in the college, he had gone into the room at three o'clock in the morning to hunt up an envelope big enough to take his major contribution to the *New Theological Quarterly*. The place hadn't been locked up *then*. It was outrageous that it should be locked up *now*. Or at least it was disheartening. For wasn't he a *member* of common room, and thus being excluded in an arbitrary way?

Suddenly there was somebody standing beside him. His eyes had got used to the gloom, and he saw that it was a young man, casually dressed. Somehow he knew about this young man instantly and exactly. He wasn't an undergraduate, but he was the next thing to it. He was a young man so extremely

47

clever—his features and his glance told George this at once—
that he had been snapped up as a Junior Fellow within days of
qualifying for a degree. To do that he had written nine three-
hour papers, had a pleasant ten- or fifteen-minute chat called a
viva with persons as clever as himself—and now here, if he cared
to be, he was established for life. George's indignation vanished.
He found himself rejoicing in this youth's good fortune just as he
had rejoiced in the benediction of Smithers' bowler hat. And the
youth hesitated only for an appraising instant before deciding to
speak.

'Of course it's the most awful nonsense,' he said. 'We're
security-mad. Burglars and so forth. Utterly bonkers! It's true
there's the Tompion grandfather clock. But who could walk off
with that?'

'Or the scagliola table,' George said. 'Hideous affair.' George
hadn't felt so at ease for weeks. 'And the strap-work bookcase
thought up by William Morris. You'd need a truck for it.'

'Exactly.' This time, it wasn't even for a moment that the
young man hesitated. 'I say! Can I let you in?' Already he had a
key in his hand.

'You're very kind.' A first twinge of misgiving beset George. It
now seemed doubtful, somehow, that beyond this bleak barrier
there would still be that respectable elderly woman prepared to
produce tea—let alone muffins. Muffins didn't go with Yale
locks. *Tempora mutantur, nos et mutamur in illis.* But already the
innovatory door was gliding past George's nose.

The two men (forty-three and possibly twenty-two) entered
the common room together.

It hadn't changed. It wasn't shabby with the shabbiness some
of the minor colleges had to affect. In fact it was very splendid.
From three of the walls there looked down on it with approval
the portraits not of obscurely distinguished scholars but of prime
ministers and persons of that sort. And George suddenly knew it
wouldn't do. To cross the room and punch a bell wouldn't really
do. Whatever his formal status, it would be a presuming and
unbecoming action. Besides which, if the elderly woman really
was there, this delightful young man would by now probably be
saying, 'What about a cup of tea?'

'I'll just take down an address or two from *Members in*

Residence,' George said—thus avoiding a positive fib. 'It's over on that table.'

'Yes, of course.' Now for the first time the young man did fractionally hesitate. 'I have to write a note or two,' he said. And he sat down at the escritoire that was said to have belonged to Marie-Antoinette.

So the truth came to George. The young man wasn't *quite* sure. He had a duty as a host to a stranger who was almost certainly an old member. But he had a duty to the college as well, and must respect its regulations, bonkers though they might be. He proposed to remain in the common room until George was prepared to leave it. It was as simple, it was as sensible, as that.

This small sad comedy came quite quickly to an end. Standing upon his years, George shook hands with the young man as he thanked him and said goodbye. They didn't exchange names. There would have been something exceeding the occasion in such a gesture.

George had reached Carfax before he remembered about Lewis, Rushdie and Storey. They were still hanging on that peg in the Camera. There was plenty of time in which to retrieve them. But what if, as he ascended those steps, the President of the British Academy, having concluded his researches, once more encountered him? George saw that he must take himself in hand. He turned round and was back in the Camera within five minutes. So, provided again with what was to constitute his 'light' reading during the inquisitions and persuasions of Father Hooker, he finally reached the railway station. He still had a quarter of an hour to wait, but he would spend the time on the platform. Reaching the man who would let him on, he felt in a pocket for his ticket. It was one of the large affairs that had become fashionable, and about the size of a luggage label. It seemed to be in rather a crumpled condition. He handed it to the collector, who glanced at it and impassively handed it back to him. He saw that it read:

THE WORLD NOW STANDS ON THE BRINK
OF THE FINAL ABYSS

II

'BUT THIS MAN told us Uncle George was going to take a cab,' Henry Naylor said.

'Well, yes.' Henry's brother Charles was fiddling with a gun he rather hoped a college friend was going to invite him to bring to Scotland in August. 'The man gave me that message as soon as I'd identified him on the platform. Which wasn't difficult.'

'But Hilda's gone to the station all the same?'

'Yes. We knew when the next train arrives, and I wasn't keen on going back there myself.' Charles tapped the gun, by way of showing that he had something weighty on his hands. 'I said I thought you'd go—just by way of enjoying your driving licence.' (It was only a few weeks since Henry had passed his driving test.) 'But you weren't around.'

'I was doing bloody calculus.' Henry, who enjoyed his maths, scowled insincerely. 'Holidays just aren't holidays any longer. Not in a post-A-level year. It's swot, swot. Why should I go after a rotten scholarship? There's pots of money.'

'Scholarships don't have much to do with money nowadays. It's just petty prestige. Daddy likes the idea of any sort of prestige. He feels he himself is a thoroughly non-prestige City character. And a non-starter so far as the constituency is concerned. He'll never win it. So he's keen on nursing that odd scrap of ability you have for maths.'

'He might do better to put his money on Hilda. Hilda's tiresome, but she has something. I'd say it's a certain command of dispassionate interest. Spectatorship as a *métier*. It's why she sometimes mutters about Flaubert and Joyce.'

'Never heard of them.' Charles was always quick to resent what he thought of as a lurking egg-head quality in his brother. 'Or was Joyce the chap who wrote some dirty books?'

'Yes, he was.'

'And the other chap, too?'

'Flaubert? I know nothing about him.' Henry had got it into his head that the distinguished thing was to have a flair for a single intellectual activity, so except when off his guard he regularly represented himself as a good deal less well-informed than he was. 'Let's get back to the current situation. Hilda and Uncle George will be here any time now. What about this minder—Hunter, is he, or Bunter?'

'Hunter was the last one. This one is Hooker. It seems he likes to be called Father Hooker.'

'Does that mean he's high church?'

'I don't know whether he's high or low. And I don't know which Uncle George is, for that matter. It's only Tweedledum and Tweedledee, isn't it? By the way, where's that Hookerdum now?'

'He told mummy he must go and dress.'

'Must *what*?' Charles was startled.

'Dress. For dinner, I imagine.'

'Good God!' Charles was horrified. 'Get into a dinner-jacket?'

'I suppose so. Or some clerical equivalent. All purple, perhaps.'

'That's only bishops and people—and for very grand sprees.' Charles spoke with authority. 'But didn't mummy tell him we don't?'

'Definitely she didn't. She was being rather inattentive, I think. He'd been talking to her for quite some time.'

'But, Henry, it's bloody awkward, isn't it? If the chap comes down like that. He ought to have asked, of course.'

'He makes old-fashioned assumptions out of books,' Henry suggested, 'because lacking actual contact with high society.'

'To hell with high society!' It was clearly not egalitarian feeling that moved Charles to this senseless exclamation. He was genuinely upset. 'Here's a wretched little black beetle turning up to rescue Uncle George—simply under the orders of some bigger beetle, I suppose—and the first thing we do is to embarrass the poor chap.'

'We could send one of the maids up to his room with a message. As if that were a routine kind of thing.'

'She'd muck it up. Giggle, perhaps.' It was true that, although servants survived at Plumley, they were sometimes scarcely recognizable as such. 'I'd better go and put on a dinner-jacket myself. Keep him in countenance. It's the usual quick dodge when there's been a balls-up. You, too.'

'Hell I will.' For a moment Henry looked merely obstinate. Then he laughed, and both brothers laughed together. 'I'll go up myself,' he said. 'Tap on the door and say, "By the way, we don't wash or dress." It should be quite easy.'

'Don't forget that Father business. It's a harmless civility. Scat, young man.' And Charles Naylor picked up his gun again.

Driving to the railway station in her own old car—declared by her brothers to have been a christening present—Hilda had been visited by a brilliant idea. This happened quite often, although it always turned out to be in a disappointingly short-term way. More particularly, it had been happening since she won her prize. It had been a startling pot to come by: well-distanced from any commercial racket, and awarded by judges acknowledged to be critics of the most austere sort. Her story had been printed in what her father might have called a prestige magazine. Publishers had written to ask whether she had a novel on the stocks, and a firm of literary agents had suggested it would be prudent to employ their services. Hilda knew that it might be just a flash in the pan—or told herself that she did. She had been overwhelmed for a time, all the same. Chiefly, she didn't want her family to know. And they didn't, since they and all their acquaintance lived as remote as Esquimaux from anything of the kind. She might have created a pride of lions to replace Landseer's in Trafalgar Square, she thought, and nobody in the Plumley world would have been aware of it. So she was keeping mum and biding her time.

The idea that had come to her turned on the arrival of Uncle George and the new minder. There was to be a grown-up family like her own, only larger, with all its members convinced of the worth and rightness of their several absorbing interests and concerns. An Uncle George, a clergyman turned suddenly agnostic, was to return among them, followed by a minder like this man Hooker. But despite the efforts of the minder—or actually promoted by them in various highly ironical fashions she'd have to work out—the Uncle-George infection spread. One by one, the whole extended family lost whatever faith it had in one mundane thing or another. Universal aboulia (a splendid word) reigned. The only survivor was the Uncle George, who simply woke up one morning with his faith restored. The direst victim was the minder. Equally abruptly, he lost all confidence in his role, and went out and drowned himself in a pond.

As a project upon which to base a successful career as a novelist, this idea proved even more short-lived than many others. It was dead when Hilda was still a couple of miles from the station where she was to pick up her uncle. For one thing, if achieved, its existence couldn't, as could that of the prize story, be kept from her family, and they would all be hurt in their minds by it. This must be a difficulty authors had to face regularly, and Hilda wondered whether anybody had written a book, or at least a thesis, about it. For a few moments she toyed with the idea herself. (Hilda had read English at Oxford.) But that kind of thing should be left to dons. And of course to critics. There *were* critics, and some of them could spot a reasonably decent short story when it was presented to them. Hilda, however, wasn't going to be a critic any more than she was going to be a don. She was going to *write*.

Uncle George's carriage came to a stop almost opposite to where she was waiting for him on the platform, so she saw him while he was still opening the door. He had a suitcase and what appeared to be a parcel of books, and the one was getting in the way of the other. She debated, as she advanced, whether she should grab the suitcase and hold on to it. Charles or Henry could properly do that, but perhaps for her to do so would be to treat her uncle as an old man. It was one of those female disabilities a gaggle of women were nowadays making a fuss about. Hilda wondered whether she was right not much to fall for women's lib. A great-aunt on her mother's side had been a prominent suffragette. Was that different? She hadn't thought about it, and it wasn't a moment to think about it now. Observation first and reflection afterwards: that was the golden rule. So now she registered how her uncle's expression as he caught sight of her contrived simultaneously to indicate pleasure and dismay.

'Hilda!' he shouted—and then gave a moment, for no apparent reason, to confusedly switching the suitcase and the parcel from one fist to the other. Almost simultaneously, however, he managed a kiss. 'But I said I'd get a taxi!' he then exclaimed. 'There *is* a taxi—quite often.'

'Charles came to fetch your friend, so I thought I'd come and fetch you. So as to be sure you were in time for dinner.'

'My friend? Yes, of course. Hooker. Do you like him?'

'No, not really.'

'Oh, dear! He isn't a friend, you know—or even an acquaintance. But he's said to be very distinguished. I rather dodged him on that train. I thought, you see, that I'd just take a potter round Oxford. It was thoughtless of me. These two car trips! I *am* so sorry.'

'Was it nice?' Effecting a judicious compromise, Hilda had managed to relieve her uncle of the parcel of books. 'Oxford, I mean.'

'Yes, indeed.' Uncle George said this with immediate conviction. 'But changed in some ways since my time. Probably not since yours or Charles's. It's a pity Charles didn't finish there.'

'Charles simply refused to pass his Mods.'

'Probably they can be very vexatious. Henry will have better luck. I think of him, you know, as a dark horse who may yet break clear of those maths blinkers.'

'I rather agree.' Hilda was now leading the way to her car. What was in her head was a humiliating realization of the trashy character of the family fantasy she had been thinking up as fit for fiction. Uncle George was *real*. To flatten him out into a manikin in a yarn would be merely wanton. Yet you were always told that the material for novels and things had to be found not in books but in first-hand experience of life. And that wasn't, as books were, easy to come by. Your family was your stock-in-trade, at least to start with.

Suddenly Hilda had another idea. Somebody publishes a novel crammed with her or his nearest relations, all satirically presented. And all the relations read it, are enthusiastic, and quite fail to spot either themselves or each other. I come out with bad ideas, Hilda told herself, as easily as a baby does with spots. 'How is the tennis court?' Uncle George asked. They were now seated in the car, and Hilda was revving up. 'It has come out in spots.' Hilda realized that this was an obscure remark. 'Patches of moss or something that produce an odd bounce if the ball lands on them.' It was like Uncle George to ask a conscientious question like this—even perhaps to think it up ahead. He was in the dumps about God and his immortal soul, both of which he now presumably believed to be old wives' tales. But he felt he had to enter into others' concerns, however trivial. The tennis court wasn't prominent in Hilda's mind, and she wasn't too pleased that it should be supposed to be so. She was going to have serious talks with Uncle George. Meantime, there was no harm in thinking of him as an old dear, although he was only in what is called early middle age. It would be a precaution against any sense of annoyance. Charles and Henry were probably going to experience just that with their uncle, particularly since he had more or less brought along the man Hooker.

'I have to be on the look out'—George said with telepathic effect—'not to be harping on my own affairs. I expect you've heard about them.'

'Yes, I have.'

'In Oxford an engaging young woman handed me something about atom bombs.' Uncle George didn't seem to offer this as an inconsequent remark. 'It's a bit frightening, all that. Yet the magnitude of a possible catastrophe is not its true measure.'

'How do you mean, uncle?'

'Or the mere neutral magnitude of the universe as science—which means no more than your brains and mine—has revealed it. The distance between star and star has no significance in itself.'

'Hasn't it?' They were now on the high road, but Hilda slowed down a little. 'Pascal . . .'

'Yes, of course.' Uncle George was pleased. 'Pascal was

scared, certainly. But it wasn't the immensities, you know. It was the silence in them. A quality, not a dimension. Dear me! We've got on tricky ground, Hilda.'

They drove on, silent for some time. Hilda, like Uncle George, was now pleased. There *were* serious talks ahead of them. The last time Uncle George had 'lost his faith' she had been too young to make much of it. There would be a difference this time. She was curious about religious feeling, and particularly about its apparent compulsiveness in some people and its total absence in others. But more interesting than that was its coming and going in a single individual—and here her uncle appeared to be a classic case. But she must be chary of taking any initiative in probing the matter. That, in present circumstances, would be indelicate. She must just watch out for a promising lead in. One had almost turned up already in that piece of chat about Pascal. And now, after the silence that had succeeded it, her uncle moved a little away from what he had called tricky ground.

'When I tumbled out of Oxford,' he said, 'and I mean not today but twenty years ago, I tumbled straight into the church. What are you now going to tumble into, Hilda?'

'A job, I suppose, if I can find one. But'—and Hilda took a plunge that surprised her—'I want to try to write.'

'Excellent,' Uncle George said. He seemed no more surprised than if she'd said she was going to take a course in cookery.

'Only I haven't told anybody at home yet.'

'Then they won't get it out of me.' Uncle George said this so cheerfully that one fear that had been in Hilda's mind was dispelled. He wasn't going to moan and groan.

'The snag, uncle, seems to me that I've seen so little. I keep telling myself that I need experience. *Experientia docet.*'

'My dear child, you've got that wise saw wrong. *Experientia docet stultos* is what the chap said. The less stupid you are, the less you have to knock around for what you need. Not that knocking around isn't great fun. I wish I'd managed more of it. Have you any plans which that way incline?'

'Not really. Only I'm just back from three weeks in Italy.' Hilda felt this wasn't much of a claim. 'With another girl,' she added. This made it sound feebler still.

'Where did you go?'

'Florence, and then Arezzo . . .'

'And San Sepolcro?' her uncle asked.

'Yes, we took a bus there.'

'Good! Where else?'

'Just Siena. As a matter of fact, it was something there that has chiefly stuck in my head.'

'Not that fancy-dress horse race?'

'Of course not. It wasn't happening, anyway, during our week there. It was something in San Domenico. San Domenico's just stuffing with Saint Catherine, you remember.'

'So it is.' Uncle George was far from solemn. 'Those awfully important steps, for instance. Only three or four of them. But I expect she took them levitating.'

'Yes, I know. I read quite a bit about her, as a matter of fact. But it wasn't the steps. It was her skull.'

'It would be that, of course.' Uncle George was now a little more serious.

'There it is, in a glass box in a very special little chapel. Glaring at you. Or not quite that, because I think they've put something dull behind the eye sockets. But what really shook me was two or three colour photographs they'd pinned up near it. You see, the Pope had been there a couple of weeks earlier. And there he was in the photographs, with an entourage of cardinals and bishops and people all in purple and scarlet. Venerating the skull.'

'It struck you as remarkable?' Uncle George asked gently.

'I think he's rather a good Pope.' Hilda paused for a moment and drove more slowly: she was abashed at having produced this patronizing testimonial. 'Highly intelligent, and all taken up with ghastly things happening all over the world. And there he was, doing this venerating.'

'Why not?'

'Pigges' bones.'

'That's good Chaucer, but not quite fair to His Holiness, Hilda. Or His Nibs, if you like. It *is* a human skull, you know.'

'Yes, of course. You get a hand-out saying that another Pope set up a high commission or something of important medical people. And they said, Yes, it is a very old skull of rather a small

57

woman and *quale si osserva nel tipo femminile senese*. Think of that.'

'It seems to have struck you in a distinctly unfavourable light.' Uncle George said this in a puzzled voice, so that Hilda realized he was feeling he must proceed with caution. He probably had no clear idea whether his niece was now a sceptic, or a devout Christian of a firmly protestant kind, or some sort of waverer between one thing and another. If this last, he would certainly not want to push his own new stance of unbelief on her. He was too diffident a person for that. 'But consider, Hilda,' he was now saying. 'It may, for a start, very well *be* Catherine's skull. The mortal remains of saints or persons tipped for sainthood were through some centuries pretty well dismembered and lodged here and there in bits and pieces.' Uncle George paused on this. 'Put that way,' he said, 'it sounds frivolous. But you know what I mean.'

'Yes.'

'Catherine of Siena is one of the most remarkable women in the history of the Christian church. Her only rival is Teresa of Avila. Catherine was the daughter of a dyer, and she ended up sorting out and rearranging the papacy. Of course, odd things, as you know, happened to her on the way. She received the *stigmata*, but concluded it would be impolitic to compete with St Francis on that particular ground, so she secured through prayer that the wounds would be invisible to other people. She can be seen as wildly hysterical and good for any number of laughs. But she *was* astounding. Over that business of getting the papal family back from Avignon she succeeded where Petrarch had failed—and Dante himself before that. And she wrote, it seems, like an angel in the purest Tuscan going.'

'All right: Catherine was a paragon.'

'Yes—but come back to your present Pope. Here, in front of him in Siena, is what millions believe to be the woman's noddle. Call it that if you like.'

'But I don't like.' Hilda was now becoming rather uncomfortable. 'I don't want to be mocking.'

'I'm sure you don't. But the point is that the Pope goes into this chapel with his clergy around him. And he contemplates the thing with respect and reverence. That's all that 'venerate' means, you know. It doesn't mean 'worship'. Your colour photographs aren't of a Golden Calf affair.'

'Yes, I see.' Hilda wondered whether to continue. She sensed in Uncle George the existence still of a divided mind, reluctant to write off the simplicities of naïve religious persuasions. He had probably been experiencing some rather desperate days or even weeks, but was cheering up now simply because he was coming home. And her knowing this did perhaps entitle her to go on. 'But the whole business of relics,' she said, 'seems quite weird to me.'

'Yes—but it doesn't to a great many other people, Hilda, my dear. It's something intertwined with centuries of catholic devotion. The Pope himself, as a child in Poland, may have been taught to venerate such things.'

'Yes, of course. But in Siena there was something else.' Hilda had resolved to be firm. 'In the basement of the Palazzo Pubblico there was a marvellous exhibition of the Gothic in Siena. *Il Gotico.* All the swells were on view: Duccio, Simone Martini, the Lorenzetti, Sodoma—the lot. But there was also a good deal of hardware. And what I chiefly noticed was a reliquary. You know what I mean?'

'Yes.' Uncle George was slightly amused by this question.

'This one was about the size of a decent bracket clock, but shaped more or less like a spire. All very golden and ornate. It had twelve uniform little circular glazed windows about as big as a man's wrist-watch. There was a tiny relic—a scrap of bone or something—in each. Of course, it was all as old as the hills. But it had been brought up to date. Behind each relic was a minute printed label telling you just what you were looking at: perhaps a paring of Saint Somebody's great toe.'

'There's a technical word for such things,' Uncle George said composedly. '*Exuviae.*'

'One had a place of honour right at the apex of the contraption. About half a centimetre of hair. And the label, the little printed label, said it was the Virgin Mary's.'

'It isn't impossible, is it? The Blessed Virgin is rather a special case. That she was carried bodily up to Heaven has never become dogma, but in the Roman Church it is widely accorded the status of a pious opinion. No end of people would be deeply

59

offended if you purported to exhibit the Virgin's skull after the fashion of Saint Catherine's. But that a stray hair or two may have floated down en route is quite in order and rather poetical.'

'Uncle George, it's all the greatest nonsense.'

'And you sound almost indignant about it! Of course there's a lot to perturb in Italy. Trollope's Mrs Proudie was shocked to hear that they were pretty weak on Sabbath observance in Rome.'

Hilda was laughing at this before she realized that her uncle wasn't quite composed, after all. He wasn't yet out of the wood, and these small absurdities (as they surely were) made part of his problem. So she had been labouring them tactlessly. She tried to get away on a lighter note.

'Of course,' she said, 'it's only sensible for an immemorial institution to keep up to date. It's how it has managed to survive century by century, after all. There was a church—I think in Arezzo, but I can't really remember—which had rows of little electric candles in some of the chapels. They were penny-in-the-slot candles. You dropped in a hundred-lire coin and on flicked one candle.'

'Sensible, as you say. And particularly attractive to the children—clutching their piaculative pence. Do you know that T.S. Eliot must have invented "piaculative"? The regular form is "piacular".'

'It wouldn't scan.'

'"Piaculary" would—which is another possibility, only obsolete.'

Hilda reflected that this was the sort of momentous information dished out in lectures she'd had to attend in Oxford. But she was also aware that, in some curious way, her uncle was temporizing.

'Arezzo and Borgo San Sepolcro,' he now said. 'But what about Monterchi?'

'I'm afraid I've never heard of Monterchi.'

'It's on the way. His mother came from there.'

'Whose mother, Uncle George?'

'Piero's, of course. There's a little mortuary chapel, with his Madonna del Parto. Iconographically unusual, perhaps unique, in Italy. The child hasn't been born, you know.'

'I see.'

'Anyway, San Sepolcro. You saw the picture?'

'Of course. It was why we went there.'

'Like many other people—since the painter became so fashionable.' There was a moment's silence. Uncle George was clearly unhappy at having produced this slightly caustic remark. Then he turned a troubled face to his niece as she sat at the wheel. 'Do you know?' he said. 'I *have* come to think it a pack of fables from top to bottom, but I'd hate to drag anybody after me into that persuasion.'

'Me, you mean. But I don't know that I need any dragging. Haven't I just indicated as much?'

'We were only talking about some of the trimmings, Hilda.' There was another silence. Then, strangely, Uncle George's expression turned from distress to mischief. 'But that picture,' he said, 'isn't a trimming. It's the one scrap of evidence I can't get away from. Odd, isn't it? Don't tell Hooker.'

After this, not much was said for the rest of the drive, so Hilda had leisure to reflect on her uncle's condition—soberly, this time, and without primitive literary designs on it. If you weren't merely an occasional church-goer, muttering the Apostles' creed on Sundays and remembering to bob your head at the right place in it, but had for long had the duty of climbing into the pulpit and saying, 'In the name of the Father and the Son and the Holy Ghost, Amen,' you had undoubtedly been in a very tight spot indeed before beginning to talk about a pack of fables. Uncle George's track-record wasn't very distinguished. There was undeniably a labile streak in his make-up. But he deserved better of her than she'd managed so far. She recalled with decent shame now, when her brother Charles had announced the present state of play, she had only managed to come out with something smart about it. She was making virtuous resolutions as she brought her car to a halt at Plumley.

'How did you find him?' Edward Naylor asked this nervously. He had waited at the foot of the staircase until Hilda came down from seeing her uncle installed in his bedroom. 'A pretty worried man, eh?'

'There's a worried man there, daddy. But other men as well.'

Edward Naylor frowned. His children were constantly making senseless remarks—even Charles and Henry, whose characters he thought he penetrated to pretty thoroughly. But most often it was Hilda. He believed that Hilda was cleverer than the boys, and as he was conscious of his own marked ability—as being the kind of man at whom others glance first when a sticky point turns up at a board meeting—he felt that he and his daughter ought to be the members of the family who fully understood each other. And Hilda tried. Whereas, when some occasion of cross purposes arose, Charles and Henry might just mutter about the generation gap and walk away, Hilda would at least stay put and continue talking. But he couldn't be certain that it wasn't chiefly on account of mere curiosity. Required to make a living—he had sometimes reflected—his daughter might go far in industrial espionage.

'But the state of play?' he asked. 'Did you rumble it at all?' (Edward Naylor probably believed this to be a very up-to-date expression, freely bandied about among the young.) 'Is your uncle in trouble over the whole bag of tricks this time: the Immaculate Conception, and all those miracles, and the Sermon on the Mount and the Resurrection?'

The man Hooker, Hilda thought, would be pained by this shocking mix up; it was clear that her father hadn't a clue as to what the Immaculate Conception was, and would feel far from enlightened if informed by his brother that as a Dominican tertiary Catherine of Siena would have been required to disbelieve in it.

'I only know a bit about the Resurrection,' she said. 'It seems to be the crux at the moment.' She was rather pleased at bringing in so apposite a word. 'Because of a painting of the thing at a little place called Borgo San Sepolcro.'

'Good heavens!' Edward Naylor was now frankly bewildered. 'You mean that just on the strength of looking at some picture—or more probably just recalling it—your uncle feels. . . ?'

'Just that.'

'That there must be something in it?'

'That it must be true, after all. At least I think that's how his

62

mind works on the thing. Daddy, just what do you want Uncle George to do? Stick to his job?'

'Don't make fun of me, Hilda.' Edward Naylor could sometimes produce an unexpected remark. 'What a man should stick to is his guns, even if it means packing in his job. I'm sticking to my own guns at the moment, as a matter of fact.'

'Just how, daddy?'

'Bingo.' Hilda's father made his transition to this topic, she saw, without the slightest difficulty. When he had on hand something that he regarded as important it was commonly in her that he first confided. 'They say there's not another six months in bingo: old women with pennies in their purses in crumbling abandoned cinemas. But it can be revamped in a perfectly recognizable form and channelled through the media. I'm certain of that. Expensive to mount and run, but lots of money in it, all the same.'

'I see. Do you know? I think I'll come into the business, just like Charles.'

This disconcerted Edward Naylor. Was it intended seriously? And Charles, ejected from Oxford in an untimely but not disgraceful fashion, hadn't exactly 'come into the business'. The business wasn't structured in quite that way, and his father had been obliged to chat up a good many cronies before edging the young man into a niche of sorts with a reasonable screw. The idea of going through the same process for a daughter was preposterous—particularly as a woman, on reaching what was absurdly called *la crème de la crème* in a secretarial capacity, was at the end of the road so far as the business world was concerned. It was *so* preposterous that he saw he could afford to be jovial about it.

'Not on your life,' he said robustly—and then his expression changed. 'But about your uncle,' he said. 'Something really awkward has happened. Do you remember a bit of talk about Prowse asking him to preach? Your mother said something about it, but didn't recall this really awkward thing. It came into her head again only when that new parlourmaid asked her some silly question about the dinner-table. It's this evening that the Prowses are coming to dine. They'll be ringing the door-bell any minute now.'

63

'Well, that's very nice, I suppose.'

'I don't feel it to be anything of the kind.' Edward Naylor was now as disturbed about the Prowses as his son Charles had been at the prospect of Father Hooker's arriving unsuitably attired at the family board. 'Here is your uncle on his first night back home. It *is* home to him, you know, since he has never got married or anything of the sort.'

'Or anything of the sort?' Hilda repeated, perplexed. But her father went on.

'And this Mr Hooker actually arrives before him. It's hardly decent.'

'But Uncle George himself was responsible for just that. He as good as confessed it was to give the man the slip for a time that he stopped off at Oxford.'

'And quite right, too. What I feel is that they might at least have let my brother have a few days quietly to himself at Plumley before coming at him. It's what happened last time.'

'Yes, I know. But now there's a new bishop, and I suppose he feels the thing to be so momentous—a single soul's eternal destiny, and all that—that no time should be lost. And anyway, daddy, I don't see what it has to do with the Prowses.'

'It's as if we were stacking up parsons against your uncle.'

For a moment Hilda found nothing to say. This, she was thinking, was what comes out of those absurd public schools. Obtuse business men like daddy, not all of them wholly scrupulous when in their offices, roam the land exhibiting a hypertrophied sense of fair play.

'But Mr Prowse is *just* a parson,' she asserted a shade impatiently. 'Whereas Uncle George, before he took to the slums and so on, was on his way to being rather a good theologian. No doubt Father Hooker is that too. Even if they get going on the thing after dinner—which is extremely improbable in itself—Mr Prowse will simply keep mum and sip your port. He sips tea with the kind of old women who waste their pennies on your bingo, and he could probably give both the others points at that. But he won't weigh in about Jesus Christ having perhaps been a sacred mushroom.'

Edward Naylor, although without the reading that might have enabled him to make something of this last crude remark, appeared reassured by his daughter's picture of the situation, and he didn't even resent that bit about bingo. The wholesale purveyors of leisure-time diversions were coming to stand where the wholesale purveyors of beer and stout had stood: in the socially impregnable position of those who make humble life bearable. He could afford the routine family jokes about the basis of the family prosperity.

'And there's the bell,' he said. 'I expect there's only that gawky girl. You go.'

The dinner started off quite well. Father Hooker, counselled by Henry, had made only slight changes in his attire. That George Naylor was in mufti wouldn't strike the Prowses as out of the way: it was normal enough in a clergyman on holiday. Christopher Prowse was in his usual frayed but well-laundered dog-collar: it was only his jacket and trousers that showed spotty in places—this because the Prowses had to think twice about dry-cleaning. The near-poverty of the Vicar of Plumley and his household was a source of embarrassment to Edward Naylor. It was difficult to do anything about it with proper tact. Edward had recently gathered that a ten-pound note put in the bag at Easter no longer goes prescriptively into the clerical pocket. The embarrassment was shared to some extent by George, who had felt unable (without ungraciousness) to divest himself of a small private income deriving from the family business. Even Mrs Naylor was not untouched by it. She had been obliged to arrange for a plain dinner on occasions like the present ever since she had heard her elder son say something coarse-grained about treating the poor devil to a square meal. To describe a clergyman as a devil struck her as peculiarly wrong.

That things went well was largely due to George, who talked with animation. Hilda saw with satisfaction that her uncle's troubles were outweighed for the moment by the simple pleasure he took in a family gathering. She backed him up by taking a larger share in the conversation than was usual with her. Asked about her Italian trip by Mr Prowse, she gave a full account of it, avoiding the awkward issues that had cropped up in her discussion with Uncle George. This was a success. The vicar had visited Italy as a young man, and was given to

65

recalling the occasion on a nostalgic note. He said it was a source of lasting regret to him that he had failed to see Assisi. The tour, he explained, hadn't run to it. Hilda saw that Mr Prowse, like most Anglican parsons, was prepared to regard as of peculiar sanctity the city that had been the birthplace of St Francis.

But at this point Henry Naylor behaved badly by announcing, plainly with malicious intent, that he had heard Assisi was a well-run little place since the municipality had been taken over by the Communists. The claim, whether fact or invention, upset the Prowses, and it had to be George who came to the rescue. He embarked on a lively account of his afternoon in Oxford. Hilda suspected that her uncle, although he had so roundly endorsed it as having been a 'nice' occasion, had really found it variously discomfiting. But it was precisely on this that he seized now with a spirited account of some ludicrous episode connected with the Bodleian Library.

Hilda enjoyed the comedy, but was conscious of discontent as well. It seemed a shame that Uncle George, who could cheerfully represent himself as a figure of fun, should be fated to take matters of belief so desperately seriously as he undoubtedly did. Hilda believed she didn't believe in beliefs. Whatever belief you subscribed to, you were left in the same spot in the end. It made no odds whether you swore by Genesis or the Big Bang: a point came at which the whole thing was incomprehensible and absurd. But from day to day you could still behave in a reasonably civilized fashion nevertheless. This, of course, was in effect the family ethos in which Hilda had been brought up, although she would perhaps have been indignant to be told so. She wondered how Christopher Prowse really felt about the human lot. He was a fairly recent arrival at Plumley, and she hadn't yet got the hang of him. It didn't seem likely to be a complicated hang. He was probably resigned to the sufficiency of the trivial round, the common task, and she ought, therefore, to approve of him. Inconsistently, however, she judged that he didn't amount to much. You couldn't say that of Uncle George.

Nor, conceivably, could you say it of Father Hooker, even although he continued at times to seem unlikeable. So far, he had been rather silent during the meal, perhaps because concerned to take the measure of this clutch of Naylors and their local spiritual guide. But now he caught on to the Bodleian business, and the other mild reverses to which Uncle George had similarly been lending a humorous turn. It had been his line that Dr Naylor would have been treated with more respect had he been properly dressed.

'I was very pleased,' Father Hooker had suddenly said to George, 'to see you enjoying your ease—as indeed you are still doing now—in flannels. *Dulce est desipere in loco.* But in general—purely in general—there is surely an abnegation of responsibility in it. Except'—and here Hooker gave a little bow to his hostess—'upon delightfully private and domestic occasions.'

For a couple of seconds silence obtained—no doubt from a feeling that the chap had said something out of turn. For one thing, it seemed deliberately to ignore the significance that George clearly attached to the shedding of clerical garments. Certainly it startled George himself. But it also prompted him to mischief.

'My dear Hooker,' he said (having presumably decided that a familiar mode of address was proper at his sister-in-law's table), 'would it be your impression that Christ turned up at the Last Supper in alb, stole and chasuble?'

'Really, Dr Naylor . . .'

'Or that the disciples went fishing in cassocks?'

Father Hooker must have reflected that here was a new George Naylor. Being doubtless a classical scholar, he may even have likened his latest apostate to Antaeus, who gained strength from planting his feet on native soil.

'It is hardly matter for a jest,' he said.

'No, indeed. It's a matter of serious and curious interest. I was reading an article about it in *Theology* not long ago. Most of our ecclesiastical habiliments were simply the ordinary wear of the upper classes in classical Rome. The clergy just held on to them. And the dog-collar, you know, which there *are* no end of jests about, is merely something we ourselves nobbled from the Romish clergy on the continent well within the present century. We're sticking to it. They're giving it up. Have you been in Rome itself lately?'

'No,' Father Hooker said with dignity. 'I have not.'

'I was there quite recently. It's one's impression at first that the whole priestly class has been driven from the streets. Not so. The regulars, of course, are as they were. But the seculars—your parish priest, and so on—have taken to mufti. They may just wear a little gold cross—rather as our athletes and footballers are fond of doing nowadays.'

Again there was silence. George's kinsfolk probably felt that they had been required to listen to something impressively learned but not quite the thing. It was Mr Prowse who first ventured to speak.

'Fascinating!' he exclaimed—if with a certain lack of conviction. '*Theology*, did you say? I must look it up. One gets terribly rusty, you know, under pressure of parochial work.'

'Particularly,' Mrs Prowse added, 'since we've had Cubs as well as Brownies.'

'I suppose that must be so.' This came from a George who looked suddenly abashed and his familiar diffident self. 'Delicious fish,' he said to his sister-in-law. 'Turbot, isn't it? You must have a marvellous cook, Mary.'

'Bream, George,' Mary Naylor whispered.

The domestic confidence pleased George. He had certainly come home.

III

'YOU DON'T THINK it's going to rain?' George Naylor asked his niece next morning. He and Hilda were first down to the breakfast table. 'I've been out on the terrace, and there's a low bank of cloud to the west.'

'No, it's not going to rain.' Hilda tried not to sound amused. There had been something wistful in her uncle's voice.

'Good! I've arranged to go for a walk, as it happens, with'— George braced himself for fun—'with this emissary from Tower Hamlets. I expect he'll appear at any minute.'

'How nice, Uncle George. I'll come along too. When I'm at home I always walk the dogs after breakfast. It's expected of me. One of my roles is kennel-maid.'

'As a matter of fact, my dear . . .'

'Yes, I know. And I won't have it. Not at this indecent pace. Daddy agrees with me. He says they ought to let you have a breather. and my taking this first walk with you will perhaps be a hint of how we feel.'

'But you mustn't feel hostile towards Hooker. You see . . .'

'Don't *you*?'

'Don't I what, Hilda?'

'Feel he's a pain in the neck.'

'Certainly not. I admit that, personally, I don't find myself terribly attracted to him. But . . .'

'So far, so good.'

'Hilda, you must simply not take that line. For Father Hooker it's a very serious matter, and we must at least be courteous to him. And I'm not sure I can quite rely on your brothers there. They might forget that he's their parents' guest.'

69

'Willy-nilly, so far as we are concerned.'

'We must put that out of our heads. And be fair to the chap.'

'We must be fair with each other. So now then, Uncle George: honour bright. Why did you get off that train at Oxford?'

'It was weak of me—and I was punished for it by finding the place isn't even a comfortable bolt-hole any longer.'

'Because its atmosphere is still heavy with Anglican piety? I can't say I ever noticed it.'

'Nothing of the kind. It was simply . . .'

But at this moment Father Hooker entered the room. Disconcertingly, he had, like Uncle George, put on a turn-down collar and a tie. In answer to Hilda's prescriptive question, he said that he had slept very well. Country air, he told her, always agreed with him and gave him an appetite. With this jocular preface, he set about foraging for what appealed to him. Whatever his shortcomings, he couldn't be called awkward or ill at ease. When the two cocker spaniels came lolloping in to claim their due he made their acquaintance cordially if inexpertly straight away. This was rather a surprise. There had been a positively awkward moment on the previous evening when he had betrayed an almost pathological aversion to the two Plumley cats. These creatures had at once detected that the visitor was no cat-lover, and after the manner of their kind had therefore proposed to climb affectionately all over him—whereupon he had repelled them in alarm and with almost unseemly violence. Now he was doing much better with the dogs. And it seemed to be with simple satisfaction that he heard of Hilda as proposing to join in the walk.

None of this softened Hilda. It was all policy, she told herself. If Church of England priests could become Jesuits, Hooker would be among the first to sign on. Although at dinner he had met another parson who was clearly on terms of intimacy with the Naylors, he probably regarded the whole household as hostile to him, and also as pretty closely-knit in any final analysis. So he had decided he must endeavour to stand well with everybody. To effect this he was prepared to be a bit of a turncoat—or at least of a turncollar. Last night he had talked about getting into mufti with that pompous nonsense about abnegations of responsibility. But now here he was doing it himself—just by way of cutting what he conceived to be an agreeable figure.

Hilda had got as far as this in her reflections before it came to her that they represented a small orgy of vulgar prejudice. If Uncle George asserted there was something to be said for Father Hooker it was her business to accept it as true. Uncle George, after all, ought to know. And if he had bolted at Oxford—which he didn't deny—she certainly mustn't make a standing joke of it.

So Hilda took care to fetch Father Hooker a third cup of coffee. Not very long after that, the walk began.

Theological discussion—if that were the right term for argument with an apostate—was ruled out. Father Hooker knew very well why George Naylor had been provided with an escort of a young woman and two dogs, and he resigned himself to the situation with reasonable address. Himself presumably unaccustomed to canine company, he could be detected, moreover, as having to give much of his mind to what he conceived as the difficult task of avoiding being tripped up by the friskings of Bill and Bess. These creatures were indeed not too well-trained. But Hilda was used to them, and her uncle appeared able literally to take them in his stride. When Father Hooker did manage to talk it was to deploy such resources in the way of rural interests as he possessed. He named trees accurately but for no particular reason. He inquired about crops and the prospects of the harvest. He commented in almost sub-Wordsworthian tones on some clouds and on the noises—presumably joyous—being made by a lark.

Hilda felt that it was going to be a pretty boring walk. She had hoped that Uncle George, who had so agreeably perked up at the dinner-table and startled Father Hooker with that nonsense about the disciples fishing in cassocks, might manage a little gamesomeness now. But Uncle George didn't have much to say. He was made both happy and pensive, his niece thought, simply by the fact of walking through Plumley village again. It was like this when they came to the church.

The church wasn't large, since at no time in its recorded history had Plumley been much of a place. But through the centuries plenty of people had died there, so there was a big churchyard, partly screened from the road by a low stone wall. There was also a lich-gate, which now served rather oddly as the front gate of the vicarage as well. Beside this there was a notice-board: quite an imposing twin-leaved affair protected by glass. Along the top of it one read in white paint:

THE CHURCH OF ST MICHAEL AND ALL ANGELS PLUMLEY
Vicar: The Revd C. Prowse M.A.
Telephone: Plumley 2

The party paused in front of this, and perused the only notice on view:

On Wed. 13th inst at 7.30p.m.
a meeting will be held at the
Vicarage to make arrangements
for
THE AUTUMN BAZAAR
It is hoped that all prepared
to organize stalls, refreshments etc.
will be able to attend loyally as before
New faces welcome

It was a lonely little notice, having something of the effect of a *cri de coeur*, but with a certain forlorn liveliness occasioned by its having been laboriously printed out in a variety of coloured chalks. Father Hooker regarded it sombrely, as if wondering what the Church Militant was coming to. Most irrationally, Hilda found herself feeling apologetic, and this expressed itself in a distinctly random remark.

'The church is quite small,' she said. 'Almost poky. It wouldn't have much room for St Michael and all the angels.'

'Ah, but—my dear young lady—remember.' It was clear that Father Hooker was about to produce a pleasantry. 'Any number of them has been judged capable of dancing on the point of a needle.'

The effect of this observation was, for some obscure reason, disheartening. There was a moment of silence and immobility. This went even for the dogs, which had so positioned themselves as to be able to sniff each at the other's behind, although surely without any expectation of novelty. The morning ramble from Plumley Park might have been felt as having reached its nadir all too rapidly. It was at this juncture that the young man appeared.

He had issued from the modest porch of the vicarage itself, and he was a *wild* young man. Hilda was aware of this incongruous fact at once. She was aware, too, of a disposition in herself to like wild young men. It was a quality not exhibited by either of her brothers. Charles and Henry, decent youths in the main, could be uncivilized and churlish, but wildness eluded them. Here, however, the quality was evident in this young man striding rapidly towards them. His dark hair, although in fact hanging in a great lock over his right eye, could be imagined as streaming in a gale behind him. He wasn't to be called sharp-featured—he was too handsome for that—but his expression suggested a mind with a cutting edge. He was dressed in stylish near-rags, just as a wild young man should be.

He came up with them as they still stood at the lich-gate. He glanced at the two middle-aged men and uttered a brisk and unpausing good morning. He glanced at Hilda and came to a halt—instantaneously but smoothly, much as if he were a Rolls-Royce.

'Miss Naylor?' he said. 'I think I ought to introduce myself. Simon Prowse. Christopher's nephew.'

'How do you do? This is my uncle, Dr Naylor. And this is Father Hooker, who is paying us a short visit.' Hilda managed this with commendable composure. There was a shaking of hands.

'I had to guess about you,' Simon Prowse said to Hilda. 'I've never been here before. You mayn't have heard of me.'

'No, I never have.'

'Quiet sort of hole to do some reading for Schools next year.'

Simon Prowse seemed to feel he ought to give this explanation without delay. It placed him, of course, as an Oxford man, and presumably still an undergraduate. So he's younger than I am, Hilda thought. I'm ageing fast. She wondered whether Simon was at the vicarage in the character of a paying guest. It was very likely.

'Christopher and Edith are very nice,' Simon said. ('Nice' was

73

an odd word for a wild young man to use. Perhaps it had occurred to him that 'quiet sort of hole' had scarcely been felicitous as the description of a kinsman's dwelling.) 'And here Christopher is. He must have spotted you through the lace curtains and the aspidistra leaves.'

Hilda was unaware of these objects as ever having been on view in the vicarage. But Simon somehow didn't sound like a snob. It was as if the disparaging flight of fancy had an ideological rather than a social implication. Moreover—at least provisionally—it would be sensible to like Simon Prowse. One dislikeable companion at a time was quite enough.

It was true that Christopher Prowse had appeared. He was hurrying down his garden path, making welcoming gestures as he moved. He seemed to take it kindly that the Naylors' theologically distinguished guest had paused even to take an interest in his autumn bazaar.

'Ah, good morning!' he said. 'That was a delightful occasion yesterday evening. I see that you have made the acquaintance of my nephew Simon. Simon is reading with me. Not quite a reading-party in the old-fashioned sense, but a pleasing approximation to it. More accurately, Simon is *going to read* with me, since we haven't quite begun as yet. His Latin set texts. Of course I have been brushing up my own Latin. For all I know, Simon is really ahead of me. If that proves to be the case, it will all be part of the game.'

Simon, Hilda thought, was taking no trouble to look as if he judged it would be *his* sort of game. Latin set texts were, after all, a poor stamping ground for wild young men. Perhaps he was a conscientious son of Prowses unknown, and was at the vicarage because obediently acquiescing in some family arrangement. But he didn't suggest himself as one much given to acquiescence or obedience. In fact there was something a little puzzling about Simon. At this moment he was looking at her frankly and openly in an appraising way. But the appraisal wasn't quite of the sort she might have expected—or so, at least, she felt. He might almost have been trying to decide whether she was—potentially —friend or foe.

'I wonder whether you would care to go into the church?' It was hesitantly that the vicar asked George this question, so that

Hilda wondered whether her uncle's defection had been hinted to him by her parents. Or it was possible that rumours of George's former backsliding had reached him from other parishioners since his own coming to Plumley.

Uncle George agreed at once that they must all look at the church. Even on the exterior, he said, Father Hooker might find matter of interest. The lower courses of the tower were undoubtedly Saxon. The long-and-short work at the corners proved the point.

So they all moved on through the churchyard, which was full of crosses and headstones and displaced lids on empty receptacles—most of them cocked at tumble-down angles in the manner of a mortuary scene by Stanley Spencer. Then they peered up at the tower. Even Bill and Bess, being accustomed to going along with human vagary, elevated their muzzles in air.

'Have a go with these,' Simon said to Hilda. Simon, although she hadn't noticed the fact, had a pair of field-glasses slung from his neck, and these he was now disengaging and handing to her. Although she had known all about the long-and-short work since childhood, she accepted this civility and focused the glasses on the tower before handing them on to Father Hooker. Simon must be a bird-watcher, and had been about to set off on a prowl. When one thought of it, there was a hint of fanaticism about him. Bird-watchers were often like that. In fact bird-watching could be so conducted as to be far from the mildest of hobbies. It might square with wildness readily enough.

They went into the church, Bill and Bess being still of the party. There was an interesting font. There were marble slabs enumerating the virtues of former owners of Plumley Park. There was a small, a becomingly modest slab commemorating George's grandfather, the Naylor who had bought the place. On the wall of the chancel some fragments of mediaeval painting continued a ghostly existence too faintly to be very confidently viewed as depicting St Michael chatting with Moses on the Mount. It was George's father who had commissioned the celebrated Professor Tristram to coax this dubious occasion into demisemi visibility.

The church had an equivocal smell, neither quite dusty nor quite musty. That there was some mammalian or avian component in this was immediately suggested by the indecorous comportment of Bill and Bess. Sniffing and faintly yelping, they were suddenly scampering in a mad excitement all over the place. Rat or rabbit; squirrel, bat, or even owl: dead or alive, there must be something of the sort around. The vicar, perhaps because of that nostalgic feeling for St Francis and his Assisi, regarded with complacency this bad conduct on the part of Brother Dog. St Francis himself, Hilda thought, would have been extremely cross, the kinetic little brutes being so evidently incapable of pausing to listen to a homily. Hilda also expected Father Hooker to be cross now, since he probably had a high standard of the behaviour required in religious edifices. But Father Hooker had been in good humour ever since his appearance at breakfast, and he continued in this vein on the present occasion.

'Aha!' he said. 'Here surely we have the *domini canes*, my dear Mr Prowse. You will recall the famous pun. And somewhere in Florence, I think, there is a pictorial representation of it popularly termed "The Triumph of the Dominican Order". You may recall that too.'

'I don't know that I do,' the vicar said nervously. 'My trip to Italy, a cherished memory, was so very many years . . .'

'The Cappellone degli Spagnuoli in Santa Maria Novella,' the vicar's nephew interrupted impatiently. 'A major thing by Andrea da Firenzi. And there the *domini canes*—or hounds of heaven, if you like—certainly are. A whole piebald pack of them, hunting down the wolves of heresy like mad. Up the Dominicans and down with Arius.'

Hilda was startled by this unexpected performance. The wild young man was also civilized! When herself so recently in Florence she had failed to sign up Santa Maria Novella, perhaps because her guidebook had discouragingly described it as near the railway station. So—much to her vexation—she couldn't join in this sudden burst of culture. San Domenico at Siena was no help at all. Uncle George probably knew all about the *domini canes*, but Uncle George was keeping mum. Perhaps he had some sympathy with Arius. Perhaps—it was a horrid thought—he was mistrusting his ability to stand up to Hooker in their coming disputation. Hilda took it for granted that any such failure would be a disaster. Never having passed through even a brief phase of religious feeling, she couldn't very well do anything else.

But now—driving Bill and Bess before them—they were in the open air again. And at once there was a parting. Simon Prowse had glanced at his watch.

'On my way,' he said, and walked off without further utterance. He must, Hilda supposed, have an appointment with some birds.

It was one of the days on which Edward Naylor went up to town. From these occasions he was increasingly prone to return in poor spirits, and when this happened—when, in his wife's phrase, he was to be regarded as 'jaded'—it had become the custom for Hilda to see him through a late cup of tea. If Mary Naylor undertook the task, she was apt to do so in a mood of anxiety which her husband didn't care for, since it was often his own mood too. Hilda could be relied on to be unostentatiously cheerful. The present occasion was like that. Edward had chaired a meeting at which it had to be decided who here or there should be promoted to this or that—a task which in prosperous times would be regarded as not all that important. But with things now as tight as they were, even a single misjudgement might have serious consequences. And there were men on the Board, Edward was convinced, who would back a misjudgement if they possibly could.

George Naylor, although he knew of this convention of a tête-à-tête, ventured to join his brother and niece. They were the two members of his family whom he found most congenial. And Edward responded to his appearance cordially enough.

'Hardly had a decent word with you,' he said. 'You're sure that fellow isn't at the keyhole?'

'No sugar, you remember,' George said to Hilda. 'My dear Edward, we mustn't regard Hooker as a spy.'

'Guardian angel, eh?'

'Not quite that, either—or not from my point of view. We mustn't forget that the poor fellow's position is a difficult one.'

'Difficult? I don't suppose he has any anxieties about his next month's screw.'

77

George was baffled for a moment by this apparent *non sequitur*. Then he remembered that the financial slant on things must be a constant preoccupation with Edward.

'I mean, in particular, his having been set on me'—George seemed to enjoy this expression—'so briskly. It must make his position with Mary and yourself feel awkward to him.'

'Really, Uncle George!' Hilda exclaimed. 'Can't you see he's not that sensitive sort of person at all?'

'I've very little idea of what sort of person he is. How could I have, after only a day's acquaintance? So I must give him the benefit of every doubt.'

Edward Naylor endorsed this with an emphatic nod—presumably as being a proper sentiment on the part of a parson, or even ex-parson. But precisely this annoyed Hilda. Uncle George should take the freedom of his new position, and stop laying on Christian attitudes so freely. He was in danger of being hung up on them.

'Of course, we all have our troubles,' Edward Naylor said suddenly, and as if his mind had strayed elsewhere. 'They're not to be avoided—in business or out of it.'

'Nothing going too badly, I hope?' George asked. He realized that he had been presented with a cue for some such question as this.

'Unemployment, George. It goes on and on, and up and up. It's a tragedy.'

'Yes, indeed,' George said soberly.

'Reached its optimum donkey's ages ago.'

'Its optimum?' George had repeated the word in perplexity. Hilda's interest sharpened. She was developing a theory that her father owned a dual personality. One personality made all the going while he was being a director of companies in London, and was entirely concerned with material interests and the main chance. The second took over here at home, where he made a very passable country gentleman, acknowledging all the proper responsibilities. With luck, Hilda thought, it might be possible to elaborate an entertaining comparison between this sort of Englishman (who must be fairly common) and those Japanese business men who were said to spend the day wearing bowler hats and carrying brief-cases and furled umbrellas, but then went home and dressed appropriately to a domestic set-up in which no hint of a modern world was permitted. What was particularly worth study in her father was the manner in which the two personalities occasionally played bo-peep or hide-and-seek. Or at least they did this at Plumley, and with pleasing effects of incongruity as a result. Perhaps this was happening now.

'Yes,' Hilda said, backing up her uncle. 'What's optimum unemployment?'

'The optimum comes just before the numbers reach the point at which government has to cut off the pocket-money element in the hand-out. Particularly to the youngsters. So long as they had time on their hands and a bit of money in their pockets, they were our best customers. And we were always coming up with something, you may be sure. The pin-tables and the fruit-machines and the one-armed bandits: they fell off a little, but along came the arcade video games. We looked like hitting the jackpot there. But they're no good without that careless little pile of tenpenny bits, or whatever you call them. I'd no more sink big money in that sort of hardware now than I would in suburban cinemas. The discos are holding up best. You pay for the part of the noise you don't make yourself, but all the fling-around is for free. Thank God we diversified there in time. They even put something in your own pocket, George, old boy.'

This was a genial reference to that little private income. George didn't like it, and a hint of this must have shown on his face.

'Not that I wholly approve of the discos,' Edward Naylor went on rapidly. 'It isn't good for morality, all that near-hysteria. No better than bawdy-houses, some of them, I'm told.'

'What nonsense!' Hilda said. 'Stick to the hard-nosed stuff, daddy, and cut out the rest.'

George now looked dismayed, but whether this was on account of what he took to be a failure in filial piety wasn't clear. And Edward scarcely paused.

'Or demos, now,' he said. 'Arid ground, if any ever was. Not a penny in them! I did try for a corner in anti-nuclear banners and badges, but a clever little oriental chap got ahead of me. And take stadium control. Bigger and better barriers on the terraces, and cut down on your police bills. Sound idea. But no sooner had we started writing the cheques than people stopped going to football matches at all, in case they got a brick or a bottle in the face. Cowardly. No longer any spirit in that whole class of society. I tell you, we've a hard row to hoe.'

'Again, it's a point of view,' George said. 'You know, I hate dire poverty. I hate the very idea of it. But it may be maintained that, in measure, it helps some people to discover that a good many of the best things in life come for free. It's a subversive thought, of course, when the growth of leisure industries is in question.'

'Well, yes. Quite worth thinking about.' Edward Naylor wasn't in the least offended by this clever, if almost incomprehensible talk on the part of his eccentric brother. Hilda, on the other hand, was not, on reflection, quite pleased. Uncle George was right to take her father's innocent spouting not too seriously. But there was something a little facile in that stuff about the best things in life not bringing a bill along with them. It was Sunday Schoolish, in fact. A boy bathing in a stream was happy, but might be the happier for knowing that his new fishing-rod was waiting for him on the bank. If he believed that the possession of a fishing-rod was going to be beyond him for keeps, he mightn't be happy at all. Hilda recalled how once at Oxford she had skimmed through something called a theodicy, written by an eighteenth-century bishop. Where the bishop might have written the word 'poverty' he wrote 'freedom from riches', and he had pointed out that if all you could afford was bread and water you weren't likely to contract gout. Hilda saw that her line of thought here pointed—although a little uncertainly—to the possibility that Uncle George might find it harder to shed certain simple habits of mind and unexamined persuasions than a belief in the Holy Trinity or whatever. Stopping off being a priest was probably a pretty complex affair.

Presently her father was talking about the iniquitous tax you had to pay for the privilege of giving some incompetent new office-boy a job pretty well for life, and Uncle George was listening with every appearance of attention. If patience was regarded as a specifically Christian virtue (but she didn't suppose it was: Stoics and people had recommended it) Uncle

George would certainly need no urging by Father Hooker to retain it. Hilda herself being not all that patient, she made an excuse of clearing up the tea things for leaving the brothers together, and then she went off to her room.

She opened her diary and made some brief notes on what she had been listening to. She closed it and thought—again quite briefly—about Simon Prowse. (He was rather an attractive young man.) After this, she decided to address her mind more seriously to the question of her vocation.

Whenever she did this, it was Hilda's habit to take the lid off the portable typewriter that stood on the desk beside the diary. She did this now—so that the machine was waiting, expectant, to record the comedy that she knew existed all round her. If only she could define it, catch it! She might begin, if not the actual composition, at least the thinking about it where she had left off, which had been with the difficulties of basing a novel on one's own family set-up. But the difficulty she had seen was a moral rather than an aesthetic one: almost no more than the silly business of good taste. Now she saw what might be called the obverse of the proposition. It would all be too damned easy. Provided she distanced and contracted the element of actual theological debate (which was going to come her way very little, in any case) there was enough in the actual goings on around her to provide the material for quite a neat job. Supposing she had set a tape-recorder going during that recent tea-drinking, supposing she carried such a thing around with her through Plumley Park and its environs: supposing this, she would be in possession of what would make, with only a minimum of doctoring and editing, a very average sort of cheerful little modern novel. And what on earth would be the good of that? Of what was simply happening, of what happened all the time, we all had quite as much as we wanted. Straight realism, mere reportage (good word again) was dead boring, and remained so even if given a comic twist or two here and there. *You had to manage a much bigger twist.* That was it! Something out of common expectation, something eruptive and belonging essentially to the imagination, had to be haled in. And in the present case, in which there lurked matter of quite grave import within the Uncle George/Father Hooker charade, what you fished out of the hat had to be somehow equipollent (*meaty* word) with the underlying seriousness of Uncle George's situation. An earthquake, Hilda thought rather wildly. A plague. An unexpected return of the Black Death.

At this point in her reflections there came a knock at Hilda's door. Knocking at doors was prescriptive with the Naylors, and as each person's knock tended to be of slightly different quality, you generally knew who was there even before the door opened. This time it was Hilda's mother. She was at once revealed as wearing what Hilda thought of as her 'vexatious little chore' expression. It would be some *quite* small thing, but the daughter of the house had to provide the helping hand.

'My dear,' Mary Naylor said, 'it's lemons. It seems that Mrs Deathridge is proposing pancakes.' Mrs Deathridge was the cook.

'And there are no lemons. I see.'

'It seems she used the last two lemons when we had those little scraps of smoked salmon the other day. Of course she ought to have put them on the shopping-list. But Mrs Deathridge, you know, is getting on.'

'Aren't we all? But I'll go. I'll go along on my bike.'

'Yes, dear—but of course there's no hurry.' Mrs Naylor looked at her watch. 'Mr Rudkin always keeps open till six.' Mr Rudkin ran the village shop, which was also the post office. 'I think you should get half a dozen, although I believe they are rather expensive nowadays.'

'They oughtn't to be. There were endless acres of the things coming along in Italy.'

'It must be something to do with the Common Market.' This was a favourite thought of Mary Naylor's. 'Mrs Deathridge says she has remembered that your uncle is fond of pancakes. So I didn't like, you see, to suggest she give us something else.'

'Of course we must support Uncle George in every way. Daddy keeps on saying so.'

'And we must be civil, Hilda, to this rather pompous Father Hooker. It is such a serious thing he is trying to help your uncle about. Don't you think?'

'Well, yes—I suppose I do.'

'I am afraid, at times, that your uncle may be tempted to

make fun of him. George can be like that, even when much troubled in mind.'

'So he can.'

'And I'm a little worried about your brothers. It's a shocking thing to say, but they can both at times be rather rude. I'm sure they don't mean to be.'

'You can't be rude without meaning to be rude.' Hilda reacted conscientiously and at once against woolly uses of language.

'No, dear—of course not.' Mrs Naylor was entirely pacificatory. 'I wonder whether you could just give Charles and Henry a hint?'

'No, mummy, I could not.' Hilda said this decisively.

'But mightn't it come best from you? You are all young, and do so wonderfully understand one another.'

'It would only be counter-productive.' Hilda didn't much care for this very current expression, but she was clear that nannying her brothers was a vexatious little chore that simply wasn't on. 'I think I'll go for those lemons straight away.'

'Good! But there is just one more thing.' There was usually one thing more when Mrs Naylor conversed with her daughter, since she would have liked a fuller confidential relationship than in fact existed between them. 'When you all met Mr Prowse at the church this morning did you get the impression that he *knows*?'

'About Uncle George's difficulties, you mean? I don't think he does. But I suppose he's bound to tumble to the situation sooner or later. I don't see that just when is very important.'

'What I'm wondering, Hilda, is whether Father Hooker may think it part of his own duty to tell our parish priest, and whether it mightn't come better from one of ourselves.'

'Christopher Prowse isn't Uncle George's parish priest. It's none of his business, I'd suppose. And, in any case, it's something that ought to be left to Uncle George himself.'

'I'm sure you are right, dear.' Mrs Naylor was quite a strong-minded woman in small patches, but with her family it was becoming one of her pleasures to do a good deal of giving in. 'Perhaps,' she added, '*four* lemons. Only the other day, your father was saying we must be careful. It was when Charles

83

started talking about a new Mercedes. But I suppose what goes for motor cars goes for lemons as well.'

'*Four* lemons, then,' Hilda said, and prepared to set out on her errand.

Mr Rudkin's shop lay at the far end of the village, just beyond the church and vicarage. On this occasion, as Hilda cycled past, there was no sign of Simon Prowse, whether peering through aspidistra leaves or otherwise. (But why should there be? Hilda judged it odd that she had thought of him.) In the shop, however, she came on Simon's hostess, carrying a capacious basket. It was almost closing time, and Mr Rudkin's messenger-boy was already fiddling with the shutters. Mr Rudkin himself was attending in an appropriately semi-deferential way upon the vicar's wife. (He would a little step up the attitude when it came to Hilda's turn.) Hilda had a notion—or perhaps now invented a notion—that Edith Prowse came into the shop regularly at this hour in the hope of acquiring at a reduced price the more perishable of its residual stock of vegetables. The Prowses had no children, so Hilda supposed they couldn't be exactly desperate. But she knew that it wasn't only mice that were free from riches (and consequently from the threat of gout) in churches. The knowledge didn't make her feel exactly uncomfortable. It did, however, make her a little wary. She mustn't, for example, embark now on her mother's comical decision that it had better be four, and not six lemons. So she was still thinking up a line of harmless talk when Mrs Prowse addressed her with enthusiasm.

'Oh Hilda, how particularly nice to run into you! To have the opportunity, I mean, of saying what a delightful dinner that was. Do tell your mother how much Christopher and I enjoyed it. In my own mother's time—do you know?—one wrote little notes, or at least left cards, after dining with friends. It's a pity, in some ways, that such punctilios have died out. And yet our own casual informalities have their merit. Don't you think?'

Hilda allowed herself to agree that casual informalities are to be commended. It was rather a line of Edith Prowse's, she remembered, to hint at small grandeurs in her family back-ground.

'My uncle and his friend Father Hooker,' she said in the correct Plumley chit-chat manner, 'were delighted to make the acquaintance of your nephew. Am I right that his name is Simon? I didn't quite catch it.' This untruth surprised Hilda in the utterance.

'Yes—Simon. A delightful young man. Quite an acquisition, indeed. And so totally unexpected!'

'Unexpected, Edith?'

'Well, we hadn't heard from him for a long time. Indeed, Hilda, I don't believe we had ever heard from him *at all*. Except, of course, for Christmas cards.'

'There are lots of people like that—who feel that a card at Christmas is a sufficient link with relations.'

'I suppose so. Christmas *does* mean something to everybody, don't you think?'

'Well, yes—I suppose it does.'

'So Simon's proposal turned up quite out of the blue: that he should come to the vicarage and that Christopher should help him with his exam.'

'It seems a very good idea.'

'Yes—but Christopher has become a little uneasy about it. I don't mean about his own ability to coach Simon. Christopher keeps up his scholarship very well.'

'I'm sure he does, Edith. Even although he's so busy a man.'

'Yes, indeed. Well, only this afternoon he persuaded Simon to produce his books, and they looked at them together. And Christopher felt that Simon has a long way to go.' Edith Prowse hesitated for a moment here. 'He doesn't feel that Simon can really have been doing any serious work at all.'

'But doesn't that make Simon Prowse's decision to have some coaching all the more sensible?'

'I suppose, Hilda, one can look at it that way.' Mrs Prowse glanced cautiously round Mr Rudkin's shop. But they were now the only customers, and Mr Rudkin himself was helping with the shutters. Even so, Mrs Prowse lowered her voice. 'We have even begun to wonder whether there may not be a *romance*.'

'A romance?' Hilda repeated a shade coldly.

'A lady in the case—and in the neighbourhood.' Mrs Prowse

now glanced at Hilda as with a suddenly inspired suspicion. 'Simon does a great deal of telephoning. But not from the vicarage. He says he doesn't want to muck up our account. He telephones from the kiosk outside this shop.'

'Well, he doesn't telephone to *me*,' Hilda said tartly.

'My dear Hilda!' Mrs Prowse seemed overwhelmed with confusion. 'I'd never dream . . .'

'Of course not, Edith. But do you really suspect that Mr Prowse may be carrying on—well, an intrigue of some sort from the shelter of your house? It would be most dishonourable.' Hilda was about to add, 'And wholly unworthy of him'. But she stopped herself, reflecting that as she had appeared to be uncertain even of the young man's Christian name she was not in a position to make so bold a statement. 'Perhaps,' she suggested ingeniously, 'Mr Prowse has been bitten by what they call the turf, and comes down here to telephone his bets.'

'Oh, dear! That would be just as bad. But we must simply hope for the best.' Edith Prowse was now looking at a single fatigued lettuce lingering in one of Mr Rudkin's boxes, and she might almost have been referring to it. Hilda felt that perhaps their conversation was over, and she walked across to another box and possessed herself of four quite healthy lemons. But Mrs Prowse followed her.

'Christopher and I both felt,' she said, 'that Dr Naylor is looking a little strained. Settlement work must be so exhausting! I hope he has come to you on quite a substantial visit?'

'I hope so too.'

'And Father Hooker—such an interesting man! Christopher looked him up in Crockford. Are they friends of long standing?'

'Uncle George and Father Hooker? I haven't inquired, Edith. I'm afraid I haven't the trick of asking questions.' Hilda was conscious that this had been an unkind and unnecessary barb to direct upon a harmless woman. 'I think they have concerns in common.'

'Of course they all do, don't they?' Mrs Prowse was here referring, a shade archly, to the cloth in general. 'Do you know? Christopher has had such a bold idea! I hardly venture to mention it. But perhaps I may be allowed to take soundings.' Mrs Prowse made a pause on this, but elicited no response.

'Christopher is wondering whether he might venture to ask Father Hooker to preach next Sunday.'

'Oh, I see.' Hilda remembered there had been family anxiety lest the vicar should make this request of Uncle George, with possibly an embarrassing result. But the Prowses now had their eye, it seemed, on what they conceived to be superior talent. Hilda wasn't pleased. 'I don't know why not,' she said. 'The man should be flattered at being asked, I suppose. And he needn't accept if he doesn't want to.'

'Yes. of course. But we could put up such an attractive notice if he did! And congregations have been so very poor recently that it's really quite disheartening.'

Hilda saw that it must be that, and was conscious that she herself had of late been doing little in the way of church-going.

'We have had considerable hopes,' Edith Prowse went on, 'from that new place at Nether Plumley, which has to do with being very scientific about animals—although we don't quite know how. A government department—is it Health and Social Security?—has bought up a lot of houses round about to provide accommodation for the staff. Very highly qualified university people for the most part, we understand. So, naturally, we might have hoped. . .'

'Certainly, you might.' Hilda had interrupted simply because she found this innocence about the drift of the modern scientific mind rather alarming. 'Look,' she said impulsively. 'If you like, I'll ask Father Hooker for you this evening. Take soundings, as you call it.'

'Christopher will be *so* grateful! And I must fly.' Mrs Prowse, deciding to reject the lettuce, hurried over to settle her affairs with a respectfully impatient Mr Rudkin. Hilda, feigning to meditate a further purchase, gave her a couple of minutes to be clear of the shop. She then paid for the lemons and went out to her bicycle.

Encounters like that, she told herself, make me feel like a character in Barbara Pym. Perhaps that's what I am: *anima naturaliter Pym*. Having succumbed to an unacknowledged passion for Christopher Prowse, I shall become his most assiduous parishioner, never absent from any of the goings-on in his church. I shall preside over tea-urns and embroider hassocks—or perhaps even slippers for the adored one—as a Victorian lady would do. I shall make an edifying end, and Edith Prowse will particularly mourn me as having been, next to herself, her husband's staunchest stay. Such is to be the destiny of Hilda Naylor, who for a brief span in youth gave promise of larger things. At the moment, out of mere good nature, I have engaged myself to ask Father Hooker to preach a sermon in St Michael and All Angels. Angelic of me, is it not.

But seriously—she asked herself as she began to pedal—might something not be done with the parish as *mise en scène?* It would be territory a little less contracted than the family, but still eminently compassable. *Cranford* stuff. Her tutor had once told her to read a book called *Annals of the Parish* by a certain John Galt. Of course she had failed to do so. But what about *New Annals of the Parish,* by Hilda Naylor? Or—to be quite splendidly old-world—*by Miss Naylor?* Or, yet again and with a splendid fantasy, *by* (some equivalent of) *Currer, Ellis, and Acton Bell?*

The church was at the head of a short rise, and Hilda changed gear: she had rather a developed bicycle, much less elderly than her car. It was tiresome to own so flippant a mind. The hopeless snag about *New Annals* would be having to accept as a datum the fact that in the parish nothing ever happens. It takes a Chekhov to get along on nullibiety (*marvellous* word) and even Chekhov takes a break: a shot is fired and a man senselessly dies; another shot achieves comic futility; there is the sound of an axe biting into a tree. No such resources in Plumley.

She was now abreast of the vicarage. It was still broad daylight on this summer evening, but there was a light in an attic window. Had a reformed Simon, inspired by his studious uncle, symbolically turned up the lamp and applied himself to his books? Even that would be quite something in this obscure village. But where are the eagles and the trumpets? Where that eruptive, that equipollent thing?

There was no light in the church, since it wasn't business hours. Hilda glanced at the familiar notice-board. *Vicar: The Revd C. Prowse M.A.* There was still the announcement about the autumn bazaar. But now there was another notice, balancing the first one on the other half of the board. Perhaps just because

Edith Prowse had made a remark about putting up a notice, Hilda's attention was caught by this. It was something brief and boldly lettered, but she couldn't quite read it as she rode. So she dismounted and took a closer look. What the thing said was:

BAN THE BOMB

'What the bloody hell!'

Startled by this exclamation close to her left ear, Hilda turned her head. Simon Prowse was standing beside her. He was staring at the notice-board, and clearly in a state of considerable indignation.

'Oh, good evening,' Hilda said.

'Hallo, Miss Naylor. Sorry if I made you jump.'

'You didn't make me jump.' Hilda resented being aspersed as a nervous female. 'It is a little odd, isn't it? That printed sticker, I mean. One sees them here and there. But I haven't seen one on a church notice-board before.'

'And you won't see it on this one for long.' Simon took a step forward and reached up an arm. It was obvious that he intended to rip the thing away.

'Hold hard, Simon!' Hilda said—and was momentarily confused. She ought to have said 'Mr Prowse' for one thing. And, for another, 'Hold hard!' was surely a peculiarly mannish expression. It had probably originated among jolly Jack Tars hauling on ropes. She ought to have managed a pleading 'Do wait a moment, please', or something like that.

'What do you mean—hold hard?' Demanding this, Simon did however lower his arm.

'Don't you think it may have been put up by your uncle? Or at least been approved by him in some way?'

'Put up by Christopher? By a *parson*? Don't make me laugh.'

'I don't care whether I make you laugh or not, Mr Prowse.' Hilda was enraged by this improper contempt and—as she conceived it—puppyish ignorance. 'Don't you know that it's a very live issue among the parsons, as you call them? There was a terrific to-do not all that long ago—surely you remember?— with letters in *The Times*, and I don't know what. Bishops and people all at jar together and by the ears.' Hilda paused for breath—and also because again in trouble with the craft of words. 'At jar together and by the ears' was hopelessly archaic and literary. 'Whether to retain the bomb or not,' she said. 'It's the most overwhelmingly important issue of our time.' She paused on this. 'And so,' she added, 'when one is beginning to think of growing up one ought to be keeping a cool head about it, and not go bloody-helling and flying off the handle.'

The effect of this outburst on Simon Prowse was marked but perplexing. He seemed at a loss for words, and even for an attitude. When he did speak, it was while eyeing her narrowly. Hilda didn't mind being eyed, simply as something that even well-conducted young men went in for in a quiet way. But she disliked what she seemed to detect as a certain intensity of regard in Simon. Perhaps he was working out just what her clothes concealed—much as a judge at a dog show (she had been told) endeavours to discern precisely what musculature underlies one or another woolly canine integument. Perhaps he was impertinently speculating about how far this simple village maiden would let him go.

'Yes, of course,' he said. 'You're no doubt right about the bomb in a general way. But I'm sure that poor old Christopher wouldn't go out on a limb about it at his own front gate. So having put up this thing *is* bloody cheek—and in a place like placid Plumley won't do any good anyway. Contrariwise, in fact. Spotlight the thing. Set people talking. Silly little bitch!'

'Mr Prowse!'

'I beg your pardon!' Very properly, Simon was much confused. 'You didn't think I was saying that to *you*, did you? I was just thinking it must be some fool of a girl who's going round advertising herself and her lofty beliefs by sticking up these things at random. That's all.'

Hilda was mollified by this, but felt at the same time that Simon Prowse was an oddly incoherent young man. She could make very little sense of his attitude.

'All the same,' she said firmly, 'I think we'd better leave the thing as it is.'

'Very well.' Simon was suddenly good-humoured again. 'It's your stamping ground, I suppose—your father being lord of the broad estates and the hall.'

'There aren't any broad estates.' Hilda had felt Simon's Tennysonian crack to have been in doubtful taste, but she was now determined not to appear censorious. So she laughed as if at a good joke, and at this the young man brightened at once.

'I say!' he exclaimed impulsively. 'May I ask you something?'

'Yes, of course.'

'Just how far would you be prepared to go?'

Fortunately—as it immediately turned out—Hilda didn't rise to another outraged 'Mr Prowse!' She merely stared at him in complete astonishment.

'What I mean is,' Simon said, 'that I can tell, somehow, that you're against the bomb: making it, and storing it, and deploying it, and everything else. Right?'

Hilda was silent for a moment. At Oxford she had discussed the bomb with friends often enough, and even debated it with strangers on some formal occasions. But she wasn't quite sure that she wanted to be challenged about it by Christopher Prowse's nephew and pupil in this oddly equivocal fashion. She wished she hadn't got off her bicycle and been found staring at that stupid notice-board.

'Well, yes,' she said. 'I'm against it in the sense that I find it wholly horrifying. Surely nearly everybody does.'

'Are you prepared to take it lying down?'

'Lying down?'

'Literally, for that matter.' There was now something almost malicious in Simon's glance. 'Suppose they decided to truck a missile of some sort into your park. Would you be prepared to say, "Over my dead body", and lie down in front of it?'

'It would be a silly and rhetorical thing to say. I'd know there wasn't going to be any dead body—only some cops, male or female, hauling me out of the way. But the actual token physical resistance has more to be said for it. About myself, I don't know. Perhaps it would depend on just how I felt at the time.'

Hilda judged that this, if a bit feeble, was at least honest. And Simon seemed quite to approve of it, although it was detectably in a rather inattentive fashion. In a different sense he was being attentive enough, collecting her bicycle from the wall against which it was leaning, and bringing it up to her. She decided that their conversation had taken the turn it had because he had supposed it would interest her, and that his more active thoughts lay elsewhere. Something of the sort now appeared.

'I say!' he said. 'Can you tell me anything about tennis prospects in these parts? I've brought my things, but they don't have a court at the vicarage. And, anyway, old Christopher doesn't play.'

As there was a tennis court at the Park, and as Simon had probably heard of it, there was perhaps something a shade shameless in this request for information. But Hilda wasn't offended. She found herself not knowing whether she liked Simon Prowse, but she was candidly aware that she liked the look of him.

'Our own court is in quite decent order,' she said. 'And both my brothers are at home just now. You must come up some time and play with them. Charles, who's the elder, is average, but it seems that Henry is going to be county standard, at least.'

'It sounds intimidating.' Simon paused, so that it was with a slightly unfortunate effect of afterthought that he asked, 'And you?'

'Oh, I knock the thing about at times. But I'm not serious.'

'Ah, but I am. So it sounds quite splendid. I'll be most grateful.' Simon glanced at Hilda, and appeared to feel that this asseveration had been lacking in conviction. 'Oh, I know!' he said. 'The Letters of Pliny the Younger and God knows what else with Christopher. I must put my neck in the collar if I'm to stick the course at Oxford and get so much as a half-blue for anything. You see, Hilda, one of nature's playboys—that's me.'

Pedalling home, Hilda was aware of perplexity which for some minutes she couldn't explain to herself. Then she got it. There was surely something to think about in one of nature's playboys who could, at the drop of a handkerchief, turn briskly informative on the Cappellone degli Spagnuoli in Santa Maria Novella. The wild young man, in fact, was disposed to make fun of her.

She wondered whether she resented this, or whether she welcomed it as something to take note of and analyse. Simon Prowse was barely an acquaintance as yet, so any sort of setting out to tease her hadn't been quite mannerly. But had that been what he was about? Had he been saying to himself, 'Here's a jolly sort of girl I can start talking nonsense to at once'—and fired off that rubbish about being a simple hearty with a mind only for things like tennis and half-blues? (It certainly wasn't *true* of him: even without that inadvertent stuff about Andrea da Firenzi she'd somehow have been sure of that.) Had he decided she was herself an uncomplicated athletic type, and did he propose embarking upon improper designs on that basis? There would be a certain faint gratification to be extracted from this, but something hinted to her she wasn't entitled even to such a crumb. Simon Prowse had no design upon her at all. Indefinably but without doubt, his mind was on other things.

This was mysterious. But then young men were supposed to be just that in the regard of maidens standing with reluctant feet etc. It wasn't a psychological fact accorded much prominence in novels and things nowadays, but it might be a fact all the same. She remembered being told—although she hadn't checked up on it—that Jane Austen had never embarked upon a scene in which young men engaged in talk among themselves. Yet Miss Austen must have had plenty of scope for observation and even eavesdropping, having been endowed with five brothers older than herself—two of whom became admirals and one of whom lived to be ninety-one. (Much conscientious note-making as a student could still burden Hilda's thinking with irrelevant detail.) She had only two brothers herself, but she didn't feel that she'd be helpless if set to reproduce a good deal of their tête-à-tête conversation.

At this point, and as she shoved her bicycle away in its shed, Hilda had one of her ideas. Why not write a novel with quite a large cast, exclusively composed of males? It would be a test of virtuosity and invention, and some reviewers would call it silly and others would call it the cat's whiskers. Its title could be simply *The Men*. Or it could be something sophisticated, like *Priapic Persons*. *Priapic Persons* by Hilda Naylor. Once more, Hilda had to charge herself as being of incurably flippant mind. It was with this weighing upon her that, rounding the house to enter by the front door, she ran into that least flippant of men, Father Hooker.

Hooker had presumably emerged to take the evening air, and possibly to engage in meditation or contemplation or some similar professional activity. He had resumed his clerical attire, no doubt in preparation for the dinner-table.

'A perfect summer evening, Miss Naylor,' Father Hooker said informatively. 'I am thinking of a little stroll through your rose garden. It is remarkable how vivid the colours become as the sun drops towards the horizon. Have you by any fortunate chance a few minutes in which you are free to join me?'

This was rather on the formal side, but Hilda didn't find herself objecting to it. Father Hooker was at least a brisk change from Simon Prowse.

'Yes, of course,' she said. 'You must see the *Moyesii*.' (Hilda had been properly brought up.) 'Bronzy-scarlet—and with marvellous red hips later on.'

'I think I know a red Cabbage when I meet one, but am not well-instructed beyond that. Like Coleridge, you see, I was a liveried schoolboy in the depths of the huge city pent.' Hooker paused on this: it perhaps intimated that he had taken the trouble to find out how Hilda had occupied herself at Oxford. 'Like Coleridge' was rather comical. But Hooker must be given his due. It was easy to see him as indecently hounding Uncle George, but she must remember that, from his own standpoint, his mission was as important as a mission could be. It was difficult to hold on to that perception. Except perhaps for Henry, Hilda reflected, the rest of her family would have no grasp of it at all.

They were now among the roses. Father Hooker sniffed at them here and there—rather as he might have sniffed at an inhalant if he had a cold in the head. Hilda remembered that she had business to transact with him, and that here was an opportunity to get through with it in decent privacy.

'I have a message for you,' she said. 'It's from Mr Prowse. He'd like you to preach at matins next Sunday.'

Father Hooker came to a halt, frowning. He was obviously very much surprised.

'Dear me!' he said. 'I am, of course, gratified. But why should your vicar think to employ an emissary—even one as charming as yourself?'

Hilda, although she thought this pretty awful, managed a friendly smile.

'Christopher Prowse is a rather retiring sort of person,' she said. 'And my uncle has preached for him once or twice. He must have thought it would be nice to have a change—and that you would be quite a catch, of course.'

'A catch, Miss Naylor?' Not unreasonably, Father Hooker suspected he was being made game of.

'I'm sorry. I mean that the chance of a distinguished preacher is probably something that particularly attracts Mr Prowse at present. Congregations have been becoming pretty thin, and he would like to see some of the new people in the district turning up. Especially the scientists from a research place of some sort that has opened up at Nether Plumley. Perhaps the Prowses are a shade naïve in their hopes there. Scientists aren't—are they?—too keen on religion as a general rule.'

'My dear Miss Naylor, that, if I may say so, is a rash remark. That there is necessarily a conflict between religion and science must be indicted, indeed, as a vulgar error. I dislike it the more because—if I may interject a personal note—my own education was scientific in the first place. I graduated as a physicist.'

'How very interesting.' Hilda really did find it to be that. And although Father Hooker laboured under the social disability of being unable to talk other than like a book, she noted to herself the curious fact that she was coming to feel a certain respect for him. 'And did you hold down a job as a physicist?' she asked.

'Certainly I did. I was twenty-seven before the conviction came to me that mine should be another vocation. Just what happens at Nether Plumley?'

'I don't know much about it. Nobody does, I think. But it's called the Institute of Animal Genetics.'

'Dear me! When I was still a boy almost every English university had a Professor of Oriental Languages. Animal Genetics suggests a similar sweep. But we stray from our subject, Miss Naylor—which is Mr Prowse's very kind suggestion. Is he aware, do you know, of your uncle's present difficulties?'

'I'm almost sure he doesn't know about Uncle George's decision at all.' Hilda came out firmly with what she judged to be the proper word. 'So if you can't act, he may invite Uncle George again. It might be embarrassing.'

'Yes. Yes, indeed. I think I had better call on Mr Prowse and discuss the matter. In the wider context we are both so painfully aware of, Miss Naylor.'

'I don't know that I feel pain about it.'

'No, no—I must speak only for myself. And I ought to say that I judge my position among you to be extremely delicate. It is not as if I were in any sense an old family friend. Or even a former college-mate or colleague of Dr Naylor's. I really don't think I ought to undertake to preach in your parish church. Of course I would make no reference whatever—no, not in the most oblique fashion—to the unhappy situation you and your parents and brothers are aware of. Nevertheless, it would be an aggressive thing to do, Miss Naylor. I should not be happy in it.'

At this point Hilda felt her newly fledged respect for Father Hooker increase. But she also—and very shockingly—felt a spirit of mischief stir in her.

'I really think you should accept the vicar's invitation,' she said.

'No!' This time Father Hooker spoke quite sharply. 'It is not my business to attempt to edify a rural congregation. I am here to bring your uncle back to the truth in Christ.'

'Yes, of course.' To Hilda this was startling language, and she told herself she had better belt up. But her sense of comedy was too much for her. 'I suppose,' she asked, 'that my uncle *could* preach, if Mr Prowse were to ask him?'

'I scarcely understand you.'

'I mean, he hasn't been prohibited or inhibited or in one way or another turfed out by a bishop or anything?'

'Good heavens, no!' Father Hooker was appalled. 'Dr Naylor remains an ordained Anglican priest. And for that matter—as you must surely know, my dear young lady—a layman may with perfect propriety be invited to preach or deliver an address from an Anglican pulpit. Your uncle could certainly preach, and indeed take duty for the entire service. But, of course, he wouldn't want to.'

'Can we be sure?'

'Sure! In his present sad state of mind it would be highly indecorous. Indeed, it would be reprehensible.'

'Father Hooker, I think you are a keen observer of human character.' Hilda produced this impertinent bouquet unblushingly. 'You must have become aware that my uncle has at times a rather dangerous sense of fun?'

'It may be so.' Father Hooker appeared cautious, even a shade apprehensive. '*Hilaritas* is a quality proper in a Christian. Our Roman friends even require evidence of it when beatification is in question.'

'What if Uncle George took *hilaritas* a bit far in St Michael and All Angels?'

'Impossible! It would be totally out of character.'

Hilda was silent for a moment, since she knew this to be true. Then she tried something else.

'But, Father Hooker, even if he remained quite serious, mightn't it turn awkard? My uncle is rather impulsive.'

'So he is.' Father Hooker was perhaps recalling that sudden question directed at the business person in the train.

'He might think he ought to explain himself to the congregation. He can be very direct, you know, and at times a little ingenuous as well. He might discuss, and rather unfavourably, what I believe are called the evidences of the Christian religion. It would be well above our rustic heads. But he wouldn't think of that.'

'You are perfectly right. We cannot be too careful. Occasion of scandal is above all things to be avoided.' Father Hooker was now seriously alarmed. 'It will be prudent for me to accept Mr Prowse's invitation. I will call on him tomorrow morning and express my pleasure in the prospect. And I am most grateful to you, Miss Naylor: *most* grateful.'

Hilda managed only a mutter by way of concluding this extravagant episode. She ought, she felt, to have the grace to be ashamed of herself. But at least there was now no danger of Christopher Prowse's inviting her uncle into his pulpit. And while it was nonsense to have pretended that Uncle George might have accepted such an invitation, it was very possible that he would have been distressed at receiving it.

Hilda was thus able to conclude that she had done one good deed for the day. She performed a second by delivering her four lemons to Mrs Deathridge in her kitchen.

IV

'DO YOU KNOW what your mother's up to?' Henry Naylor asked his sister next morning. The Naylor young often said 'your mother' and 'your father' to one another, since it sounded amusingly old-world. 'Garnishing the torture chamber for friend Hooker.'

'What do you mean: the torture chamber?'

'The smoking-room, as it used to be called. Nobody ever goes near it. It's to be where Uncle George and the minder talk things out.'

'I've gathered they're more likely to do that during quiet walks on the downs.'

'Well, yes. But when there was a religious caterpillar called Hunter here before, it seems there was a spell of bad weather during which the Inquisition applied the thumb-screws in the smoking-room. So your mother's busy adorning it with roses now—just in case. She thinks it may assuage the agony.'

'What a laboured joke. And Hooker won't notice the roses unless they're cabbages.'

'Cabbages?'

'Cabbage roses. Hooker recognizes them at once.'

'There can't be roses called cabbages. Not even gardening females can have thought up anything so silly as that.'

'Well, there are.'

'Hilda Naylor, you lie.'

Absurd conversations of this sort were prescriptive between Hilda and her brothers from time to time. Hilda was commonly prepared to be amused by them. And although she felt merely impatient on the present occasion, she continued the game almost by rote.

'Henry Naylor,' she said, 'you are an ignorant baboon.'

'You'll be telling me next that cabbage roses are an unhealthy green.'

'They're round and red and compact and double, as a matter of fact.'

'Double? And a lot of toil and trouble?'

'You can do sums, Henry. But that apart, you have a rag-bag mind.'

'I haven't, as a matter of fact.' Henry appeared to offer this by way of whimsical confidence. 'Any more sisterly chat?'

'No—except that a young man wants to come and play tennis.'

'With us, you mean?'

'Yes, of course. He's staying with the Prowses, and he pretty well invited himself.'

'Wasn't that a bit forward? What's his name?'

'He's a Prowse, too—a nephew of the vicar's. Simon, I think I gathered.'

'Does he look any good?'

'Oh, definitely. A clean-run athletic type, without much between the ears.' Hilda remembered that this was a judgement that had to be qualified. 'Though with some scraps of civilized information,' she added concessively. 'He's to be coached or crammed by Christopher Prowse for Schools next year. Something involving some gobbets of Latin if he's to scrape through. At least I rather gathered it's like that.'

'You mean he's an undergraduate at Oxford?' Being himself a postulant for that condition, Henry couldn't give this question too censorious a tone.

'Yes—but I haven't gathered at what college.'

'One would expect a Prowse to be somewhere pretty obscure.' This reflection put Henry in immediate good humour. 'I suppose we'd better have him along. But three men, and one woman getting on in life, aren't much good on a tennis court. We'd need another wench, and I can't think of any of the locals I'd particularly want to encourage. Do you think this Prowse could bring a girl with him?'

'It's most unlikely, I'd say.' Unconsciously, Hilda spoke with a hint of satisfaction. 'He only arrived a day or two ago, and he hasn't ever been to Plumley before. Call on him this afternoon, Henry, and fix something.'

'Call on him—me?' This from Henry was mere ritual. Although only a woman, Hilda Naylor had learnt not to be submissive to her younger siblings. In fact she gave them orders when she wanted to.

At this moment the elder of them came into the room. Charles Naylor appeared to be in a bad temper. He had been oiling his gun, and then shoving it out of sight and mind. His invitation to Scotland had arrived. But, outrageously, it was for the first week of August and a bit of fishing.

'Here comes young Sunshine,' Henry said. Henry had got wind of his brother's misfortune. 'Lucky that we have this Hooker to hand. He can lay on the comforts of religion.'

'To hell with Hooker and black-beetles all,' Charles said morosely. 'And we needn't even except Uncle George, since he's asking for his cards. A blameless ex-black-beetle henceforth.'

'We can't be sure of that yet,' Henry said. 'Hooker may win. The previous chap did. I don't know that it was a calamity.'

'I wish we could send Hooker packing. A regular pain in the neck is Hooker.'

'I think, Charles, that we ought to stop talking about Father Hooker like that.' Hilda, as she said this, wasn't failing to remember that she had herself applied this expression to their guest in the not very distant past. Her view of the man was undoubtedly changing. 'If we do it behind his back, the feeling will begin to show through in his presence. And that would be disgusting—let alone distressing Uncle George no end.'

This virtuous speech didn't surprise the young men. They would have spoken of it as a turn Hilda sometimes put on, but were chastened by it, all the same. They may even have felt occasionally that their sister supplied something their mother came a little short on. But Hilda now felt she had been a bit of a prig, and sought to redress the balance.

'As for the comforts of religion,' she said, 'they're going to be offered you, Henry, on Sunday. Hooker is going to do Christopher's preaching for him.'

There was a short silence while the brothers digested this, and then Henry spoke.

'Good God!' he said. 'We'll have to go.'

'Certainly we shall. And considering that your father is the vicar's churchwarden, that pew with its little stick has been untenanted recently more than is decent.'

'What *is* a churchwarden?' Charles asked. 'I've never understood. And there's another little stick on the other side of the aisle.'

'That's the parishioners' churchwarden's.'

'Who's he?'

'Mr Rudkin, of course. You really are a shocking ignoramus, Charles.'

'Naylor and Rudkin,' Henry said. 'The two commercial pillars of Plumley are its religious pillars too. What could be more proper?'

'It seems that Christopher hankers after a few scientific pillars as well,' Hilda continued. 'He'd like to see some of the people from that affair at Nether Plumley show themselves in church.'

'To profess themselves Christians?' Charles asked. 'Why, they don't even profess themselves drinkers. Never seen in the pubs. The godly Christopher is being unreasonable.'

'You'd certainly know about the pubs, Charles ,' Henry said ungraciously. Henry had only very lately attained the age at which pubs become legal territory, and being fresh-faced and consequently rather juvenile in appearance could still attract a misdoubting glance from a barman or (even more humiliatingly) a barmaid. Hilda, when annoyed with him, would quote a tag from some poet about the distress of boyhood changing into man, the unfinished man and his pain. Henry didn't care for that at all.

The weather continued fine, so the smoking-room wasn't brought into use. Nor did Uncle George and Father Hooker take those secluded walks over the downs. They either sat in a little arbour in full view of the house, or strolled up and down the terrace, similarly exposed to view. The terrace was the most impressive feature of Plumley Park, having been constructed by some past owner with ideas above his modest squirarchal station. There was a balustrade, somewhat inconveniently continuous in the interest of enhanced consequence, and terminated at either end by broad flights of shallow steps. There were half a dozen statues, three of which had worn quite well; and a further embellishment had been admitted in the form of several large if not very meaningful stone urns. What saved the terrace from seeming pretentious was the view to be obtained from it. The view stood up to the terrace, and the terrace stood up to the view.

Plumley village, although quite close by, was concealed by a patch of rising ground, but even in summer respectfully intimated its presence by a few spirals of blue-grey smoke from the humble hearths of its inhabitants. Across the park the vista was interrupted only by the Plumley oaks: a senatorial company which seemed to have drawn unusually close together as if in resistance to a disturbing condition of things in the world without. Beyond this the terrain sloped down to Nether Plumley at a distance convenient for remarking through field-glasses that not much seemed to happen there—except, no doubt, in the scientific establishment lately planted down on its outskirts: a functional and graceless building like a large white plastic toy, from the centre of which rose a single tall dark chimney-stack suggestive of a finger pointing menacingly into the heavens.

Watching her uncle and his companion perambulating before this backdrop, Hilda found herself speculating with some uneasiness about just what was cooking. Nothing that could confidently be diagnosed as a dispute made itself evident. Disputation in the mediaeval and technical sense of the word was another matter. Each of the two scholars involved (to employ a term equally applicable, no doubt, to both Uncle George and Father Hooker) tended to speak at some length, his interlocutor listening attentively the while. There would then be a considering pause, which might last throughout a stroll from one end of the terrace to the other. Then there would be an equally long and obviously carefully phrased reply, similarly received with courteous concentration. The performance was occasionally varied by the two learned persons coming to a stop, turning to survey the landscape at large, and seemingly offering each other remarks of a topographical rather than a polemical order. Oxford dons—it occurred to Hilda—had probably behaved in this way in their quadrangles and gardens long ago, before the sick hurry and divided aims of the modern world had reduced them to a ceaseless scurrying here and there just like other people. There were eighteenth-century engravings and aquatints of the academic scene that exactly caught this effect.

It came to Hilda that Uncle George and Father Hooker were enjoying themselves! Could such a monstrous state of affairs really have arisen? (For the moment Hilda saw it as precisely that.) Could her uncle, hard upon passing through as searing an experience, surely, as could befall a serious man, possibly be deriving pleasure from theological chit-chat with Hooker? Did Hooker, whom her brothers regarded so confidently as an utter ass, and whom she herself had so lately been laughing at, have it in him to engage the respectful attention of Uncle George? Hilda hadn't got far in asking herself these rhetorical questions before she identified what was actually vexing her. Was Hooker saying things like *'Certum est quia impossibile est'*, and was Uncle George responding with *'Distinguo'* —or perhaps with the merely vernacular 'I reject Tertullian's dreadful sentence'? She hadn't a clue. She was going to be a writer. But to project herself into the minds of either of these men, to find words for them to say, was totally beyond both the range of her knowledge and the twitch of her imaginative tether. Even her uncle, whom she had known since a child, was a sealed book to her. Both of them were that. *Fontes signati*, as some wormy old phrase had it. Were those two, facetiously typed by Henry as at opposite ends of the stick in a torture chamber, birds of a feather at heart? Hilda didn't know. She was without a net to cast over them and find out.

Quite soon she had to restrain herself from compulsively peeping through windows at the discoursing pair—almost as if through those aspidistra leaves and lace curtains which Simon Prowse had associated with observations undertaken in the vicarage by his uncle. And she continued struggling to supply them with plausible theological remarks. If the Fall—she made Hooker say—is to be regarded simply as a potent and persuasive aetiological myth, does it necessarily follow that the Incarnation or the Resurrection must be relegated to the same category? Hilda was quite pleased with 'aetiological'—it showed that she wasn't exactly a dunce—but was cross that invention failed her when it came to providing Uncle George with an adequately learned reply. She had to acknowledge that her attitude to the whole thing was essentially emotional. She wanted Uncle George to 'win' partly because religious scepticism was an element in the received and unthinking stock-in-trade of her generation, but more essentially just because she was fond of him. She could see that whether it would do him any good to 'win' was an open question; that if Father Hooker 'won' as Dr Hunter had 'won', George Naylor might be a happier man for the rest of his days. It was all very well for Uncle George to speak robustly of 'a pack of fables from top to bottom'—but what if that sort of judgement had its origin in a comparatively superficial level of his mind? Wasn't Uncle George, who could regard as profoundly evidential a picture by Piero della Francesca, quite as much *anima naturaliter Christiana* as she herself feared to be *anima naturaliter Pym?* All this was perplexing and disturbing. Hilda hated being out of her depth, and saw that she must turn to practical affairs. She went outside, avoided the terrace, ran to earth the garden boy, and commanded him to reline the tennis court.

The tennis party was a success, although not an unqualified success so far as Hilda was concerned. This was because Simon had, after all, found a girl and brought her along. Since he was, as Edith Prowse had explained, a stranger in those parts, it had to be inferred that he was a quick worker. There was, moreover, something enigmatical about his relationship with his recruit, since whether Simon had known her for long and in some different part of the country remained obscure. She went by the name of June Gale, and about this there was a disturbing element too. You told yourself that one scarcely expects gales in June: something like that. Otherwise June was an ordinary sort of girl—or she was that if you ignored the fact that she was attractive and would strip pretty. She played decent tennis, but didn't give the impression that it was much her sort of thing. Hilda suspected that she was just one more Oxford character. It was odd that the fact didn't transpire in such casual talk as took place. Eventually, and when play had come to a stop in the interest of a well-furnished tea-table set out in open air, Hilda went fishing about this. There had recurred to her Edith

Prowse's quaint persuasion (as it had appeared to be) that her parlour-boarder at the vicarage might have turned up at Plumley less for the purpose of mastering some Latin texts than in pursuit and furtherance of romance. The vicar's wife was a silly woman, and it seemed a silly idea—besides being no business of Hilda's. Hilda fished, all the same.

'Have you known Simon for long?' she asked, in what she took to be a 'casual' voice.

'Only off and on,' June said. 'Have you?'

'Far from it. I met him for the first time only the other day. It seems he hasn't ever been to Plumley before. Have you?'

'Only off and on.'

Before reiterating this useful phrase, June—or so it had seemed to Hilda—had glanced towards Simon, who was sitting nearby, almost as if for instructions. This was mysterious and unsatisfactory. Hilda, who had lately snubbed Edith Prowse for asking a string of questions, herself asked a third one straight away now.

'Are you at Oxford, June?'

English idiom admits of only one interpretation of this; it means, 'Are you a student at Oxford University?' But June, after giving it a moment's consideration, seemed to receive it in a more general sense.

'Oxford?' she reiterated vaguely. 'No, I don't live in Oxford. I know it a bit. Do you?'

This was sufficiently vexatious to make Hilda feel quite cross. She offered a brief affirmative, and fell to examining the handle of her tennis racket with care. What was the meaning of such uncivil reticence? It did really look as if something covert were going on between this girl and Simon Prowse—and perhaps something better to be described as an intrigue than a romance. But if Simon had come to Plumley in pursuit of June, this surely made it necessary to suppose that her home was not very far away. Yet again, if this were so, Simon was at least not fortune-hunting, since all persons of any substance were known to the Naylors for many miles around. In any case, 'fortune-hunting' was an obsolete idea, existing nowadays only in the vast and depressing acreage of 'standard' English plays and novels. It was more probable that Simon and June were having a love affair about which—and again the notion was an old-fashioned one—they wanted to keep quiet. But then why had Simon gone out of his way to parade the girl at the Naylors? Vanity and impudence, Hilda told herself at the conclusion of these discreditable and idle speculations.

So she avoided further conversation with June during the rest of the afternoon. But she did keep an eye on the supposed lovers, and believed herself to detect a further oddity in their relationship. June wasn't altogether in Simon's good books. At least he was keeping a wary eye on her, as if at any moment she might put a foot wrong—and had even, perhaps, done so not long ago. This was again tiresomely mysterious. It had nothing to do with social comportment—a trivial aspect of life which June commanded as sufficiently as did Hilda herself. And there was another thing. Neither Uncle George nor Father Hooker was playing tennis (although she suspected that Uncle George would have rather liked to do so) and they were sitting side by side in deck-chairs in a silence more companionable-seeming than Hilda at all cared for. But what chiefly struck her was that Uncle George seemed to be as interested in June Gale as she was herself. Interested and *puzzled*. The puzzlement was reassuring in a way. She wouldn't have liked to think of her uncle as taking a certain sort of specific interest in a pretty girl. Anything of the kind would have made her feel jealous. And jealousy, for that matter, must be at work in her in all this brouhaha about the Gale female and Simon Prowse—a young man with whom she had exchanged no more than ten minutes' conversation. This was humiliating—especially in one, like herself, dedicated to the dispassionate observations and appraisals proper in a promising novelist. The tennis party, she told herself, was a stupid affair.

Simon seemed to get on best with the youngest of the Naylors. This was perhaps because he and Henry were the strongest players on the court by quite a long way. Simon was first-class: the sort of player who, in any humdrum tennis, is obliged unobtrusively to contain his game in the interest of a general agreeableness. Simon himself was aware of this better than one might have expected in the light of other facets of his behaviour. Hilda found further perplexity here. The mindless hearty who had neither will nor ability to get up a batch of the Younger

Pliny's boring letters was, if quite amiably, in evidence, and there was no glimpse of the young man who knew what to look for in the churches of Florence. It was almost on what she thought of as her professional side that Hilda found herself worried by this small puzzle. When you were writing fiction it was possible suddenly to discover that you had committed yourself to making some quite important member of your dramatis personae behave 'out of character', and that you couldn't see how to pull him or her together. But that in real life there should be alternative versions of Simon Prowse on offer made no sense.

Tea was followed by a singles between Simon and Charles, and Hilda watched it with interest. It didn't last long, since Simon—naturally enough—abandoned the skilfully unaggressive game he had at times put up when playing mixed doubles. There were no more of the graceful but unpugnacious lobs which he had occasionally employed to mask his superiority. He was out to kill Charles's game—but not quite outright. He had Charles running around, red-faced and sweating, rather more than was necessary simply to take a point. Hilda, who didn't much go in for sympathizing with her elder brother, might have watched this exhibition with satisfaction if it hadn't been for June. June was following Simon's superior dexterities with goggling admiration. So was it really a matter of predatory girl chasing desirable boy? But whatever was going on—Hilda had to repeat to herself—was no business of hers. She was annoyed by it, all the same. She was also, and even more absurdly, annoyed that Simon in unrumpled flannels no longer very adequately suggested the wild young man of her initial impression a few days before. She decided not to see much more of him during the remainder of his stay at the vicarage.

When the game was over Charles had almost ceased to be in decent command of himself, although he did just manage the requisite casual word or two to his opponent. Then, rather surprisingly, he made a bee line for his sister and flung himself down beside her.

'This bloody racket,' he said. 'I'll have to have it restrung.'

'You'll need more than a restrung racket if you're going to make much impression on Simon Prowse. You're not in the same street—and don't you know it.' Hilda was without any impulse to offer consolatory words.

'Barging in—and bringing that trollop with him! Damned cheek.'

'Miss Gale isn't a trollop. You do mishandle words dreadfully.'

'I admit *she'd* handle nicely. Jointed just right for this way and that.' Charles, whose sexual experience was probably still all inside his head, occasionally tumbled into speech as gross as this. 'What's that chap Prowse doing in Plumley, in any case?'

'You know perfectly well. He's come to be coached by his uncle, Christopher Prowse.'

'Good God!' It was seemingly for the first time that Charles was taking in this information. 'In how to write sermons?'

'In some Latin texts, and stuff of that kind.'

'Latin texts? It's enough to make the cat laugh.'

'Why not?'

'Why not? Because I've recognized him, of course. But naturally he doesn't recognize *me*.'

This, although it had the appearance of a further puzzle, didn't entirely baffle Hilda.

'Are you talking about Oxford?' she asked.

'Of course I am. Prowse was two years ahead of me at Trinity, and wouldn't ever have noticed me. But he was quite the star, and must be there still—hogging all the prizes.'

'Prizes? For high jumping and long jumping and hurdles and that kind of thing?'

'Christ, no! For writing poems in ancient Greek, and rubbish of that sort. I suppose he'll be taking Greats in June and becoming a Fellow of All Souls and what have you. Coached by Christopher Prowse? Coached by my arse! I'm going to have a shower.'

With this archaic impropriety, Charles hurried off to the house. Hilda wasn't worried about him, knowing that he would quickly feel ashamed of himself, and inside fifteen minutes be back on parade in a dry shirt and a better mind. Just this did happen, and the tennis continued until six o'clock. Hilda didn't play too well, being distracted on more fronts than one. Uncle George and Father Hooker were now conversing again, and although Uncle George occasionally interrupted himself to produce an appreciative 'Good shot!' or 'Well served!' it was clear that the serious debate had been resumed. And that this time the resumption should be virtually in public struck her, if irrationally, as ominous. It somehow suggested that they must be coming together at least in some degree. And as she couldn't believe that Father Hooker was at all likely to be seduced into infidelity she had to conclude that it was Uncle George who was beginning to give way. Perhaps this was to be expected.

But Hilda's more urgent thoughts were on another topic. She had, she persuaded herself, detected from the start something disingenuous in the picture of himself which Simon Prowse had offered her. Nevertheless what Charles had now revealed about the young man's academic standing was little short of astounding. It was true that Charles didn't remotely know his way about in the world of Fellowships of All Souls and the like, and he might be exaggerating the extent to which Simon was a high flyer in that field. But the essence of his account must be true. Simon was the kind of young man who quite naturally took Andrea da Firenzi and the Cappellone degli Spagnuoli in his stride, and he no more needed his uncle the vicar to help him through Tacitus or Pliny Junior than he needed a governess to teach him his *ABC*.

What followed from this? It could, indeed, only be the sort of disgraceful deception that the idiotic Edith Prowse had fleetingly thought up a milk-and-water version of. Young men do, of course, pursue young women under various degrees of difficulty from time to time. In romances and comedies and farces such as clutter up literature they disguise themselves as clowns or dotards or serving-men or even serving-wenches, and get away with it amid general applause. But to pass oneself off on one's uncle as an unlettered lad, mad as the mist and snow. . .

Hilda pulled herself up before this wild plunge into her favourite poet. The plain fact was that Simon Prowse had gone to extravagant lengths to disguise the true occasion of his need to be in the vicinity of Plumley—which was also, almost equally mysteriously, the vicinity of June Gale. *Simon* was definitely after *her*. One had to go back to seeing it that way on. Simon must be very *much* after the girl to have cooked up so crazy a situation. It couldn't just be the ordinary thing of disapproving parents, and so forth. Was June, perhaps, already a married woman? Was there an adulterous relationship that had to be kept dark until a divorce or something had happened? Had Simon and June the misfortune to have been born brother and sister, like characters in a Jacobean melodrama? Or at least with one common parent, like Byron and what-was-her-name? These lurid speculations produced from Hilda two double faults in succession. She was glad when the tennis was wound up.

But the two visitors didn't immediately take their leave, since this would not have accorded with Mary Naylor's notions of proper hospitality. The tea things and the soft drinks had been cleared away and replaced by sherry and the like. Americans, Hilda seemed to recall, were fond of calling this fading of the day the Happy Hour. She didn't want a Happy Hour herself, or even a happy ten minutes. A brief spell of solitude, she felt, would be useful in getting Simon Prowse and whatever nonsense he was involved with out of her system. But when the party did break up she found herself hailed by her uncle, and in consequence drawn into conversation with Father Hooker as well.

'Hilda, my dear,' Uncle George said, 'do you happen to have Tolstoy's *War and Peace* on your shelves? And, if so, might we borrow it?'

Hilda didn't think much of that 'we', but she offered to fetch *War and Peace* at once.

'Would you say,' her uncle pursued, 'that it's a very great novel indeed?'

'The greatest ever written,' Hilda said firmly, and turned at once to Father Hooker. 'Would you agree?'

'It is rather a stiff question.' Father Hooker seemed surprised but not displeased at being thus abruptly invoked. 'And I fear my acquaintance with fiction in general is insufficiently extensive to admit of my embarking on large generalization.' Father Hooker didn't say this in a snubbing way, and he sounded less pompous than his syntax might suggest. 'What your uncle and I have been trying to recall is the argument of the long concluding section.'

'A kind of philosophical essay?' Hilda said. 'I seem to remember not making much of it.'

'Tolstoy is examining the concepts of freedom and necessity in the context of a theory of history. And your uncle and I have been discussing the issue of determinism and acts of the will.'

'I see.' Hilda now recalled a good deal. 'What Tolstoy says is that the closer we are to an action in place and time, the more we are aware of the free will in it. And the further away we are, the more we see it as determined and unavoidable.'

'Just so—and your uncle and I judge it might be of interest to revive our memory of the contention. Our own concern is with a related matter: the question of divine intervention in human affairs. We are wondering whether we are in agreement that, failing the acceptance of that intervention as veridical, a total fatalism or determinism is the only view of the nature of things that may rationally be entertained. Would that, my dear Naylor, be a fair summary of our position?'

'No doubt,' Uncle George said—almost absently. 'But what really puzzled Tolstoy was why hundreds of thousands of men should march from west to east and east to west across Europe, slaughtering hundreds of thousands of other men as they go. And nowadays the slaughtering doesn't even require the marching men. It's a more urgent problem than whether I can, or cannot, raise my arm of my own free will.'

Hilda was about to say, 'So it is'. In fact she said nothing, and went to fetch and hand over Tolstoy's book. Actually to become involved in such discussions wouldn't be her sort of thing at all. But Uncle George and Father Hooker were professionals, and it had now to be faced that they were equally in a state of intellectual satisfaction as they talked. At their own sort of tennis they were probably quite in the Simon Prowse class.

But if the amenity, almost the cosiness, of Uncle George's developing relationship with the minder was a surprise to Hilda, another surprise was sprung on her by her uncle later that evening. Dinner was over, and Father Hooker (who was proving to be not without gleams or glints of social tact) had declared his intention of taking a solitary stroll beneath—as he expressed it—'that beautiful harvest moon'. The harvest moon was still a good many weeks ahead, but Father Hooker was not to be mocked because of that. If Sherlock Holmes was to be admired for knowing nothing about the Copernican System, an eminent theologian was not to be aspersed for getting lunar matters a little wrong. There *was* rather a splendid moon, and he was entitled to go out and enjoy it. And it gave George Naylor the opportunity for a comfortable chat with his niece.

'My dear,' he said, 'can you tell me what a coincidence is?'

'Something surprising brought about by chance.'

'Why should we be surprised by anything brought about by chance? Chance is blind and mindless pretty well by definition isn't it? So why should any of its operations seem surprising?'

'It's something to do with statistics and probabilities.' Hilda was accustomed to whimsical catechisms of this sort from her uncle, but rather suspicious on the present occasion. 'Is this to be more about necessity and free will and divine intervention?'

'I suppose it might connect up that way, but it's not what I'm thinking of. Coincidence is a notable coming together of X and Y counter to any probability—although probability, mark you, is an uncommonly tricky counter—and without distinguishable cause. Suppose Hooker and I are strangers. . .'

'I rather wish you were.'

'And suppose each of us happens to have a wooden leg. And we meet.'

'But not at the club or clinic for wooden-legged men.'

'Exactly!' It was evident that Uncle George was delighted that his niece should be so promptly on the ball. 'We may never have so much as heard of one another, but be attending the burial, say, of a common friend. So there we suddenly are, standing shoulder to shoulder at the graveside: two wooden-legged men. *That's* a coincidence.'

'So it is. But just what are we getting at?'

'The girl who came to tennis.'

'June Gale has been to a funeral?'

'No, no: there's no analogy of that sort. I simply felt this afternoon that she reminded me of somebody. I couldn't place her, and was quite bothered about it. Then I realized that I'd actually run into Miss Gale herself a few days ago. It was in Oxford when I was on my way to Plumley. I rather think I told you how it was.'

'You mean that June Gale was the girl'—Hilda was gazing at

her uncle round-eyed—'who. . .who landed you a hand-out on the bomb?'

'Just that. And her bobbing up on me again within the week in an out of the way place like Plumley certainly rates as a coincidence. And no causality at work. No link. A completely random thing.'

'Well, no.' Hilda sought for further words. 'Or, rather, perhaps not quite.' She paused again, conscious that large new vistas may suddenly confront the inward eye. 'Do you think that this afternoon she recognized you as somebody she'd canvassed in that way?'

'I'm not all that striking, my dear.' Uncle George must have found this a gratifying reflection, for he chuckled happily. 'No doubt she was handing out those leaflets like mad. She wouldn't know me from Adam.'

'Masaccio's Adam.'

'Whatever do you mean by that?'

'Something I *did* see in Florence. In the Carmine. It's called *La Cacciata*, meaning the expulsion of Adam and Eve from Paradise. The Angel with his sword is above them. But what's ahead is the bomb. It's why Adam is shielding his eyes. I saw it that way at once.'

'My dear child!' For a moment Uncle George was silent. 'Are you,' he asked gently, 'by way of thinking a good deal about the bomb?'

'Not inordinately. But my whole generation, I suppose, gives a thought to it from time to time. One sees, perhaps, some children playing around in a field, or a street. And the bloody old bomb rears its ugly head.'

'Yes.' George was silent again, so that from the next room a faint quacking could be heard. It was the BBC entertaining Hilda's parents to the nine o'clock news. 'How have we got on to this?'

'I was going to tell you about Christopher Prowse's notice-board. You know it. Vicar: The Revd C. Prowse M.A.'

'Of course I know it.'

'Well—just the other day, it must have been—somebody stuck up a notice on it. BAN THE BOMB. Simply that.'

'Might it have been the vicar himself?' This came from Uncle

113

George almost on a hopeful note. 'A good many of the clergy—and of the Christian laity, too—are showing themselves ready to take a pretty stiff line about any sort of preparing for nuclear war.'

'I suppose so.' Hilda felt awkward; she hadn't failed to register a kind of forlorn pride in this last remark. 'But, no—it wouldn't be Christopher Prowse. Nor his wife, either.'

'Then who. . . ?'

'I came on the thing almost in the same moment that their nephew did. We stared at it together.'

'The young man who's going to be coached?'

'The young man who says he is. Not-so-simple Simon. But what happened was this: Simon was absolutely furious, and wanted to tear the thing down. I had to stop him.'

'Why did you want to do that, Hilda?'

'Because I thought a church notice-board was a very reasonable place for such an injunction. Aren't we told about a Prince of Peace, and so on?'

'Yes.' Uncle George's silence was longer this time. 'But this Simon's reaction is quite a common one. Plenty of people see the anti-bomb folk as virtually emissaries from Moscow.'

'Yes, I know. But it wasn't that way with Simon. I'm *sure* it wasn't. He was feeling that somebody had made a false, give-away move. And I believe now that it was that girl.'

'That girl?' For the moment, Uncle George seemed merely puzzled. 'What girl? I don't know what you're talking about.'

'June Gale again, his inept apprentice—who's presumably hand-out and sticker mad. And therefore in danger of blowing the gaff. Uncle George, can't you *see?*'

'As far as my nose, I suppose. But, Hilda, aren't you perhaps seeing rather far beyond yours? And may it be a matter of professional instinct? I mean, to think up a plot, and generally to get things moving in sleepy old Plumley by dumping some dark design on the young man at the vicarage and his friend, my Oxford acquaintance. And you're promisingly quick off your mark.'

Hilda was a good deal taken aback by this, with its devastating suggestion that she went around concocting novelettes in her head. Uncle George had been entirely serious about his Church's (or his late Church's) attitude to the bomb. It was too bad that he should now take to making fun of her. But she gave a swift glance at him and was a little reassured. Perhaps he was really testing her out.

'I know it sounds absurd,' she said. 'But listen. That coaching stuff at the vicarage is nonsense. Charles has turned out to remember something about this Simon Prowse at Trinity. He seems quite clear about it. The vicar's nephew was, and is, a high-flying Mods and Greats type, and probably as good as booked for All Souls. He could coach the lights out of his uncle, if he wanted to. So he's here under false pretences.'

'I see.' Uncle George hesitated for a moment. 'Would I be right in thinking you find this Simon rather attractive?'

'Well, yes—in a mild way.' Hilda wasn't comfortable. She was also guilelessly surprised that her uncle had an eye open on this kind of territory. 'But don't think I'm other than quite fancy-free.'

'You can see my point. If Simon is deceiving those innocent vicarage people, the spectacle isn't merely freakish but rather disagreeable as well. And its most likely occasion is. . .'

'Yes, I know. That's how I've been seeing it up till now. Some sort of irresponsible sexual escapade. Miss Gale is really Mrs Somebody, perhaps. But no doubt that's just my inventive mind again. Let's get back to the bomb. And Nether Plumley.'

'And *what*, Hilda?'

'That new Institute. Doesn't "Institute" sound peculiarly innocuous? One thinks of Women's Institutes at once! "Establishment" is the sinister word. So there are no new Establishments. Just Institutes.'

'My dear, isn't your imagination now running riot?'

'Just *think*, Uncle George, and you'll see it's doing nothing of the kind. What did that girl hand you in Oxford?'

'A nuclear disarmament thing. Vigorous in its expression.'

'Good. Point one. And here she is at Plumley. And here's our Simon, pretending to be mastering the details of Pliny's stupid villa, and in fact snooping around with field-glasses.'

'And furious when our June rashly surfaces, so to speak, on that notice-board?'

'Capital, Uncle George. That's just it! The Institute,

incidentally, is a Government Agency. That means there can be any amount of clamping down on it. And—again incidentally— it now has a tremendous-great perimeter fence. *And*'—Hilda had suddenly remembered another recent accession of know- ledge—'its people don't go into the pubs. So there's a hush-hush suggestion about the whole thing. What goes on is supposed to be a ploy called animal genetics. But nobody has ever seen any animals.'

'They keep out of the pubs, too?'

'Do be serious, Uncle George. And you see what I think. They pretend it's animals, but it's really something about bombs.'

'But wouldn't that be an imposture very difficult to sustain?'

'And you see what's brewing.' Hilda had happily ignored her uncle's distinctly cogent question. 'Simon and that girl belong to a group proposing to expose it in some way, or do a demo or even a sit-in. Simon with his binoculars is spying out the ground for something of the sort. He may even be the prime mover in the whole plan.'

'Perhaps you're right.' Uncle George did now appear to be serious, but nevertheless not greatly concerned. 'I don't quite see that it's any business of ours.'

'The bomb-thing ought to be everybody's business.'

'I agree with you there. And there's a sense in which everybody has to take sides about it. Do you want to *do* something, Hilda?'

This question pulled Hilda up.

'What do you mean—*do* something?' she asked evasively. 'In this immediate context, I mean. What *can* I do?'

'Communicate your suspicions to the local bobby. Or, alternatively, chase up Simon and tell him you want to sign on.'

'Yes. And—do you know?—Simon virtually challenged me. I've just remembered that too. It was when he and I had come on that thing on the notice-board, and I wouldn't let him tear it down. It led to our having a short, random sort of talk about the whole nuclear mess. He struck me as rather incoherent, as if he was confronting an unexpected situation and feeling his way in face of it. Then he asked me if I'd be prepared to lie down in front of a truck. A truck conveying the things, he meant.'

'Quite so. And did you. . . ?'

Rather abruptly, Uncle George broke off. Father Hooker, having conversed with the moon, had returned to the house and entered the room.

'A magnificent night,' Father Hooker said. 'How astounding seem the heavens! The moon must be felt as neighbourly now, but even Mars and Venus are another matter—although lately, indeed, brought within the reach of projectiles contrived by Man. Yet we must view the planets of our little solar system as merely jostling one another in the street when we consider the stars. Were I to travel—I remind myself—at the speed of light for millions of years I should barely come up with them. Nevertheless, meditated on, these immensities but call my mind home to quietness.'

Hilda recalled Uncle George saying something about those immensities. He didn't think them all that important, but he hadn't said they called him home to quietness either.

'A thousand ages in thy sight,' she said, 'being like an evening gone?' Even as she spoke, she was abashed at having uttered so pert and senseless a quip. Uncle George, she felt, would be ashamed of her. But then Hooker wouldn't decant this sort of stuff so copiously on Uncle George's head. With him, he presumably talked hard theology—pious reflection being for old wives at tea parties, and ignorant girls.

Father Hooker, however, gave no sign of taking offence. He even glanced at Hilda as if he were genuinely capable of feeling amused.

'Ah,' he said, 'Isaac Watts! Lewis Carroll very properly made fun of him—just as you make fun of me, Miss Naylor.'

'Please call me Hilda.' It was impossible not to be irritated by Father Hooker's inappropriate formalities.

'I shall be only too happy. Do you by any chance know the good Isaac's *Divine Songs for Children*, Hilda?'

'I'm afraid not.'

'Some are merely comical. "How rude are the boys that throw pebbles and mire" is no doubt a virtuous reflection for well brought-up children to indulge in. But consider this:

Lord, I ascribe it to Thy grace,
And not to chance, as others do,
That I was born of Christian race,
And not a Heathen, or a Jew.'

'I think that's rather comical as well,' Hilda said.
'It may be so. But again:

There is a dreadful Hell,
And everlasting pains;
There sinners must with devils dwell
In darkness, fire, and chains.

Is it not extremely shocking that innocent children should have
been required to mouth such stuff?'

'I suppose it is.' Hilda wondered whether it was orthodox in
Father Hooker to regard children as innocent. 'But it's very
mild, in its way. You should read the Jesuit's sermon to
schoolboys in *Portrait of the Artist as a Young Man*.'

'But I have.' Father Hooker said this in a quite neutral tone;
again he was unoffended by a gauche performance. 'A good deal
of Joyce ought to be recommended reading for Christians.
Naylor, you would agree with me?'

'Certainly. And it's always a satisfaction, Hooker, to agree
with you now and then.'

All this rather silenced Hilda. Just what was the relationship
—the intellectual and the personal relationship—developing
between these two men appeared to be something she was more
and more losing any sense of. It was a puzzle: another puzzle to
add to the Simon Prowse one.

'But, if the hour be not too late, there is something I'd value
advice on.' Father Hooker had sat down comfortably between
uncle and niece. 'It is a matter upon which you can both help:
you, Naylor, from your pastoral experience, and you, Hilda,
from your knowledge of local feeling. The vicar, as you know,
has rather surprisingly asked me to preach for him on Sunday. It
was with some hesitation that I decided to accept.' Father
Hooker paused on this, and Hilda reflected, as she had done
once before, that he could give a full-blooded Jesuit points from

time to time. Hooker had agreed to preach because she had herself persuaded him (very absurdly) that Uncle George might otherwise do so, and to some embarrassing effect. 'It is commonly supposed,' Father Hooker went on, 'that parsons carry sermons in their pockets, or at least in their suitcases. I do not. I happen to believe that every sermon should have its due and immediate occasion.'

'John Donne,' Uncle George said, 'preached his own funeral sermon. I suppose that would fill your requirement well.'

'I must not think to equate myself with a Dean of St Paul's. Nor am I virtually in my shroud quite yet. Donne had himself depicted in his.' Father Hooker lingered again on this—which he would classify, Hilda supposed, as a pleasantry. 'And I always bear in mind an apophthegm of Archbishop Whately's. "Preach not because you have to say something," the Archbishop enjoins, "but because you have something to say." '

'Pretty good,' Hilda said. 'It goes for writers, too.'

'Undoubtedly. So I am looking for a subject which I myself feel to be of special urgency at the present time, and which there is some reason to feel may be of equal interest to my hearers.'

Across Father Hooker's chest, Hilda and her uncle exchanged an astonished glance. Was it conceivable. . . ?

'The other day before luncheon,' Father Hooker went on, 'I happened to take a short stroll through the village. The church notice-board caught my attention. Affixed to it was a small placard calling for the banning of the bomb.'

'The bomb,' Hilda said—and wondered what on earth had made her produce this stupid echo.

'Indeed, the bomb. The word, I believe, is now chiefly taken to mean any long-range nuclear missile. Naturally, I debated with myself the likelihood of the placard's having been posted by Mr Prowse himself. He might well have judged it to be his duty to do so.'

'So he might,' Uncle George said. 'But I don't think it was he who put it up, all the same.'

'It came to me as a matter of some delicacy.' (Delicacy, Hilda thought, was rather a thing with Hooker.) 'I had half a mind to call at the vicarage and inquire. On weighty issues—and this issue is weighty indeed—one ought to know where one's fellow labourers stand.'

'Most certainly,' Uncle George said.

'I decided, however, on another course. It might be described, jestingly, as taking the temperature of the flock.'

'The flock?' Uncle George queried wonderingly.

'The parishioners, Naylor. The cottage folk. I dropped into the pub.'

Had Father Hooker announced that he had stripped and plunged into the village pond he would scarcely have achieved as startling an effect as with this. It was true that he had been judging it tactful—'delicate', perhaps—to continue wearing mufti for the greater part of the day. But that he should think successfully to hob-nob with smock-frock'd boors over a mug of ale in the local pot-house strained credulity. Was this the man—Uncle George might have asked himself—who had kept that outspread copy of *The Times* between himself and the plebeian world of Mrs Bowman and Mrs Archer, Len and Ron? Apparently it was. And it could be detected, moreover, that Father Hooker was unobtrusively entertained by the effect his disclosure had now created.

'My dear Hooker,' Uncle George asked wonderingly, 'are we to understand that you entered into a discussion of nuclear fission, and unilateral disarmament and the like, with whoever happened to be at the bar?'

'Certainly. There was a little resistance to be overcome at first. I believe it arose from a knowledge that I was staying here at the Park. Nor could I find that there was much interest in the little placard on the church notice-board. I gathered that the notice-board seldom engages the attention of the village people at all. One odd fact, however, did appear—and it makes me feel that the dangers arising from nuclear proliferation are, although it may be very obscurely, stirring in the minds even of rural societies. An elderly man of respectable if humble appearance assured me that the new Institute at Nether Plumley—about which you and I, Hilda, had a word lately—were nowt to do with animals, but only with such things as them atomics and the like. I believe I reproduce his precise words. And another elderly man agreed with him. It is, of course, most clearly a grotesque misconception, but not insignificant as suggesting that real anxieties about the arms race and so forth are abroad in other than intellectual circles.'

Father Hooker paused on this, perhaps only to take breath. But Hilda spoke at once.

'Did you say something to us about seeking advice?' she asked.

'Yes, indeed. What has occurred to me is this: that on Sunday I might usefully speak in a measured way about the peculiar perils of our age, and the duty of Christians in confronting them. And I might take occasion to mention, lightly but firmly, the folly of indulging in absurd suspicions of doubtless beneficent activities which we are not well qualified to understand. What do you think?'

What Hilda thought was that the pulpit in St Michael and All Angels was not exactly an advantageous perch from which to reach the ears of Plumley's populace at large. At matins on Sunday the congregation would consist of something under ten per cent of the local gentry and of nobody else whomsoever— except, indeed, for Mr Rudkin and an aged hireling who took the collection and rang the bell. The respectable if humble patron of the pub and his coeval supporter would not be present to be instructed.

'I don't see why not,' Hilda said. 'I, for one, would very much like to hear what you have to say about it all.'

'And you, Naylor—what do you think?'

'I think that if you manage to talk sense about those peculiar perils, Hooker, the occasion will be a notable one. I wish I could be there to hear it. But you and I have our meetings on that terrace, after all.'

So a question she had been asking herself—Hilda thought— was answered. Uncle George didn't intend to go to church. And she saw—it is to be feared with satisfaction—that the two men were, for the moment, distanced again. Father Hooker got to his feet, made one of his impossible little stiff bows, and intimated that he would seek his host and hostess, to say good night to them before going to bed. Hilda watched him out of the room, before turning to her uncle.

'Never mind,' she said. 'I'll listen most attentively, and bring you the heads of the sermon.' But she saw that Uncle George wasn't very amused. 'You really won't come to church?' she asked.

'My dear, I must let Thomas Hardy speak for me. With that bright believing band I have no claim to be.'

V

GEORGE NAYLOR BEGAN the following day with a feeling of holiday. This was because it was Saturday, and Father Hooker had explained that he must devote it entirely to the composing of his sermon. The privilege of preaching, he said, came to him all too rarely, and he regarded every occasion of the sort as a heavy responsibility, to be prepared for with care. It was a statement not wholly consistent with what Hilda had reported of his attitude upon first hearing of Christopher Prowse's invitation to edify a rural congregation. But George didn't quarrel with it, being rejoiced (he believed) at the prospect of a day's freedom. Almost as soon as breakfast was over, he took himself off to a corner of the garden for a long immersion in what Hooker would have described as light reading: the promisingly lengthy novel by Salman Rushdie he had picked up in Blackwell's.

Mr Rushdie, it seemed, was an Oxford man, who chose to write about his native India. Rather well, George decided after a dozen pages. Very well, indeed, he told himself after a further dozen, and he settled back in his deck-chair with every prospect of complete absorption until lunch-time. But then, and very strangely, the mystery of midnight's children ceased to command him. He took time off from it to think of something else; he did this not once but several times; eventually he had to recognize that what was distracting him was the behaviour of Father Hooker.

He was feeling annoyed with Hooker. There was nothing new about this. The man had annoyed him from the start—from the very moment, it might be said, of his first lowering *The Times* from before his nose in the corner of that railway-carriage. But now it was a new sort of annoyance, and a surprising one. He was annoyed that Hooker should be wasting his time concocting a sermon for a gaggle of retired army men and garden-prattling women. Hooker's proper business was discussing theology with George.

George wasn't particularly alarmed by this discovery of how his own mind was moving. Hooker was making no headway with him, and almost certainly knew that he wasn't. It was merely that Hooker represented something George had been going short of for several years: well-ordered discourse from a well-stocked mind. In his East End mission George's speculative intelligence had slumbered; he had spent himself being wise and understanding and avuncular to immature and ill-informed and touchingly helpless and bewildered people. Hooker, although undeniably of a somewhat rebarbative personality, was a top man in his line. He would probably end up as Nolloth Professor of the Philosophy of the Christian Religion at Oxford.

This was no doubt to exaggerate Hooker's abilities. George really knew this. But he also knew that his liability to error in the matter was an index of the extent to which he had fallen out of touch with learned and scholarly persons. Yet he had been finding, in the course of his talks with Hooker, that Theology, if the Queen of the Sciences, is also to be likened to a bicycle. Once proficient, you are proficient for keeps. Mount even after long desuetude, and you don't positively tumble. In arguing about Christian dogma with Hooker he had no sense of having to keep his end up. It was level-pegging most of the time. And on all sorts of interesting by-roads they were apt to look about them and discover common ground.

Having thus reasoned things out, George decided it was amusing rather than sinister that he should want to hog Hooker. So he returned contentedly to Rushdie's India, emerging from it only when the single syllable 'Nosh!', bellowed at him across the lawn by his nephew, Henry, told him that luncheon was on the table.

It was a dull meal, not accompanied by much conversation. Hilda tried a topic or two, but with, for her uncle, the detectable aim of eliciting absurdity in aid of professional note-taking. Charles was glum, perhaps wondering whether he could decently tote that gun as well as his fishing-rod to Scotland, just as a hint that he would like to be asked to stay on until the Glorious Twelfth arrived. Nor was Henry cheerful, and George asked himself whether his discontent was a matter of intellectual malaise. To a casual regard Henry was almost as Philistine as his brother. But it was evident that he worked hard at his maths, and perhaps he had got far enough with the discipline to realize that his own little play-pen therein had its bars; that being 'good' at maths at school, and even at a university, doesn't make one in any weighty sense a mathematician. So Henry might well be feeling it was a waste of effort.

George had been thinking a good deal about waste. Waste had become one of his talking points with Hooker. The sheer vast wastefulness everywhere evident in nature was one of the things hardest to square with the conception of a beneficent creator. George had instanced (perhaps hoping to discompose his opponent) the spermatozoa: millions of the little brutes elbowing and jostling and wriggling in completely futile effort, with perhaps not one of them making it in the end. Hooker had welcomed the spermatozoa as affording a striking instance of the Divine Abundance. An empty phrase—George thought—but a resonant one. He again perceived that he was becoming rather addicted to Hooker as a disputant.

The children's father, too, was pretty silent during the meal. Several times, indeed, Edward Naylor made as if to address his brother, and on each occasion failed to do so. There was something about this that alerted George, although he couldn't quite tell why. And he was unprepared for what followed.

He had returned to the garden, proposing in Mr Rushdie's company to make a further passage to India and its perplexing inhabitants: a far-away place, far-away peoples, about which and whom, after some centuries of messing around, we know less than we should. This sombre thought, perhaps a consequence of that general gloom at the luncheon-table, was quite comfortably with George as he settled himself again in his deck-chair. But the book remained unopened. It was because he observed his brother to be bearing down on him.

This description wouldn't have satisfied Hilda. 'Tacking towards him,' was more accurate. Edward, that is to say, was approaching in a strolling and criss-cross fashion designed to suggest that actual contact with his brother would be unpremeditated and virtually fortuitous. When it had been achieved, however, Edward drew up a second chair and sat down on it.

'It seems that chap Hooker's going to preach tomorrow,' he said.

'Yes. He is.'

'A bit out of turn, wouldn't you say?'

'Hooker rather felt that himself. But the Prowses were very keen on it, I gather, and he has allowed himself to be persuaded. At least he'll be a change from your vicar. Prowse can't exactly be described as having a very striking mental endowment.'

'Certainly not.' Edward Naylor's tone was that of one who concurs in rebutting an aspersion. 'Awkward fellow, though, in some ways, Hooker.'

'He hasn't come to Plumley, Edward, to display social accomplishments.'

'No, no—one must grant him that.' Edward was silent for a moment following this not wholly lucid remark. Then he apparently decided that he had been offered what might be termed a legitimate lead.

'But as to what the beggar *is* here for,' he said. 'How do things go? Do you feel that you're likely to. . . ?' Edward broke off for a moment. The words he had been about to use were 'give in', which seemed not quite felicitous. But he found himself seeking for some periphrasis in vain. '. . . give in?' he said.

'Dear me, no!' George seemed to find this question merely surprising. 'Hooker and I remain, I fear, sadly far apart. But we are having very interesting discussions, all the same. There are areas of contemporary thinking in which he is much more at home than I am. He even seems to me to possess a certain innovative power. I have been much struck by some of the things he has said about the kerygmatic Christ.'

'Is that so?' To Edward Naylor it would not have been surprising to learn that this personage inhabited an ashram in Mr Rushdie's subcontinent. But he listened respectfully to his brother nevertheless.

'And there's another striking thing about Hooker. He is very much a kenoticist—which I take to be unusual in orthodox Anglican theologians today. He has even said to me. . .' George broke off—perhaps as conscious that Edward himself might never much have reflected upon whether Jesus Christ was aware of being the Second Person of the Trinity. 'But about what you were asking,' he said. 'About caving in and knuckling under. Definitely not.'

'Capital!' The vicar's churchwarden appeared to experience no difficulty in uttering this decided commendation. 'After all, it's not a disaster, you know.'

'A disaster?'

'My dear fellow, you do have that small income from the shop. It's not much, but it will serve to tide things over until I can get something fixed. It took several months with Charles, but I managed it. The only trouble in that quarter is that the boy doesn't turn up very often. It worries the little managing chaps.' Edward paused—almost as if expecting his brother to say, 'They won't have that trouble with me'. Not receiving this assurance, he went on, 'I don't know whether I've told you about Fiesta?'

'Fiesta? I'm sure you haven't.'

'It's the Italian word for a jollification of a churchy sort.'

'Or might it be the Spanish?' George suggested diffidently.

'That's right—the Spanish. Saints' Days and the like are fiestas. Carnivals, you might say, with lots of entertainment laid on. Actually, I thought for a time of calling the company "Carnivals Limited". But it sounds not quite right. Carnivals ought to be unlimited, don't you think?' Edward laughed happily at his own wit. 'So I've chosen just "Fiesta" instead. Catches the eye better. The advertising wallahs have a saying, you know: "Six letters catch the eye". Perfectly true.'

'My dear Edward, whatever are you talking about?'

'And do you know what put the whole idea in my head? Simply keeping my own eyes open on the Plumley home front. The Prowses and their unending bazaars and jumble sales. Dismal affairs—but the only church activities for which the village people turn out *en masse*. Scrabbling for rubbish from the lumber-rooms of their slightly more prosperous neighbours—but really rather wanting to let their hair down as well. You remember Jim Fenwick, the padre we had before this dim Christopher Prowse?'

'Of course I remember Fenwick. He baptized all the children.'

'A stout fellow, and a parson of the old school. Do you remember what he always took along to the bazaars and so forth? You might call it a gambling machine.'

'A gambling machine?'

'A kind of rustic roulette.' Edward Naylor was plainly delighted with this linguistic happiness. 'People bought numbered tickets at a bob a time. Then Fenwick would twirl a kind of arrow-affair on a board with the numbers disposed like the figures on a clock. If it stopped on your number you got a bottle of whisky or packet of tea or pin-cushion or whatever it was. The ploy would go on all afternoon with no shortage of takers. I suddenly saw it as a promising thing, just asking for development. That's where Fiesta will come in. Hire out suitable arcade-type equipment to parishes on a short-term deposit and percentage basis. With a discreet religious slant to some of it—and that's where you'd be invaluable, George: as religious adviser. For instance, I've thought of an electronic contraption with a string of mineral-water bottles seeming to pass across the screen. Press the right button at the right split second, and one of them turns to wine and bobs out on the winner. Endless scope for invention of that sort. Watch the Waves as Jesus Saves.'

'*What?*'

'You move him forward on a zigzag, trying to dodge the waves. You can't control the waves, which are randomized, but only Jesus. If you let him hit one, he begins to sink, but if you get him in the clear again quickly enough, he walks on happily. How do you feel about it?'

'I rather think Prowse might jib at having Plumley latch on to Cana—or to high jinks on the Sea of Galilee.'

'Not in too good taste, perhaps?' Edward Naylor, a reasonable man, considered this possible view of the matter soberly. 'But that's just where you'd be so much a key figure!' he then said loyally. 'So do think about it, old boy.'

An adequate response to this plea to think about the

unthinkable eluded George for the moment, but he was saved from awkwardness by the arrival of his sister-in-law.

'Edward,' Mary Naylor asked, 'do you happen to have seen Jeoffry and Old Foss?'

'I don't think I've set eyes on them either yesterday or today.'

'I'm just a little worried about them.'

'My dear, they do wander off from time to time. But here's Hooker. We can ask him.' Father Hooker was indeed approaching. He bore an abstracted air, and was perhaps going over in his mind the successive heads under which he would order his discourse on the following day. 'Hooker, you don't happen to to have run into Jeoffry and Old Foss?'

'I beg your pardon?' It was almost with a start that Father Hooker had become aware he was being addressed. 'Run into whom?'

'Not exactly whom,' George said with some amusement. 'Jeoffry and Old Foss are the cats.'

'Ah, the cats. I may perhaps be forgiven for being a little astray. The names are somewhat surprising, are they not?'

'Far from it,' George said. He was welcoming this diversion from his brother's monstrous vision of a new-style church bazaar. 'Two very distinguished cats have been so named, and it was my niece who called ours after them.' (George said 'ours' entirely without self-consciousness, since at Plumley he knew he was at home.) 'Edward Lear, who tells us that he has a runcible hat, tells us also that Old Foss is the name of his cat. But the original Jeoffry was more august. He belonged to Christopher Smart. "For I will consider my Cat Jeoffry," Smart says.'

'So he does—in the *Jubilate Agno*.' Father Hooker, whose dislike of cats in real life had made itself evident on his first evening at Plumley, was quite on terms with poetical cats—and moreover had a weakness for exhibiting himself as a well-read man. 'Smart sees his cat as duly and daily serving the Living God.'

'How very interesting!' Mary Naylor said. 'But it *was* rather odd of Hilda to choose such names, all the same.' Mary was in fact rendered uncomfortable by this unaccountable bobbing up of religion in a domestic feline context. 'And you can see that it *is* rather worrying,' she went on. 'Not their names, I mean, but their having disappeared for so long. So many get killed on the road.'

'I wish I could reassure you,' Father Hooker said. 'But, unhappily, I have seen no cats of late.'

'Happening all the time,' Edward Naylor said robustly. 'And there's another thing. A car or van comes along, kills your cat, and leaves the mangled body in the middle of the road. Presently another fellow comes along, stops, and thinks he's doing the decent thing by picking up the corpse and chucking it over a hedge or into the ditch. One of the farmers told me of its occurring only last week. He's lost his cat, and knows pretty well what's happened. But his kids are still hunting for the body. Old Foss and Jeoffry may have gone the same way at one swoop. Not but that, ten to one, nothing of the kind has occurred, and they'll turn up again as usual.'

'You don't think,' Father Hooker asked—and distinguishably with a faint wistfulness—'that they may have been devoured by a fox?'

'My dear sir, foxes don't devour cats.' Edward was vastly entertained. 'Foxes devour hens and geese. And all brutes are choosey. Cats themselves, for instance. A cat will stalk a pigeon right across the garden, but usually ignore a pheasant a couple of yards away. Unless it's a wounded pheasant. I've known a cat go for one of them.' Edward was very much the countryman as he produced this scarcely recondite information. 'Is that the damned telephone?' It was certainly the damned telephone, just audible as it rang in the house. 'Both boys have gone off, and Hilda ignores the thing on principle—so there's probably only that useless girl.'

'I'll go, dear,' Mary said—and added, in case her husband's evident immobility might appear a little lacking in propriety: 'It's sure to be Mr Rudkin about the bacon. He promised it for the week-end, but I expect Hilda may have to fetch it.'

Mary hurried away, and the three gentlemen continued to converse, perhaps more out of civility than inclination. George wanted to return to Rushdie, and Father Hooker to his sermon; Edward would have been quite content to chat, but couldn't think of anything much to chat about. Surprisingly quickly, however, Mary reappeared on the lawn, and hurried towards them with the unmistakable air of one who brings information of moment.

'Rather an extraordinary thing,' she said. 'I don't know quite what to make of it. That was Edith Prowse. She rang up to ask whether, by any chance, Sinbad was paying a kind of visit to Jeoffry and Old Foss.'

'Sinbad being a cat?' George asked.

'Yes, of course. And Sinbad has disappeared. But what's really odd is about the Rudkins. The Rudkins' boy has just delivered something at the vicarage: scrag-end, I think Edith said. And he's on his way here with the bacon now—which is one comfort, at least. But what he told the Prowses was that Peter has vanished.'

'Peter Rudkin?' Father Hooker asked, suitably shocked. 'A little boy?'

'No, no—of course not. Peter is the Rudkins' cat.'

Noon on the following day, Sunday, found George back in the garden. Again he had Mr Rushdie for company. Or he carried the possibility of that, at least, under his arm. But the book, although so beguiling, once more remained unopened. George was barely conscious that this was so. What he was conscious of was simply that he was waiting. He was waiting for the return of the Park contingent from church. And, more particularly, he was waiting for his niece. He recalled that on these occasions the Naylors frequently collected appropriate fellow-worshippers and brought them home for a glass of sherry by way of recruitment after the fatigues of devotion. He hoped this wouldn't happen on the present occasion.

Nor did it. There was a small bustle from the direction of the house, and then Hilda came across the lawn alone.

'Well?' George said. 'How did it go?'

'I hardly know where to begin.'

'Have a man come through a door with a gun,' George suggested with a determined lightness of air.

'That's only for when one's stuck.' Hilda was still carrying a prayer-book, and this she now laid carefully on top of Mr Rushdie on the grass before she sat down.

'Then start,' her uncle said, 'with what will prove to have

131

been a pregnant utterance on the part of a major character.'

'Very well. The people that walked in darkness have seen a great light: they that dwell in the land of the shadow of death, upon them hath the light shined.'

'You mean that Hooker took that as his text? No one quite like Isaiah for texts.'

'It was certainly Hooker's text, and I suppose a perfectly ordinary one. It was the application that rather surprised people. Would "application" be the right word?'

'Certainly. One applies one's text—or handles it.'

'Hooker handled it, all right. His great light was first seen over some desert in America, and then over Hiroshima. And we all dwell in the land of the shadow of death.'

'So he was as good as his word.' George said this soberly. 'And how did it go down?'

'Not too badly—except with what you might term some of the regulars. They clearly judged it uncalled for. But there was quite a congregation. It was really rather odd. There wasn't much time, after all, for word to get around that there was to be a noted metropolitan preacher.'

'I hardly think, my dear, that Hooker would care to be thought of as just that. Perhaps the sticker on the notice-board about banning the bomb had stirred curiosity a little. There was a large crowd?'

'Good heavens, no! Where would a large crowd come from in Plumley? But on one side of the aisle there were half a dozen young people, male and female, one had never seen before. And on the other side there was a small clump of more elderly women who were also total strangers. It made me think of a wedding, with the bride's and bridegroom's parties similarly disposed and glowering at each other.'

'Were those people doing that?'

'I did feel there was some kind of mutual hostility—or something like hostility—in the air. And Edith Prowse seemed to be feeling it too. The wretched woman was all of a twitter.'

'Was she supported by Prowse's nephew?'

'No, there was no sign of Simon, nor of his female friend. But it was all mildly perplexing—even without the two men from the Institute.'

'Without *what?*'

'Yes, wasn't it odd? At the end, you know, Christopher Prowse was standing at the door as usual, shaking hands and modulating into secular conversation. And with Hooker beside him. I was almost the last out, so Christopher told me about it. He was quite thrilled, and called it a breakthrough—meaning that at last he'd attracted the intellectual classes, and not just people like us. One of the boffins had introduced himself to Christopher. He's called Scattergood, it seems—which is a rather overpoweringly beneficent name to go about with.'

'So it is.' Uncle George was amused. 'Do you know? There was a Scattergood in my House at school. And a boy in the same year with the unfortunate name of Chumworthy. They used to be addressed as Do-You and Are-You. And—what was more extraordinary—there was a House Tutor named Rainwater. We called him the Drip.'

'Goodness, Uncle George! What a coruscation of juvenile wit.'

'Yes, indeed—and now I must be turning senile to reminisce about such nonsense. Go on about the after-church affair.'

'Christopher gathered that the obliging Scattergood is the top boffin at the Institute, and when he told Hooker he'd delivered a most thought-provoking address our friend was as pleased as Punch. Uncle George, just how are you thought-provoked by all this?'

'It occurs to me that these non-pub-frequenting gentlemen were rather belatedly trying to integrate themselves with the respectable church-going community.'

'Well, yes—perhaps. But I think—although I know you'll say I'm plot-mongering—that they'd heard about June Gale's sticker on that notice-board, and come along to discover whether St Michael and All Angels is a centre of anti-nuclear ferment.'

'And they actually got something like that from Hooker?'

'Well, no—not exactly. Hooker was most judicious. Almost Laodicean, I'd say.' Hilda paused to admire the appropriateness of this ink-horn term, and then saw that it wouldn't do. 'But that's not quite fair,' she said. Hooker did speak up.'

'As I'd expect him to do. For I don't, you know, share your sense of surprise whenever he gets a good mark.'

'You think I'm prejudiced against him.'

'Not exactly that. And if you do rather disapprove of him it's my fault for not greatly taking to him at the start.' George paused to consider whether this was an adequate account of the matter. 'And I mustn't pretend that I adore him now,' he added humorously. 'All the same, if he threw up the sponge and packed his bag tomorrow, I'd positively find myself missing his company. Not that I'm other than very happy just with the family. I'm very happy, indeed. And about Hooker I've been rather anxious, in a way.'

'You've wanted him to acquit himself well in poor Christopher's pulpit?'

'Yes, I have. During the last hour I've been distinctly in suspense about it. I'd hate the Prowses to have landed themselves in any way with something other than they'd bargained for. But it seems to have gone off fairly painlessly. We may relax.'

'Relax, Uncle George!' Hilda was abruptly scandalized. 'When we've discovered—you and I—the most frightful things about Simon Prowse, and the Gale girl, and the place that claims to be harmlessly engaged on something called animal genetics when it's probably thinking up bigger and better bombs? Lies and humbug all round us, and something that looks like civil commotion dead ahead! What do we *do*?'

If George was surprised by this sudden vehemence, he was far from displeased by it. Nevertheless he produced what was perhaps a discouraging reply.

'I don't know about myself,' he said. 'I've done in my time a fair amount of labouring against disabling ignorance and stupidity, not to mention what are thought of as the evil passions. I have the habit of it, and perhaps I ought to go on. But isn't it rather your thing to stand back and observe and record? Aren't you the chield amang us taking notes?'

'Don't make fun of me, Uncle George.'

'Certainly I will make fun of you whenever I can. But do just consider. One can't tell how to act until one has decided where one stands. And that may be difficult when an issue comes at one out of the blue. It's different if one has lived with it, off and on, for a long time. That's my own case, you know—which has nothing to do with bombs. And this particular affair—a possible demonstration by young people which may be against a fair target or against a totally mistaken one—is intriguing, no doubt, but not of the first significance in itself. The real issue—and it's a huge one—seems to me to require a good deal of thought before one starts running around.'

'Simon Prowse may have given it a good deal of thought.'

'That is certainly so. So, conceivably, may Miss Gale—although it's also conceivable that she represents people merely going in for rather unfocused rebellion.'

'So you're not going to do anything?'

'I didn't say that. I was suggesting you don't yourself throw your cap too hastily into the ring.' George was aware that he sounded feeble. At bottom he felt that this unexpected local mystery, now so urgent in his niece's mind, was a distraction from the issues that he and Father Hooker were committed—and now with an occasionally distinguishable co-operative intent—to clarifying to the best of their ability. It was all, he saw, rather bewildering. And bewilderment (although he regarded the condition as one of his chronic liabilities) was something George had been surprisingly little aware of in himself since the moment of his stepping off the train and being met by Hilda. It had dropped from him, just as had those bouts of amnesia. But its brief return now produced rather an odd reaction. 'I'll tell you one thing I'll do,' he said. 'I'll keep an eye on Hooker.'

'In heaven's name, Uncle George, what is there to keep an eye on in Hooker?'

'There's the fact that he's a mystery man.' Thus obscurely committed to talking nonsense, George persevered with it. 'Or perhaps a mystery woman. Don't you notice a hint of the transvestite in him? Perhaps he's a witch. Think of those cats. Hooker seems to be the sort of person who has a pathological fear of cats. But that may be a blind. He may have a kind of malign power over the creatures, and be organizing a cats' coven. Thrice the brinded cat hath mewed, you know.'

'Uncle George, are you making fun again of the kind of

nonsense you think goes on in my would-be inventive head?'

'No, no—and I apologize.' George saw that his niece was a little offended, and he was quickly repentant. 'It must just be that I'm developing an elderly and unseemly sense of comedy. As for doing anything, I don't know. But I do think Simon Prowse's imposture as practised on his uncle ought to be dropped on at once. If the young man is really organizing something—whether laudable or not—which may run into trouble with the law, Prowse—who is a first-rate innocent—might be suspected of complicity in whatever the dark design may be.' George found himself on his feet, and with that fleeting sense of bewilderment gone. 'In fact, I'll try hunting him up now.'

'Jolly d.' Hilda's displeasure had vanished. 'And I think I'll hunt up something, too. Where did those odd bods in church come from? Nobody had a notion about them, but they must be lurking somewhere. I'm going to look. And I'll take Henry with me. He badly needs time off from his infinitesimals, or whatever they are.'

'You walk Henry,' George said, 'and I'll hunt down Simon.'

It had been an impulsive resolution on George's part, prompted by a wish to show his niece that he wasn't wholly compounded of wise passiveness. But he was determined not to go back on it, and he therefore set off at once and before turning cool on the project. As a result, he was half-way down the village street before realizing that his mission wasn't a simple one.

Its entire basis, to begin with, rested on his nephew Charles's assertion of the advanced character of Simon Prowse's classical studies. What if Charles had got it all wrong—perhaps muddling one man with another? What if he had even made the whole thing up out of a misplaced sense of humour? If one accepted his story as true, one was accepting something the full freakishness of which George had perhaps failed to take the measure of. Even if the young man did want to be in the neighbourhood of Plumley in a picturesque undercover way, would he really have sought out this uncle and represented himself as a dunce in need of elementary tuition in construing Latin texts? The deception would be far from easy to sustain

136

even for a couple of hours; and only a decidedly perverse delight in play-acting, surely, could prompt to it. Organizing a demonstration against the proliferation of nuclear armaments —if that was really Simon's concern—seemed to George a ticklish matter, properly to be entered upon only in a spirit of high seriousness, and this didn't cohere at all with the prank he had been induced to suspect as going on at the vicarage.

George was so struck by the importance of this point that he actually came to a halt to consider it further. His conclusion was that he might well be wrong; that the very gravity of the main undertaking could be felt, in certain minds, to be wholesomely mitigated by a streak of outrageous fantasy. But this didn't end his sense of the complexity of what he was undertaking. Why, for instance, was it *he* who was undertaking it? What standing in the matter did he possess, and mightn't he fairly be told to mind his own business? Again, did his proposed interposition involve him to some extent in violating a confidence made to him— indirectly, it was true—by Charles Naylor? This particular scruple George was able to dismiss as fanciful, but at once yet a further question arose. Ought he—and actually within the vicarage—to tackle Simon Prowse himself head-on? Would it not be more proper to have a quiet talk with the young man's uncle, and gently intimate a suspicion that things weren't quite as they might seem?

Perpending these problems, George walked ahead. From cottages on either side of the road came occasional wafts as of incense which spoke of housewives basting the Sunday joint. On little driveways, or on the road itself, conscientious car-owners performed another of the day's ritual duties, cleansing their vehicles of the week's accumulated stains of mud and dust, washing them clean, assoiling them in preparation for another week's contact with a fallen world. These activities, George reflected, went some way towards accounting for Christopher Prowse's vacant pews. But even the intellectually unassuming classes must still wrestle at times with old-fashioned doubt. They hadn't heard of the myth of the incarnate god, but reckoned there was a lot in the Bible that would seem uncommonly improbable if presented on television. So with the bright believing band they had no claim to be either.

But these sombre thoughts were aside from the business of the moment, which was the bad conduct of Simon Prowse. And suddenly Simon Prowse was in front of George, head-on—debouching from a side-road close to the church and vicarage, in which, it seemed, one bought Sunday papers: Simon had a sheaf of them under his arm. Thus confronted, George forgot about the perplexities he had been mulling over. He came to a halt before the young man, and then spoke.

'Mr Prowse,' he said, 'can you extenuate in any way the gross deception you are imposing upon your uncle and aunt? If so, be so kind as to let me hear it.'

Abruptly taxed in this forthright fashion, Simon Prowse might well have been discomposed. Alternatively, or in addition, he might have been extremely angry. Had he there and then said, 'And what the devil have my affairs to do with you?' he would have been well within, if not his rights, at least the bounds of common expectation. But Simon took a moment before saying anything at all. He also removed from his head, with brisk and unconscious deference, a battered but serviceable straw hat.

'Now, just who,' he asked, 'has been telling tales?'

'My nephew, Charles Naylor, with whom you played tennis the other day, happens to have been an undergraduate at Trinity until a couple of terms ago.'

'I can't say I remembered him. I ought to, if he was in his third year.'

'He was in his first, but has now gone down. That, however, is neither here nor there. May I have an answer to my question?'

'I'm not quite sure.' Simon Prowse now seemed entirely at ease—and this despite a certain pallor which had made itself evident upon his features. 'I did enjoy playing tennis at your brother's house. But I don't quite see, sir, that it obliges me to stand and chat with you now. For one thing, it's almost lunch-time, is it not?'

'Come, Mr Prowse.'

Although there was no hint of indulgence in George's manner of saying this, the effect was somehow composing. George Naylor, after all, was an old hand with young men.

'I've been bound over,' Simon said. 'Are you shocked?'

George certainly wasn't shocked. Again with young men—
and occasionally with young women—who had been bound
over in one sort of law court or another, his acquaintance was
extensive and spread over a number of years.

· 'And what,' he asked, 'would it be next time?'

'A suspended sentence, I suppose. It would be a great
nuisance, that.'

'May I ask, Mr Prowse, whether this at all—well, affects your
academic career? I understand it to be extremely promising.'

'I'm most obliged to you.' Simon made this eighteenth-
centuryish response quite cheerfully. 'And, no. The dons don't
mind a bit. They'd like to have the guts themselves.'

'To march, and demonstrate, and sit in, and throw eggs?'

'I wouldn't be quite confident about the eggs. But, in a
general way, yes. I expect you've met the sort of people, rather
like your brother, only much more so: squirarchally disguised
but really bankers and so forth in a hereditary way, who
honestly believe that all professors and such like cattle are
innately subversive? They're probably quite right. Superficially,
nothing looks more utterly conservative than, say, an Oxford
senior common room. But in point of training and economic
status, the whole clerkly class is essentially Jacobin, wouldn't
you say? Which means uncommonly dangerous.'

Thus urbanely invited to engage in intellectually sophisticated
conversation, George was momentarily put to a stand. But he
managed to come back to business.

'Your being bound over to keep the peace,' he said, 'would
debar you from taking part even in peaceful demonstrations?'

'The beaks would certainly take that view. They'd say that a
demo was inherently an invitation to disorder, or some
rigmarole of that kind. And the fuzz, you know, have taken to
picking you up on film, and filing you as having been in one
place or another. They'll even come at you from the air, like
bloody recording angels. So I have to keep my head down, you
see—and not even bowed in prayer in Christopher's church,
which is why I didn't have the pleasure of listening to your friend
this morning. That's the whole thing.'

George couldn't agree that it was the whole thing, or even
approximately so. He was about to return to something like,

'And does all that justify the disgraceful imposture you are practising upon your uncle?' But he now saw that this, at least, *was* no concern of his. It wasn't even as if he were an intimate of the Prowses. Moreover, any immediate *éclaircissement* on this front—his now entering the vicarage and denouncing Simon, for instance—would inevitably have the effect of exposing Christopher Prowse as a guileless ass, for what man of reasonably acute perceptions could be taken in by such a piece of nonsense for long? But the situation had, as it were, its public as well as its private aspect, and he ought now perhaps to tackle it from that direction. George was considering just how to do so, when Simon spoke again.

'I understand about your nephew Charles,' he said, 'and his lately having been up at Trinity. But what puts it into your head to be on about marches and demonstrations?'

George wasn't sure that the young man's describing his being 'on about' something was altogether courteous in point of expression. But Simon, in addition to being clever and therefore attractive, was exhibiting decent manners, and the question was fair enough in itself.

'It's a matter of odd coincidence, Mr Prowse. Miss Gale, your slightly mysterious friend, happened to hand me a leaflet about the bomb in Oxford a few days ago.'

'Ah, yes. June was staying in Oxford with an aunt. But she just can't take time off the anti-nuclear activity.'

'Nor can you?'

'I manage a certain number of other things as well.'

If there was a hint of intellectual arrogance lurking in this, it was sufficiently dissimulated to be inoffensive on the young man's part. So George tried again.

'Just what are you aiming at—or organizing against? Is it that place at Nether Plumley?'

'I'm afraid, Dr Naylor, that I have nothing more to say.'

'I think I have some right to be informed.' George was about to add, 'You and Miss Gale, after all, have been my brother's guests.' But he realized that this would be artificial and silly. And he had, in fact, got himself into a false position, and was in danger of talking nonsense. He had no right whatever to badger this young man, and by running round like an excited spaniel he was only making himself ridiculous. There wasn't the slightest evidence that Simon Prowse and his friends proposed either to endanger life or damage property. They no doubt believed themselves—and it was an open and arguable issue—to be acting exactly in a contrary interest. George had been legitimately indignant over the prank played on the ingenuous Christopher Prowse; he had got this tangled up with his niece's not very rational persuasions about what might be going on at Nether Plumley; and as a result here he was in the middle of the village street, doing his best to have a row with a young man he knew very little about.

In falling so abruptly for this revulsion of feeling George was not perhaps being quite fair to himself. Simon had shoved in among the Naylors and banged their tennis balls around most definitely under false colours, and with no other aim than to propagate in the district the conclusion that he was a harmless and agreeably athletic dullard. There was every justification for taking a good hard look at him. But it was George's liability to have a lively sense of the other fellow's point of view. And as the main business of his life at the moment was moderating this proclivity in the area of his debate with Hooker, it was perhaps to be expected that he would let Simon Prowse get away with something—and with rather more than Hilda would approve of. George saw this clearly enough, but was resigned to making no further progress with the young man. He was casting round for some reasonably seemly way of bringing the interview to a close when the matter was taken out of his hands in a rather disconcerting fashion.

The entire colloquy had occurred on the spot where the two contestants had suddenly encountered one another: beside the churchyard wall and opposite the side-road in which Simon had been buying his newspapers. This was little more than a lane ascending from Plumley village to a road that followed the line of the downs overlooking the vale in which the Plumleys lay. Up the lane George was conscious that Simon had suddenly turned a sharpened gaze. What had apparently attracted this was the roof of a car, still several hundred yards away, which would not become fully visible until it had advanced beyond a dip and a bend now immediately in front of it. But it could already be seen to be either a police car or an ambulance, since perched on top of it was that kind of diminutive lighthouse which can be set imperiously flashing at need.

'On my way,' Simon said abruptly. And George had just time to recall that he had heard these words from the young man spoken on this spot before when Simon turned round, vaulted over the wall behind him, and disappeared amid the various graves. George peered after him in vain. It was conceivable—he weirdly thought—that he had secluded himself within one of those lidless stone receptacles, somewhat larger than a cabin trunk, that witnessed to rural burial customs some centuries ago.

But more probably, of course, Simon had simply made his way rapidly back to the vicarage. George realized that he himself ought to make similar haste in returning to the Park, where luncheon would be on the table in some ten minutes' time. He set off, therefore, at a brisk pace—and the more gratefully, perhaps, because he was leaving so unsatisfactory an episode behind him. But actually it was not a successful get-away. *He was being pursued!*

George was instantly persuaded of this, although for no better reason than that the car that had occasioned Simon's rapid departure had itself turned in the direction of Plumley Park and was now behind him. He glanced at it over his shoulder and saw that it was indeed a police car. There were uniformed constables in the two front seats. He walked on for some 20 paces, and realized that the car ought by now to have overtaken him and gone on ahead. He again looked over his shoulder, although it was a jumpy and almost guilty-seeming thing to do. The beastly car was kerb-crawling! There was no other expression for the thing. George found himself experiencing very much the sort of justified indignation that might be experienced by a virtuous female actually exposed to this indignity. More rationally, he had to suppose that there was some intention to alarm him; that these two policemen conceived themselves to be engaged in a war of nerves.

But now the car accelerated very slightly and drew level. George was constrained to look at it again; in face of its unaccountable behaviour it would have been unnatural not to do so. And both the policemen looked at him. Even the man at the wheel—surely very improperly—held him for whole seconds under a fixed regard. George couldn't recall ever having been looked at quite like this before—unless it was by some abominably sadistic prefect in chapel at his public school. It occurred to him that what are called identikit portraits of wanted miscreants are probably best built up on the basis of professionally penetrating scrutinies such as he was going to be subjected to now.

George and the car continued to move forward at the same pace. The policeman on the near side—still keeping up that steely stare—lowered his window. He called out to George as a motorist may do who seeks information from a pedestrian. Involuntarily, George halted and looked at him inquiringly. The policeman said nothing more, but raised an arm. There was a faint click, and George oddly found himself wondering whether he had been shot. Then he realized he had been photographed. The window went up again, and the car accelerated and was gone.

George had not been so indignant since the regrettable incident at the entrance to the Bodleian Library.

The family was already at table, so George had no immediate opportunity to communicate to Hilda either the unsatisfactory character of his interview with Simon Prowse or the upsetting episode that had followed upon it. He felt, however, that this was just as well, since he might have exhibited himself as more nearly flustered than was sensible. And although he had arrived a little out of breath, nobody asked him what he had been up to.

This was perhaps because Father Hooker was proving to have a lot to say. Unlike those prudent divines of an earlier age who took an hour-glass into the pulpit with them, Hooker, it seemed, had been in trouble over the length of his sermon. He had been conscious, he said, of the danger of speaking at too great length to a simple auditory—he seemed unaware that his congregation had not included a thronging peasantry—and equally fearful that he hadn't adequately satisfied the expectations of the better-informed. He had been particularly sketchy in the provision of historical background to his argument. His host, he said—with one of his shattering little bows to Edward Naylor at the foot of the table—may well have expected at least a passing reference to the Council of Narbonne. That had been in 1054—the year, as it happened, in which Macbeth (and here Hilda got a bow) had been defeated by Malcolm at Dunsinane; and the year, for that matter, in which, on the 16th of July, there had occurred the definitive split between the Roman and Greek Churches. But the immediate point was that the Council of Narbonne, wrestling with the problem of the Just War, had enjoined that even such a blameless war must not be waged on Fridays, Sundays and Feasts of the Church—which was presumably about half-way to banning it altogether.

Edward Naylor, who was being particularly addressed, managed occasional weighty nods and monosyllabic acquiescences. When Hooker found something to say about the *De jure belli* of Grotius, Edward positively managed to repeat the name 'Grotius' as if he had been expecting it to turn up for some time.

All this made George uncomfortable. He realized that social tact wasn't Hooker's strong point, and that he had been elevated in more senses than one by climbing into a pulpit: perhaps because it was very little his weekly round or common task. When not sent by fiat from Tower Hamlets on missions like the present, he probably sat in solitude in a book-lined room and did theology all day. This was a depressing picture—but at the same time George was conscious of nursing something like a growing loyalty towards Hooker, who could surely be more profitably employed than by sitting awkwardly at the Naylors' board in the interest of recapturing a most unimportant fugitive priest. Were his niece and nephews ten years younger—George reflected—they would by this time be struggling, as reasonably well brought-up children, to repress their giggles before so odd a guest. When his present afflatus sank in him Hooker would probably feel rather lonesome and out-on-a-limb. George hated the thought of this, and searched around in his head for suitable references to Origen and Aquinas in order to give some colouring of general discussion to Hooker's inopportune performance.

No great success attended this endeavour, but at least the impulse was amiable. Nevertheless, George Naylor's character at this point is not to be aspersed as improbably exemplary. He could be taxed with the frailty of harbouring weakly contradictory attitudes. He was still lurkingly disposed to resent the graceless expedition with which the Bishop of Tower Hamlets' emissary had turned up on him, and even those aspects of Father Hooker's comportment which seemed to verge, if not on the unmannerly, at least on the boring and insensitive. But while thus failing to rid himself of his sense of Hooker as a pest, he was increasingly coming to assume that he himself was the sole proper object of the man's concern. Hooker, in fact, was being seduced into neglecting him a little. It could almost be said that the bomb—George thought of it as Hilda's bomb—was threatening to take over the story. Of course it was abundantly entitled to do so—supposing it to be, so to speak—really *there*. Even after his encounter with Simon, and in spite of what Hilda had apparently come to believe, it had remained his own conviction that it wasn't; that although Simon and an unknown number of presumably young people were certainly planning a demonstration against the Institute at Nether Plumley, it was on the strength of a totally mistaken notion of what went on in the place. What had happened to him on his walk back from the village had shaken his confidence about this, however; policemen, he felt, didn't behave in quite that way except in circumstances of an exceptional order.

At the close of the meal there came into George's head something he had read as a boy nearly 30 years before. An American novelist—it must have been William Faulkner—had been given the Nobel Prize for Literature and had made a speech. There are no longer problems of the spirit, he had said. There is only the question: When will I be blown up?

It occurred to George that Hilda—an author in search of a theme—might very fairly place her uncle at the centre of a small comedy turning on this proposition.

'And we must keep a look out for the cats,' Hilda said. She and Henry had set off immediately after lunch, armed with binoculars, to scour the countryside.

'The cats?' Henry repeated this absently and with a frown. He wasn't yet sure that he thought much of the idea of hunting down potential demonstrators. He had come along, he told himself, only because he hadn't yet managed to shake off the habit of taking orders from his sister. It was something he'd better get cracking on. 'I don't think we'll see your wretched cats again,' he said.

'Don't be so dismal. Jeoffry and Old Foss are much too clever to get run over.'

'But not clever enough to avoid the stew-pots of our friends.'

'And don't be so silly.'

'There's nothing silly about it. Or not unless you're imagining things, as you probably are. Camped in some mysteriously invisible way around the Plumleys is a horde of crackpot characters preparing for what's called a riotous assembly. It stands to reason they're living off the land. We'll come on a bunch of them at any moment, asleep after a tremendous gorge on cat collops.'

'How disgusting can we get.'

'There's that saying about cats having nine lives. Obsolete. Archaic. Do you know that in London nowadays no cat has as much as half a life? Your pussy has only to put a whisker outside the door never to be seen again. The pie-shop, the furrier, the lab: they're all after poor puss. The going rate is fifty pence.'

'Henry, you're as idiotic as Hooker, who would like to think that cats are eaten by foxes.'

'Hooker talked a good deal of tripe in that sermon.' Henry had exhausted his interest in cats. 'But he stopped short of ignominy. I think that's the word. He didn't say that we should turn up our moral noses at the thing and leave using it to the Yanks. I suppose that's what your friend believes.'

'Just what do you mean: my friend?'

As Hilda made this demand, she came abruptly to a halt. They had reached the end of the Plumley Park drive, and surroundings which witnessed to the consequence not of Naylors but of proprietors who had departed long ago. There were lofty and elaborate iron gates, decently painted but never to be coaxed or wrenched shut again; these hung from bulky and flaking stone pillars which were no longer quite perpendicular, and on each of which was perched what might have been a football, or a plum pudding, or even a bomb from the days in which such things enjoyed a primitive simplicity; on either side of the drive there crouched an untenanted lodge so diminutive that it might have passed as a commodious dog-kennel. To have this ensemble between oneself and the world always struck Hilda as depressing. That she should now have paused beside it suggested something particularly arresting, even offensive, in her brother's conjecture.

'Your friend Simon,' Henry said. 'Essentially, it seems to me we're yearning after him now. Or you are. I can't really see any other explanation of this jaunt. What he and his Gale girl and his elusive legion are up to isn't any affair of ours.'

Hilda gave some moments to trying honestly to decide whether these were penetrating remarks. Alone of the family, after all, she was aware that Henry, although he could talk nonsense, was rather an able boy.

'You mean,' she said, 'that you think I think him marvellous?'

'Pretty well that.'

'I don't.'

'Good. Let's go on.'

Hilda realized that Henry had simply believed her at once. So *he*, in a way, was marvellous. And she felt some further explanation was due to him.

'As a matter of fact,' she said, 'I was rather taken with Simon. No doubt you spotted my young palpitating heart. But I've come to think of him as a bit of a showman. What he's up to—if he *is* up to it—seems a bit elaborate. I'm probably too stodgy for him. But we mustn't conclude he isn't serious about the bomb and stopping it. More serious than we are, if we pass by the mess on the other side.'

'As Uncle George would say, it's a point of view. And a point of view's just what we need. We'll take our field-glasses up to Tim's Tump. From there you can command the whole terrain—Animal Genetics and all.'

Having thus taken command, Henry set off with long strides. Tim's Tump was a long barrow, and it was improbable that a person called Tim had ever had anything to do with it—or not in any sort of respectable antiquity. It lay longitudinally on the crest of the down, and against the skyline suggested the proportions of a furry caterpillar. It had been excavated or rifled long ago; the Department of the Environment tidied it up from time to time; you could enter it, and even—on a wet day—hold a crouched sort of picnic in its interior. Arable land had crept up and around it in recent times, but here and there in the fields thus created lay great sarsen stones which no farmer had ever toiled to fragment by fire and remove. A few of them stood mysteriously erect, having been thus heaved up for unknown ritual purposes some thousands of years ago, and these had the air of sentries or outlying pickets set to guard an immemorially numinous region against intrusion. But all this still lay some 500 feet above the heads of Hilda and Henry, and there was a stiff climb to it. They were yet in the vale, and moving through a scattering of near hovels inhabited—Hilda declared—by retired witches and worn-out and discarded hinds and clowns, which nevertheless went by the imposing name of Plumley Ducis.

'Agreed,' Henry said suddenly, 'that we're not chasing the attractive Simon. What *are* we chasing? What's this in aid of? It isn't clear to me. This demo, or whatever: are you for it or against it?'

'I don't know. Uncle George seems to feel I ought to be one or the other. But, really, I just want to have a look. To see how it ticks. There isn't much to watch ticking in Plumley. I've felt that, rather, since I came back to it.'

'Then get away again. Find yourself a job. Or even a husband, if you can land a passable one.'

'Thank you very much.' Hilda paused, and decided not to be offended. 'It's a matter of a breathing-space, I think, and of looking around.'

'The fact is, my girl, that the short story has gone to your head.'

'What do you mean—the short story?' Hilda had come to a halt, and was staring at her brother in dismay.

'A chap at school showed it to me. As a matter of fact, I thought it rather good. Not that I'm a judge. It's not my kind of thing.'

'Henry, you haven't told anybody?' Hilda's perturbation was now tinged with pleasure. Actually to *hear* even an off-hand commendation was something new to her.

'Of course not. A gentleman can be trusted to conceal his sister's shame.' Henry paused for a moment. 'Does one,' he then asked curiously, 'feel very protective about that sort of progeny?'

'Yes.'

'I wonder whether I'd feel like that if I discovered something? In maths, I mean. Probably not. Do you know what was the most marvellous moment in human history?'

'You'd have to ask Hooker to get a quick answer to that one.' Hilda was now walking on. 'I suppose you'd say it was when some Arab, charging around the Sahara on his camel, found he'd invented the multiplication sign, or spotted that nought comes before one, two and three.'

'Amazingly well-educated young women are nowadays. But, no—it wasn't quite that. It was when scientists—experimental philosophers, as they said—stopped feeling protective about their achievements, and started letting on about them. Even mathematicians had imagined that their equations and things were valuable private property, to be held on to right to the grave. I suppose that was because most of them were astrologers as well, or could flog you the sums telling you how to aim a cannon or a catapult. *Publishing* your discoveries: that was the great turning-point in history.'

'So now anybody can read about the bomb.'

'Right! Of course there's a lot more to it than reading up. But, by and large, any little tin-pot dictator or junta or what-have-you can get busy on the thing. If you want to think about the bomb at all—which isn't particularly necessary in your case—you'd better begin from there.'

'A woman's sphere is the home.' Hilda said this without much attending to it. She was digesting the fact that she had a more or less grown-up brother, and that it wasn't the harmlessly oafish Charles. 'If you begin from there,' she asked, 'how do you go on?'

'Not by giving three cheers for Master Simon. Or I *think* not that, although one oughtn't to be in a hurry to be dogmatic about it. In a way, it doesn't much matter what one thinks. Catastrophe is so near-certain that thinking up ways to avoid it isn't much more than an intellectual exercise.'

'Henry, do you really believe that?'

'Oh, probably. But one has one's gut reactions as well as one's wretched little brain.'

'If enough people could be brought to think and act as Simon does . . .'

'Yes—but they never will. The thing's there—targeted on Paris, London, Moscow, New York. What's also there is the balance of terror. Its less terrifying name is the balance of power. If one country wins too many battles, enough other countries get together to slow it up. That way, you got something that used to be called the Concert of Europe. There's perhaps a faint gleam of hope in the balance of terror.'

'Which you don't think Simon much enlarges.'

'Bother Simon. He's not important. He wouldn't be, even if he weren't barking up the wrong tree.'

'What do you mean by that?'

'It's rubbish that the Nether Plumley place can have anything to do with bombs. But I'll tell you what's important—or, at least, interesting. It's the question of orders of magnitude. In that war with Hitler and the general nastiness surrounding it, about fifty million people were killed before Hiroshima was heard of. Just old-fashioned bullets and T.N.T., with occasionally a gas-chamber or the like thrown in, were adequate for the job. How many of your camel-jockey's noughts have you to add if you'd get the sum right when the bomb drops now? Is it just a quantitative question, or something quite different? Oh, God! Look who's bearing down on us.'

What had interrupted Henry Naylor's lecture was not really sufficiently disconcerting or surprising to have justified him in thus invoking the Deity. It was no more than the appearance of Christopher Prowse and his wife, taking the afternoon air in Plumley Ducis. But there was something questing in their manner of looking around them, and Hilda noted this.

'Not a single child,' she said, 'has turned up at Sunday School. Christopher and Edith are hunting down the truants.'

'Sunday School? Surely that sort of thing doesn't still happen?' Henry was entirely sceptical. 'I remember how as kids we agreed to go along once a month at five bob a time, and were told we were setting an example. But T.V. and video must have killed it stone dead.'

Hilda made no reply to this. She was engaged in reciprocating

150

those gestures of gratified recognition which were automatic with the vicar on first sighting a parishioner.

'I know!' Henry suddenly went on. 'They're searching for Sinbad. Sinbad or Tinbad or Jinbad.'

'Or Vinbad the Quailer or Linbad the Yailer.' Momentarily, Hilda ignored the Prowses; she was recalling how, a few days before, Henry had incautiously admitted familiarity at least with the name of the author of *Ulysses*. It was another dimension in which her nearly-grown-up brother was revealing himself as a dark horse. If Uncle George went away—whether back to his mission or not—Henry might turn out to be a substantial conversational resource. They could, for instance, have further civilized talks about the bomb.

'Hallo!' Henry was saying with a cheerful and correct informality. 'We're guessing that you must be looking for Sinbad. Is that right?'

'Well, Henry—yes.' Christopher Prowse was oddly hesitant. 'At least Sinbad is in our minds. Yes.'

'We can't help being a little anxious,' Edith Prowse said.

'That's only natural.' Hilda, whose mother was frequently a little anxious about one thing or another, produced a practised look of moderate concern. 'But it's my belief that those cats have gone off in a body about their own affairs, and will drift back discreetly one by one.'

'But it isn't only the cats.' Mrs Prowse suddenly discovered herself as under a burden of anxiety which she was unable longer to conceal. 'It's Christopher's nephew as well.'

'Simon!' Henry exclaimed. 'He's vanished with the cats?'

'At least, *like* the cats.' The vicar didn't seem to offer this correction with any humorous intent. 'It's really rather disturbing. Simon has been restless ever since he came to us. Hurrying off here and there with very little explanation. We thought perhaps that he had archaeological interests.'

'Or ornithological?' Hilda asked. 'That's what *I* thought.'

'Or perhaps it's music,' Henry said. 'Perhaps Simon's like the chap in Hamelin town: a latter-day Orpheus.' (Henry thus revealed yet another dimension.) 'He pipes, and the brute creation follows. He and all the cats of Plumley have now gone under the hill.'

The Prowses fortunately made nothing of this irresponsible mockery, their agitation being such that it passed over their heads.

'Simon didn't turn up in church,' Christopher Prowse said, 'and not to lunch either. And of course it has all interfered with his work most disastrously. If, indeed, it *is* his work.'

'What do you mean?' Henry asked quickly. 'If it *is* his work?'

'I wonder whether I may confide in you?' The vicar asked this in a yearning sort of way which Hilda didn't at all like. She asked herself whether she could hastily declare that her brother, although lately showing himself to be rather clever and well-informed, was not altogether wholly serious. But, in the name of family solidarity, she decided against this. Christopher Prowse must look after himself.

'Yesterday afternoon, you see,' Christopher went on, 'when Simon was out, it occurred to me to go into his room and take a look at some of his notebooks.' Christopher paused, as if aware that this was a shade awkward. 'It had come into my head that I might get some notion of the more common errors to which his Latin is prone, and assist him in that way.'

'A very helpful idea,' Henry said. 'So what?'

'It was most perplexing, most unexpected. For instance, there was a whole notebook devoted to the *Bacchae*.'

'Baccy? Something to do with smoking?'

'No, no.' Christopher seemed merely bemused before this extraordinary question. 'The *Bacchae* is a tragedy by Euripides. And the notes were on some of the knottier problems in the Greek text.'

'Oh, I see! But that's your nephew's line, isn't it?'

'Far from it. Simon professes to have elementary Latin, and no Greek at all.'

'The other day,' Edith Prowse interposed, 'I *did* just *hint* to Hilda that we thought there may be a *romance*.'

Hilda, unlike her brother, was not here confronted by anything new. But, more forcibly than before, the disingenuous behaviour of Simon Prowse towards his relations struck her in an unfavourable light.

'There's no romance,' she said. 'There's a plot. And you must face it, Christopher, that you could be represented as uncommonly easily taken in.'

'I'm sure it will all resolve itself in time.' Christopher produced this vague response without conviction; he was plainly regretting the domestic disclosure he had offered. 'But to return to the cats. Their disappearance is not connected with my nephew in any way. In fact, there is only one explanation—and it is a most distressing one, I fear. The hyena is active again.'

'But of course!' Henry said instantly. 'How stupid of me. The hyena it is. Poor pussies.'

It was clear to Hilda that her brother didn't believe in the hyena. Nor did she. Nor, for that matter, in the region of the Plumleys as a whole, did perhaps a majority of those who would at one time have been described as of the better sort. These regarded the brute as a phantom merely: a product of the kind of instant folklore that is created and propagated by the popular press. There had, indeed, twice appeared in print intelligence that the hyena had been encountered in broad daylight (and promptly ascribed to its species) by reliable members of the public: on the first occasion by William Pidduck, aged six, as he was walking home from school, and on the second by Mrs Goslin, aged eighty-three, while drawing water from a tap conveniently located at the bottom of her garden. These persons had become local celebrities for a time, and their photographs had even appeared in a national newspaper. And to a very large number of people over the months had come at least persuasive hints and intimations of the creature's near-presence, commonly in the dark. The hyena had been heard snarling; it had been heard purring; it had been heard doing deep-breathing, like a maniac on the telephone; most frequently, of course, it had been heard giving vent to demoniac laughter. Its eyes had been observed burning bright in the copses and dingles of the vicinity.

One didn't, perhaps, have to be wholly gullible to believe in the veridical status of the hyena. Wild beasts—or at least beasts that could plausibly be so described—did escape from time to time from private zoos. People who once had kept homing-pigeons or guinea-pigs in their back yard had many of them switched to lions and tigers. Indeed, at one point Edward Naylor, ever alert to the movement of plebeian minds, had briefly wondered whether it might be possible to promote packaged Adventure Playgrounds for Big Cats. So the Prowses are not to be ridiculed at this point in our story.

'But this time, at least, the police have consented to be alerted,' Christopher Prowse said. 'Someone must have apprised them of the situation, and they have turned out half a dozen patrol cars at once. There goes one of them now. Just in front of the inn.'

This was true. Such a car, cruising slowly, was visible from where the Naylors and Prowses stood.

'Did you say half a dozen?' Henry asked.

'Yes, indeed.'

'You haven't, perhaps, been seeing the same car several times?'

'Certainly not.' The vicar took the opportunity of avoiding unchristian irritation as he offered this firm denial.

'In other words, just because somebody has reported to the police that the hyena has gone pussypophagous. . .'

'Has *what*?'

'Has taken to eating cats. Just because of that, the police have turned out six cars and a dozen men?'

'Yes—and it shows most commendable thoroughness, does it not? No doubt they are armed. But it is to be hoped, of course, that they don't have to kill or maim the creature. That would be most distressing.'

'Particularly on a Sunday.' Henry had the grace at once to be ashamed of this unseemly gibe. 'Perhaps they have nets or things,' he added rapidly.

'Or darts carrying an anaesthetic charge. I have observed them in use in the great nature reserves of Africa. On television, of course. I sometimes regret that as a young man my thoughts didn't turn to the mission field. One would have seen so much more.'

'Well, yes—I imagine so.' Henry, whom this irrelevant and wistful note suddenly rendered awkward, glanced at Hilda for help. 'I suppose we should be getting along.'

'We've promised ourselves to climb to the Tump,' Hilda said. 'It's a marvellous afternoon for a view.'

'And we must get back to the vicarage.' Edith Prowse had glanced at her watch. 'Simon may have returned there by now, and it may all prove to have been some stupid mistake. Even about the cats and that horrid hyena.' The vicar's wife, who spent much time urging desponding female parishioners to look on the bright side of things, appeared to extract genuine solace from these hazy hopes. 'Please give my love to your parents, Hilda. It was delightful to see them in church this morning. And such a good congregation, too.'

There were further civil exchanges after this, since the Prowses seldom took their leave of anybody except in a lingering way. They were, Hilda supposed, a lonely couple. They had no children to return to—and on the present occasion not even a cat. Christopher Prowse, although a conscientious man, had little talent for being easily *en rapport* with his parishioners in their several classes, occupations, and domestic circumstances, and in addition to this the mere fact of being a clergyman nowadays involved a certain alienation from secular society. At the moment, the vicar and his wife had the company of their kinsman and parlour boarder. But even if they found Simon at home again on their return, he could no longer represent for them more than a vexatious and even alarming enigma. There was, of course, something irresistibly comical in the thought of Christopher with his rusty Latin suddenly finding himself confronted with a pupil well-seen in the text of the *Bacchae*—and when Henry once or twice guffawed as he and Hilda resumed their walk it was no doubt this that was amusing him. But the entire situation was uncomfortable. Hilda, although she must have been aware of it as holding out unexpected promise for the exercise of literary talent, didn't care for it at all.

They surmounted a stile, and walked diagonally across a field containing a herd of moodily munching bullocks. A number of these interrupted this tedious occupation and came nosing after them in a kind of stupid curiosity. Hilda had the discouraging thought that stupid curiosity was at present her own key-note. Simon Prowse was at least up to something, whether laudable and well-considered or not. As soon as they were back at the Park Henry, with whatever affected discontent, would take himself off to his all-absorbing maths. Even Charles would be busying himself purposively with his fishing tackle and his injuriously uninvited gun. As for Uncle George and Father Hooker, they were now—even across what must surely be the vast gulf sundering belief and disbelief—contentedly debating something they might call the philosophy of religious experience. She herself was simply wandering around in the interest of no sort of action whatever. Perhaps she had better take Henry's advice, and set about landing a passable husband.

'That hyena,' she said abruptly. 'You don't believe in it, do you?'

'Of course not.' Henry was contemptuous. 'And the police don't believe in a cat-eating cat, either. Which doesn't mean the fuzz don't have to be explained. Good God! What's that?'

'That' was a sudden loud noise overhead. They both looked up, and what they saw was a helicopter. It was coming from behind them, and flying low. For a moment they were actually in its shadow. Then it was hovering directly above them, and dropping lower still. It made a terrible din—a kind of dry clattering that set the bullocks bolting in all directions. Then it rose again, and flew away across the vale.

'Bloody silly affairs,' Henry said. 'A jet can be shot to bits all round you, and you still have a chance. But if a rotor goes on one of those things, it's curtains within five seconds. Icarus just not in it.'

'Bother Icarus.' Hilda was unimpressed by this further unexpected instance of her brother's cultivation. 'The thing pretty well buzzed us. Week-end skylarking idiots!'

'I don't think so.'

'What do you mean by that?'

'Not play. Business. In fact, the fuzz again. They're out in force, expecting trouble. No, don't come to a stop and gape, girl. We go on to the top and have our own aerial view.'

Hilda obediently kept walking—and at a pace which for some minutes effectively discouraged speech. By this route it had become almost a scramble to gain Tim's Tump. The smooth downland turf, pleasant to the tread on gentler inclines, now felt slippy and treacherous. Hilda told herself it was quite amusing to take orders from the younger of her brothers—and of course there was nobody present to witness this anomalous disposition of things.

'So you agree it's all true?' she presently managed to gasp.

'No, not all of it. It remains nonsense that they make bombs at Nether Plumley. You might as well imagine they make battleships. But they do *something*, and your friend Simon disapproves and is planning—or at least participating in—a massive protest on the spot.'

'I don't see how it can be massive. So far as we know, there's only the Gale girl within the horizon. Of course, there was that scattering of strangers in church.'

'Members of a kind of vanguard, perhaps, who happen to be given to devotion as well as demos. Two little batches of them.'

'And not on very good terms with each other.'

'Rival enthusiasts, no doubt. And I grant you that, apart from them, there's no sign at all of strangers being around. Just a bunch of cops, drawing overtime and wasting petrol. Or so it seems. But—as I say—they're expecting something. Here we are.'

They had scrambled across a ditch and through a hedge, and were standing on a high road. It was perhaps the most ancient of its kind in England: a broad ribbon of grass, here and there much rutted and muddied by the passage of agricultural machinery, which ran in gentle curves and undulations along the ridge of the downs as far as the eye could see in either direction. Primitive peoples, dressed in skins and reputedly daubed with woad, had created it through ages of tribal wars and small migrations; the Roman legions had tramped it; in the great days of the wool trade vast flocks of sheep had been driven on it from county to county. On either hand it was now lipped by a prosperous agriculture: cornfields and pasture, conifer wind-breaks, byres and barns. Beyond this, and on lower ground, it commanded peopled vistas: farmsteads and hamlets and villages and even distant towns; striding pylons; reticulated roads and lanes, and at one far remove a motorway.

From the motorway minute points of light flashed briefly like random heliographs as cruising windscreens caught the sun. On roads in the middle distance the sauntering traffic of Sunday afternoons, scaled down by distance to a Dinky-toy parade, was abundantly on view. Nearer at hand, on a winding and steeply-rising lane that quickly lost itself in a first fold of the downs, a line of cyclists, some in brightly-coloured T-shirts and others in sweaty semi-nakedness, dragged a slow length along in the manner of Pope's wounded snake. It was (in the words of another poet) a field full of folk. But here on the immemorial ridgeway was solitude, day-long emptiness. Determined walkers, equipped with rucksacks and spiked sticks and compasses, bestrode it in clumpy boots from time to time. Intermittently, hordes of mechanic youths on Hondas and Suzukis drenched it in petrol vapour in the performance of a moto-cross. But that was all. It never occurred to the citizens of the Plumleys that here was a territory in which to walk abroad and recreate themselves. Was it not up a terrible great hill? Even in secure skylarking bands, the schoolchildren, too, avoided it. There was a spooky feel about Tim's Tump and the forgotten artery that flowed past its mystery.

At some time in the eighteenth century the Tump had been improved by a local landowner (conceivably known to his intimates as Tim) with developed antiquarian tastes. Conjecturing, probably correctly, that here was the burial place of a personage even more important than himself—a Druid, perhaps, but of good family, as the higher clergy ought to be—he had embellished the site and enhanced its consequence in various appropriate ways. He had begun with a clump of oaks. But these being slow to mature, and showing small promise of answering well to the soil, he had added a short avenue of beeches, oriented to lead directly up to the entrance of the barrow. He then felt that the Druid's ghost, surveying his demesne from beneath the massive capstone to his front door, would not be well served if the beech avenue simply ended off without display. He therefore caused two of the largest sarsens on his estate to be hauled up to the Tump, and there erected as if to support the two leaves of an adequately imposing iron gate. An actual gate would have been an absurdity, but the impulse to provide the seat of an important person with a suitably imposing approach was the same that displeased Hilda at the entrance to Plumley Park.

Hilda and Henry were not, at the moment, much interested in the Tump, let alone in these subsequent tinkerings. They had climbed to this eminence for the wide prospect it afforded, and upon that Henry was already directing his binoculars with all the gravity (which his sister didn't fail to remark) of a great commander surveying the ground upon which whole armies must presently engage. But when he spoke it wasn't to any warlike purpose.

'All very agreeable,' he said. 'The coloured counties, and so forth. But just a little dull. Small effects of bustle here and there—or at least of distinguishable activity. A retired gent trimming a hedge, or dutiful young people taking granny on her Sunday jaunt.' He swung the binoculars. 'And if Plumley's quiet, Nether Plumley's quieter still.'

'Nothing happening at the Institute?'

'Nothing at all. A few cars parked inside their ring-fence. The building itself doesn't seem much to go in for windows. Perhaps that's sinister.'

'It's not much to go on.' Hilda was focusing her own binoculars. 'From up here,' she said, 'you'd almost think Nether Plumley a bit less unimportant than we are. More of the little roads—the older ones—converge on it. Those coming through the woodlands to the north, for instance. It had a market once, you know, and was quite a place. I seem to remember reading in the *Victoria County History* that Camden or somebody calls it *emporiolum non inelegans*. It's a miserable little dump now.'

'Can you see any of those police cars?' Henry was unimpressed by this exhibition of learning.

'None at all. Perhaps they're having their tea.'

'Or have gone into ambush.' Henry turned away from the view and faced the Tump. 'Hell's bells!' he said. 'What are you doing here?'

This unmannerly demand was made of June Gale, who had appeared as if from nowhere. But that (Hilda might have told herself) was a facile cliché and inaccurate as well. To be thus suddenly on the scene, June must have emerged from the Tump itself. There was plenty of room for her there. The barrow could hold, indeed, a whole committee of conspiring persons.

'Oh, hallo!' It seemed that Miss Gale was less aware of the

tone in which she had been addressed than of the mere surprising fact of the Naylors' presence. And to this her reaction was a not very intelligent question. 'Has Simon sent you?'

'Yes, he thought we might lend a hand.' Henry said this promptly. 'Are any of the others here?'

'Oh, no. Just me. Manning the command post.' Miss Gale spoke with a complacency judged by Hilda to be highly absurd. But if the expression was extravagant it was nevertheless evident that Simon Prowse had indeed entrusted the girl with some job of a responsible character. And as she was (as Hilda believed) thoroughly thick, and as she had only recently earned herself a bad mark for her assault on the church notice-board, it was impossible not to conclude that Simon was besotted with her. Even potential Fellows of All Souls, it seemed, could be fondly overcome with female charm. Hilda was more scandalized by this aspect of the situation than she was even by her brother's high-speed command of a blank lie. Henry, moreover, had committed her to some course of deception herself—which she must now sustain, since it was unthinkable to let him down. But for the moment she thought to temporize, and she searched for something to say of a non-committal sort.

'Have you been here long?' she asked.

'Only Simon at the vicarage—you know about him—and myself with friends about ten miles away. Oh, and some people camping up on the downs somewhere: rather an elderly and churchy lot. We have all sorts.'

'I believe the churchy ones were in church this morning. But what I meant was, have you been up here long?'

'Since just after dark last night. So that we shouldn't be observed, you know.'

'Do you mean you slept here?'

'Yes—in that tomb-thing.' June pointed back at the Tump. 'Of course I had my sleeping-bag and a thermos of coffee and some sandwiches. It was quite snug.'

'The associations of the place didn't disturb you at all?'

At this, June looked first blank, and then faintly suspicious, as if such a question could occur only to an alien mind.

'I didn't know you belonged,' she said. 'To us, I mean.'

'Ah! It's the principle of the cell, you know.' This was Henry in immediate top gear again. 'Small groups unaware of each other's identity. Simon must have told you about it.'

'Yes, of course.' June had hesitated for a moment before producing this, since she lacked Henry's facility in uttering fibs. 'I thought,' she said, 'you might be tied up with the other lot.'

'Oh, them!' Henry had, unhesitatingly, a contemptuous view of the other lot.

'They're quite idiotic, of course, and not our sort of thing at all. But Simon believes some of them are around.'

'Elderly and churchy, too?' Hilda asked.

'Oh, yes—a good many of them.'

'Then I think they were in the congregation this morning as well.'

'So they were—the silly old creatures!' Henry said robustly. 'But just what would *they* be up to, do you think? The same as us?'

To these questions—unfortunately, since answers would have been so informative—no answers came. June had looked at her watch, and as a result she gave a screech of dismay.

'But you've made me late!' she cried. 'Three minutes late! Come on! Oh, *come on!*'

With this, June Gale turned and ran the length of the barrow, tugging at something in the pocket of tight-fitting jeans as she went.

'Best from behind, I'd say,' Henry said. 'And when in brisk movement. There's one of your learned words for it. Callipygous, I think.'

'Don't be so revolting, Henry Naylor. And we'd better follow her, as it seems to be what she wants.' And Hilda began to run.

'It certainly is.' Henry caught up with his sister in a stride. 'June's big moment has come. God knows what it is—but having an audience for it is a bonus we mustn't cheat her of. Well, I'm damned!'

It was nothing very startling that had elicited this exclamation. Just beyond the far end of the Tump was a sizeable plot of ground which had some appearance of having been artificially levelled long ago. Perhaps the eighteenth-century improver had effected this with the thought of erecting a belvedere or gazebo from which to survey the broad prospect beneath. Or perhaps the operation had been of much higher antiquity, and here was a kind of bowling-green expressly created for the funeral games of some monarch of the Megalithic Age. Positioned precisely in its centre there now lay a pile of brushwood such as might result from a hedging operation near by. Only there were no hedges within several hundred yards. Henry's surprise had resulted from his making a simple inference. Here was preparation for a bonfire—or, better, for a beacon.

By the time Hilda had absorbed these facts, June was bending over the pile with a box of matches in her hands.

'Isn't it cunning?' she cried out excitedly. 'You'd never think! Just a heap of twigs and leaves and things. But the real stuff's scattered underneath. Simon says it's absolutely fab. We'll see.' She struck a match and poked it rather gingerly into the foot of the pile. The twigs and leaves and things weren't much interested. Nevertheless, there was almost instantly a small puff of smoke. It grew so rapidly that June had to jump back from it. It thickened to the girth of a barrel, rose to the height of a house. Incredibly, it had become a great shaft in the sky. For a moment some downward draught of air flattened it, squashed it at the peak, so that it mushroomed out into a similitude of the most sinister image known to modern man. Then it was a clear white pillar again. It was as if the empyrean had become a kind of St Peter's Square, and from a celestial Sistine Chapel cardinals like demigods were signalling the election of Christ's new Vicar on Earth.

'Pulling out all the stops,' Henry said. 'Your blasted Simon ought to be in film. He has the touch.' Henry paused on this, and scowled at June. 'Well?' he said. 'The cue's been given, hasn't it? So what?'

'Wait!' June was staring out over the vale. 'There!' she said, and pointed into distance.

All that had appeared was a motor-coach: a toy motor-coach to the naked eye, and presumably carrying toy people. It had emerged from the woodland territory to the north, and was heading towards Nether Plumley. But now there was another one, moving at a brisker pace along a road similarly oriented. One after another, further motor-coaches appeared, and the extent to which Nether Plumley was indeed at the hub of a small system of unimportant thoroughfares became plain. Hilda found herself trying to remember whether she had read of ants or beetles behaving in this way—converging in columns upon the stronghold of some adversary. Of course the present spectacle was much more simply military in suggestion. Almost, while one looked, one transformed those harmless conveyances into armoured vehicles, pumping out shell-fire as they moved.

And now there was a hint of real confrontation. Some of the police cars had appeared: two of them shooting out from some lurking-place within the perimeter fence of the Institute, and two more from the direction of Plumley itself.

'Far too much barging around to make a happy afternoon,' Henry said, and raised his binoculars. 'Christ! Just take a look.'

Hilda focused her own glasses, and surveyed what was happening. There had been a collision between two of the coaches at an intersection; one of them had been tipped on its side; people, apparently uninjured but angry, were tumbling out of both—some of them awkwardly burdened with placards attached to long poles. It was evident, even at this remove, that a furious altercation was developing between the two parties. Some of the placards were waved defiantly in air; others were being used as outright weapons in deplorable breach of the Queen's peace. A police car drove up hastily; three or four constables tumbled out of it, and began waving their arms as if dealing amateurishly with a flock of sheep. And a faint bruit came up to the Tump, so there must have been a great deal of shouting as well.

'Have a dekko at your pals,' Henry said to June, and handed her his glasses. 'Perhaps you can tell if all's going according to plan. I'm not sure there isn't a spot of civil war.'

'There can't be anything Simon isn't prepared for.' Having made this loyal declaration, June surveyed the scene presumably in security of mind. 'No end of pigs,' she said. 'There'll be splendid pictures in all the papers tomorrow. Even in *The Times*.'

It took Hilda a moment to realize that the pigs were not the research material of the animal geneticists but merely the police. But presumably there *were* members of the brute creation incarcerated in the Institute, since it would scarcely be possible to geneticize without them. She was surprised that she hadn't adequately reflected on this before. She lowered her binoculars and stared at June.

'I say!' she said. 'Are you Cruelty to Animals people? Is that it?'

'That's *them*.' June said this with a good deal of contempt. 'Dumb Friends' Lib.'

'Then I ought to tell you that I'm all for libbing dumb friends. It's a much simpler issue than the bomb.'

'But a damned sight less important. Cease your chattering, women.' Henry must have been a good deal excited by the spectacle of turmoil at Nether Plumley. 'Time to join the party. So get moving. We can be home inside twenty minutes, and in Nether Plumley five minutes after that. Even in your awful old car. Are you game?'

'Yes, of course.' Hilda spoke with a firmness she didn't quite feel. Dispassionate observation—she may have judged—wouldn't have much of a spin in the middle of a riot. 'We'd better see the thing through.'

'And will you take me?' June asked. 'I'm expected to get back on my own.'

'Why not? We'll restore you to the arms of your great commander. Just yank your sleeping-bag out of that bloody great coffin, and I'll carry it down for you.'

'Oh, Henry, I think you're fab!'

This was not, of course, quite Hilda's estimate of her brother. It was true that Henry showed signs of being, as Uncle George had prophesied, her family's dark horse. But he would be very much a donkey if he signalized his growing up by falling for the callipygous June Gale.

VI

GEORGE AND FATHER Hooker had also gone for a walk, accompanied by the spaniels, Bill and Bess. Their route was along a field-path leading to Nether Plumley, and they had not progressed far before Hooker embarked upon what was to prove, for George, a disconcerting line of thought.

'I was much impressed,' he said, 'by the Director, Dr Scattergood—and, indeed, by his younger colleague as well. The younger man was Younger.'

'I beg your pardon?'

'Of the two men, the former was Scattergood and the latter was Younger.' Hooker appeared unaware of anything odd about this information, which recalled to George the fact that Robert Elsmere and *Robert Elsmere* were not the same person. George also wondered whether there was in all England another man liable, like Hooker, to use expressions like 'the latter' and 'the former' in a conversational way. 'And both Scattergood and Younger,' Hooker went on, 'appeared to me to be intelligent men.'

'As one might rather expect, don't you think?' George suggested innocently. 'Animal genetics isn't likely to be run by donkeys.'

'Certainly not.'

'Or whatever animal genetics may stand in for.'

'My dear Naylor, I scarcely follow you.' Father Hooker had paused momentarily in his measured perambulation. 'You can hardly believe in these wild rumours about the Institute that appear to be circulating among the uninformed?'

'Well, you know, *interdum vulgus rectum videt*. Or is it *interdum stultus opportuna loquitur?*' It amused George that the learned

Hooker—perhaps because of his early education as a scientist—was sometimes not too quick at picking up simple Latin tags. 'And, for that matter. . .' But George broke off. That there was a perplexing and alarming police presence round about the Plumleys was a fact bound up with his own encounter with that cruising car and its photographer. And in the incident there had been something ludicrous that he hesitated to embark upon. Father Hooker at once filled the momentary silence.

'It would appear that Scattergood and his colleague, although at the Institute since its inception, happen not to have worshipped in your parish church until today.'

'So I gathered.' George wasn't sure that St Michael and All Angels should have had that 'your' attached to it.

'I must admit to feeling it a gratifying circumstance.'

'Naturally you would. Church-going isn't what it was—is it? You must always be pleased to hear of anybody turning up.' George knew very well that it wasn't exactly this that was in his companion's mind. But it was hard not to make fun of Father Hooker from time to time—the more so since, as now, Hooker could be unaware it was going on.

'It must be presumed that they had heard I was to preach. And Dr Scattergood expressed himself very courteously at the end of the service. We had a little chat in the churchyard. Unfortunately both men had to plead pressure of their affairs when your sister-in-law invited them to come and take sherry at the Park.'

Hooker, George noticed, had taken to saying 'the Park' like this with a kind of naïve satisfaction curious in a distinguished theologian. But powerful minds may go astray in more directions than one, and George suspected that Hooker was overestimating his pastoral appeal. Those two scientists had gone to church for much the same reason that Hooker himself had gone into the Plumley pub: to take (as Hooker had expressed it) the temperature of the flock. They had heard about June Gale's injudicious little placard; like the police, they knew there was trouble brewing; they had decided to vet the natives. But it would be ungracious in George to put this point of view to his brother's guest, and George therefore held his peace and looked about him.

He also looked up at the heavens. From these there came no voice, such as Hooker seemed almost disposed to expect, saying something like 'Well done, thou good and faithful servant'. What did come was the noise of a helicopter. And there a helicopter was. It wasn't (what George understood to be the common occasion of such appearances) scurrying across country from A to B, conveying a hard-pressed industrial magnate from the scene of one important activity to another. It was simply cruising around—either that or hovering, and hovering low. In fact it was behaving rather as that police car had behaved.

'So I think it might be proper to pay a call. That it would be the graceful thing.'

'Proper to *what?*' George realized that he had been wool-gathering.

'To call on Dr Scattergood, my dear Naylor. I gathered that he has his living-quarters within the curtilage of the Institute.'

'I see.' George wasn't enthusiastic. He was chiefly conscious that 'curtilage' was another instance of Hooker's peculiar notions of colloquial English. 'But don't you think he's probably a fairly busy chap?'

'Undoubtedly. Indeed, he had to intimate as much when he was unable to accept that invitation to the Park. He may well be unable to be at home to us. But the courtesy call will have been made. And we can leave cards.'

'So we can.' George was now almost dazed. A 'courtesy call' made within a few hours of what had occasioned it was surely on the excessive side of things. Diplomats and similar distinguished persons undoubtedly 'paid' such calls, but at a different tempo. Even the most extravagant Victorian manual of etiquette would frown on such brisk despatch. George reflected, however, on the small and yellowed scrap of pasteboard he had thought to produce for the Admissions lady at the Bodleian. No doubt it was still on his person. But he didn't at all relish the idea of leaving it on a species of in-tray at an Institute of Animal Genetics. 'I think,' he said disingenuously, 'it would be more becoming if you paid this visit by yourself. It flows from Scattergood's having turned up to hear you preach, and that's something I didn't manage myself. So there would be a kind of awkwardness, would there not?'

It was George's hope that he had here hit upon a consideration likely to have weight with Hooker, a man to be described as owning a flair for punctilios. But it turned out not to be particularly successful.

'Let us be guided by circumstances,' Father Hooker said.

'Well, yes—by all means. And there is already a circumstance which I think I ought to mention to you. It looks very much as if, this afternoon, there is to be some sort of demonstration outside this rather mysterious Institute. Just what it is about isn't clear to me, and I realize the implausibility of supposing the place to have anything to do with the production of nuclear weapons. But I do have evidence that the local police are concerned about something, and it seems reasonable to conclude that Scattergood and his colleagues are also on the alert. If so, I think our paying a social call might be distinctly inopportune.'

This was surely a succinct and sensible speech, but Father Hooker's response to it was not quite what George had hoped for.

'My dear Naylor, I should have been inattentive to much that has been in the air were I to be altogether surprised by what you say. May I hope that you are yourself without any intimate anxiety in the matter? Your charming niece is not, by any chance, involved?'

'Hilda?' George was a little startled by this question. 'I can't be sure she isn't at least interested. But a person who may indeed be involved—and even perhaps a moving spirit in the design—is Prowse's nephew, Simon.'

'The young man who came to tennis the other day?'

'Yes. There has been a good deal that is unaccountable in his behaviour while at the vicarage.'

'Again, I am not altogether surprised. His tennis, it seems, was extremely good. But is he also intelligent?'

'Very definitely so. He has been pretending to be in need of help with elementary Latin—while being in fact a strong candidate for a Fellowship at All Souls.'

'Then we must think again.' Father Hooker had come to a halt, and George had only to glance at him to see that he was, in fact, thinking quite hard. He was not a man under whose feet—metaphorically speaking—the ground could readily be seen to shift. Nevertheless, something of the sort was happening now. Conceivably because he owned an exaggerated regard for academic distinction in the University of Oxford, what he had just heard about the promising career of Simon Prowse had considerably shaken him. He was, in fact, in process of a volte-face.

'Dear me!' he said. 'I have been inclined, as you know, to regard the entire notion of this Institute's being in any way significantly involved with modern warfare as no more than so much frying eggs by moonshine.'

'As *what*?'

'A common phrase, my dear Naylor, which I borrow from the simpler classes. Nonsense, in other words. An absurd mis-apprehension which I was passingly concerned to refute in my sermon this morning. But now we have something quite remote from idle chatter in pubs. An able and highly educated young man, participating in, or even instigating, a demonstration of the kind you describe! Such a one is surely unlikely to have gone wildly astray. It must be within his knowledge that this Institute, contrary to my own persuasion, is indeed engaged in activities which, if only in some tangential fashion, connect with the kind of nuclear technology which so frequently nowadays generates mass protest of one sort or another. Do I carry you along with me, Naylor?' And Father Hooker, having achieved this very characteristic piece of expository syntax, paused for a reply.

'Well, yes—you do. And I may say that Hilda has been pretty sure about it for some time.'

'Your niece, in my opinion, has a very clear head. As for myself, I confess to having been dogmatic in reiterating, almost until this very moment, that the idea is absurd. But the truth is now apparent to me. And it is apparent, too, that we must press forward. We have a duty.'

'A duty?' George repeated—detectably to a feebler effect than he at all cared for.

'Certainly. The main burden of my sermon this morning— and I deeply regret that I had not the privilege of submitting it to your judgement—was the extreme difficulty of accommodating the concept of the Just War to the possibility of nuclear holocaust. All those exercised with the problem, whatever their convictions about it, one way or another, merit our respect. And guidance. We must afford it as we can.' Father Hooker paused, and looked quite sternly at George. 'And by "we" I mean the Church.'

Nether Plumley now lay immediately before them. It was not at all an inspiriting hamlet. Whatever small consequence it had once owned seemed long ago to have been ploughed deep into the soil. If it had contracted, it must have been while sullenly effecting a kind of scorched-earth policy; cottages that had decayed and given up appeared to have carried their foundations away with them, so that only here and there an oblong of ground showing an extra luxuriance of nettle and thistle marked the minute demesnes of a vanished peasantry; Plumley Ducis itself must have seemed the abode of a vigorous and affluent community to such inhabitants as Nether Plumley quite mysteriously supported still. Bill and Bess, no doubt at the beckoning of scents unknown, had scampered hopefully ahead to explore the scene. But they were now returning in plain dejection, like the scouts of some nomad tribe with no good report of water or shade ahead. There hadn't been in evidence even a child to chuck a stone at these four-footed foreigners, and in the small scattering of cottages along the lane the few senior citizens of the place were presumably asleep. They hadn't been to church, since there wasn't one; they weren't looking forward to the pub, because there was no pub either; they weren't even sucking peppermints, because there was no village shop.

Before this spectacle, or lack of it, Father Hooker came to a halt, and George saw that he was about to make a pronouncement. When it came it was surprisingly without the portentous quality one had come to expect from him.

'Surely it's a little puzzling?' Hooker asked. 'English agriculture is said to be doing quite well—which can scarcely be said of almost anything else. Why a depressing scene like this?'

'It certainly isn't at all cheerful.' George felt thoroughly apologetic on the part of poor Nether Plumley. 'Long ago, I believe, it was a fairly thriving village, and then it lost heart and decided to turn dismal. After that, cars and motor-bikes finished the job, here as in similar places. Agricultural labourers have become more mobile, and tend to clump where one thing and another is laid on—as in Plumley itself, for instance. And landowners and farmers quite approve, and increasingly have their tied cottages and so forth in the larger villages. So here and there you get such run-down spots as Nether Plumley. My brother says it's of very little economic significance.'

Father Hooker received George's explanations—rather oddly —with one of his little bows, perhaps as indicating that he was open to, and perhaps grateful for, being thus clued up on secular affairs.

'All the same,' he said, 'the only thing I can see to be thankful for in Nether Plumley is that from it one can lift up one's eyes unto the hills.'

'From whence doth come our aid.' George was delighted with this. 'Yes, indeed. I always find myself turning that way.'

Both men had, in fact, turned round—and naturally the dogs did so as well, so that all four visitors were facing the line of the downs.

'It is rather fine, isn't it?' George asked. 'It's surprising that so gently undulating a skyline can create such an effect. Wouldn't you say?'

'Yes, indeed.' Hooker's head indicated grave assent. 'I like that little spinney just breasting the crest. And there, just to the left of it: is that some sort of tumulus?'

'Yes, it's rather an impressive chambered tomb, now called Tim's Tump, and well worth a visit. It's curious how unfrequented all that stretch of the ancient trackway is. There's probably not a soul up there now.'

They moved on, and the Institute of Animal Genetics came into view. Perhaps because seeming so deliberately pitched in depressing surroundings, it suggested at a first glance a large receptacle for the indigent aged—a high incidence of senile dementia among whom might explain the necessity of its being enclosed within a perimeter-fence some ten feet high. In such establishments it may often be remarked that facilities for mass-incineration have for some reason constituted a high priority in the design, and it was so here, Crowning the Institute there was a chimney-stack of surprising height, and from this arose into the sky a faintly quivering column of oily black smoke. Nothing else moved. It seemed clear that the Institute rested from its endeavours (whatever those endeavours were) at the week-end with an absoluteness that was reassuringly British. Through the fence before which Father Hooker and a misdoubting George now stood were to be viewed lawns and flower-beds of the unimaginative and by-the-yard sort purveyed by contractors. Partly concealed behind a corner of the main building was a large asphalted area on which were parked several modest cars, including a couple of police panda cars without occupants. At one point on the grass three thrushes, immobile and hopefully listening for worms that weren't in fact at home, might have been viewed as inadequately standing in for birds of ill omen. All in all, it was a slightly dreary but entirely peaceful scene.

'It is clear,' Father Hooker said, 'that casual intrusion is unwelcome, and not easy to effect.' He tapped the wire mesh in front of his nose with a walking-stick which could almost have been described as of clerical appearance in itself. 'The demonstrators will not make much of this. But demonstrators, my dear Naylor, are there to be? It is difficult to believe in them amid this decent sabbath repose. Perhaps, after all, we have too readily come to believe in a piece of nonsense. Your vicar's nephew may be no more than the perpetrator of some foolish hoax. Or do I vacillate?'

George judged that he did, but refrained from saying so.

'As we're here,' he suggested, 'hadn't we better push ahead, and see if this fellow Scattergood is around? I'm quite sure about the police, you know. They took my photograph, as a matter of fact, from a passing car much like one of those parked over there.'

'Naylor, you astound me!'

'I confess I was a little shaken myself. It may just be, of course, that this Institute is so hush-hush an affair that there are routine precautions of the sort seven days a week. But it's most unlikely, isn't it? If it were so, my family and everybody else would be aware of it. The odds remain with some kind of emergency. There must be a gate somewhere in this fence. Let's go on and find it.'

So they went on. Bill and Bess, however, did so with marked reluctance. With the irritating ability of certain species of the brute creation to put on a turn suggesting a startling command of extra-sensory perception, the dogs were making panicky noises, tucking their tails beneath their bellies, and dragging all eight of their feet. George, who had brought with him the kind of leash adapted to controlling two animals at a time, was obliged to bring this device into operation, and the party, thus impeded, made a huddled progress along the fence. Round its first corner, however, they did come on a gate.

It was quite an imposing gate, and apparently the main entrance to the large compound within which the Institute stood. In addition to the gate proper, the two halves of which stood half open and as if ready to be closed at any time, there was an affair like the barrier at a level crossing, and this seemed to be mechanically operated from inside a kind of capacious sentry-box constructed of some glass-like material. There was a man—presumably a porter or commissionaire—inside the box. Lounging at ease, he was improving his mind with *The News of the World*. This journal he now momentarily lowered for the purpose of inspecting the postulants before his portal. Having done this, he very composedly fell to reading again. Not unnaturally, Father Hooker was incensed.

'Good afternoon!' Hooker said in a loud voice. And when this was without effect, 'My man!' he said commandingly and in a voice louder still. This did have some result. Very deliberately, the porter got to his feet and set down his paper on a small table beside him. He then further studied it, as if to fix in his mind the precise point at which he was breaking off from its discourse. This achieved, he emerged from the sentry box, and from across the barrier eyed Father Hooker and George, Bill and Bess, with equal and comprehensive disfavour.

'Not today,' he said.

'My good man,' Hooker said (for he was still offended), 'will you please. . .'

'Take the brutes away,' the porter said. 'There's nobody here on Sundays. Bring them back tomorrow, if you like. But I can tell you it won't be more than a couple of quid for both. That's the going rate at the moment. A quid for a dog and fifty p. for a cat. Talk of a black market! Every brat in the district has been collaring the creatures and bringing them along.'

How the gentlemen from Plumley Park would have proceeded in the face of this astounding intelligence will never be known, since their colloquy with this rough-hewn but not unhelpful person was abruptly terminated by a brisk toot upon a motor-horn immediately behind them. It had the effect of making the porter bob back into his box and throw up the barrier. A car then glided past; its driver glanced at the visitors, drew quickly to a halt, and at once jumped out to confront them.

'Scattergood himself,' Father Hooker murmured hastily to George. 'A most fortunate circumstance.'

George had his doubts about this. Dr Scattergood was glancing at his companion with, for the moment, no sign of recognition. Only a few hours earlier, Hooker had preached at the man and subsequently received from him a polite expression of gratitude for his performance. So this blankness, however brief, could not be other than mortifying. And even the blankness was not quite entire, since Scattergood was scarcely concealing a sense of irritation at the untimely intrusion he had come upon. But then his glance turned from Father Hooker to George, and at once his expression changed.

'Good Lord!' he said. 'George Naylor, surely? I have wondered whether the local people were relations of yours. Delighted to see you.'

'Do-You!' The ancient familiarity came to George's lips at once, and he found himself shaking hands with this recovered school-fellow. Then he remembered what had just been happening. 'Do-You,' he repeated on a sterner note, 'do you go in for vivisection in this place? Your porter seemed to think we wanted to sell you those dogs.'

'How very absurd!' Dr Scattergood—a dried-up and cerebral kind of man—instantly endeavoured to extend to Bill and Bess a regard indicative of sympathy and esteem, and to this the spaniels as instantly responded with piteously feeble tail-waggings, *oeillades*, and speaking looks. 'Vivisection? Definitely not. But post-mortems, of course, often enough. We do have rather a high mortality, so far—which is why we're in the market for any strays that are brought along. And I can assure you they have a whale of a time.'

George found no immediate reply, no doubt because he very reasonably suspected that Jeoffry and Old Foss were among the creatures enjoying a whale of a time at the moment, and that the same hospitality would be extended to Bill and Bess at the drop of a handkerchief. Father Hooker, who was clearly displeased at being a little left out of all this, took advantage of his silence.

'May I reintroduce myself?' he said to Scattergood with some formality. 'Adrian Hooker.'

'Yes—yes, of course.' Scattergood's glance had strayed away beyond his perimeter-fence, and it was evident that he was suppressing with difficulty a certain apprehensiveness as to what might lie there. 'Yes, indeed,' he said. 'This morning. Yes, of course.'

'Naylor and I have been walking the dogs, and had intended no more than a call. But various circumstances have invited in us the persuasion that something untoward may be afoot of which it might be well to apprise you. Naylor has even been photographed.'

'Naylor has been photographed?' Scattergood was perhaps as baffled by this apparently inconsequent announcement as by the unfamiliar choiceness of Father Hooker's phraseology.

'By the police.'

'Oh, I see. We know that a spot of bother may be coming along. But the police are making too much of it—at least if it's no more than the animal cranks. DFL, they call themselves. Dumb Friends' Lib, I believe. Harmless enough. But we're keeping a low profile, with everybody off the premises except the fellows who get our dumb friends their supper.' Scattergood appeared to have reassured himself with these remarks. 'I wonder,' he said, 'whether you'd care to look round? I believe there's been growing gossip about the Institute. You'd perhaps be able to tell people that we don't run to atrocities.'

George found himself not particularly attracted by this invitation, which he judged to be a little on the casual and graceless side. And, even so, he and Hooker had no title to receive it, since they had barged in on the place in the most unwarranted way. He saw, however, that it attracted Hooker,

175

who had been some sort of scientist at the outset of his career and owned perhaps a lingering fondness for labs and stinks. So George declared that it would interest him to see something of what went on in the name of animal genetics. Then he wondered about Bill and Bess. It seemed peculiarly unsuitable that they should be included in the invitation, and at the same time difficult to see how they could be left behind. But this problem solved itself at once. They had been let off the leash, and had taken the opportunity to withdraw discreetly from what they plainly regarded as an insalubrious environment. In fact they could just be seen, already a quarter of a mile away, ambling composedly back to Plumley Park.

Determining this had taken all three men, together with the porter, beyond the gate. As they returned to it, Scattergood glanced up at the line of the downs.

'At least we have a view,' he said. 'A lab with a view. It's something. . .Dear me! Look at the Tump. Somebody having a picnic, I suppose, and letting a fire get a little out of hand.'

They all looked at the Tump—or, rather, at a small column of smoke rising close beside it. And, even as Scattergood spoke, the column broadened, thickened, climbed. It was a great white shaft in air. Momentarily, it mushroomed and spread; became as a cloud in the heavens shaped like the hand of Man. Then it was again a simple column of smoke, white in the sunlight. Almost to an effect of dialogue, of drama, it confronted, across the vale, the black smoke still issuing from the tall chimney-stack of the Institute of Animal Genetics.

'Odd sort of effect,' Scattergood said indifferently. 'Now, come along inside.'

The interior of the Institute at once reminded George of a hospital. He was familiar with hospitals—not as ever having been a patient in one (since he had reached middle life without serious illness) but as having frequently visited in them sufferers having some claim—although frequently a slender claim—to be regarded as within the sphere of his mission. He had thus sat at the bedside of numerous men, women and children just not in sufficient pain to make the company of fellow-mortals meaningless, and of others who, although free from such immediate

176

physical affliction, had been left by one trouble or another in a state of impenetrable depression. Despite these sombre experiences, George had always managed to like hospitals. They were surprisingly cheerful places on the whole. They were beautifully clean. And, whether or not it was consciously identified as such, there was a great deal of the Christian conduct of life going on in them.

The Institute had, for a start, the true hospital smell: one of common disinfectants in the main, but to the lay mind seeming to incorporate intriguing whiffs of chloroform or ether escaping from operating theatres and drifting down corridors. Yet in this place, somehow, they were disturbing smells, and George, as he walked round in the wake of Dr Scattergood (formerly prone to be addressed as Do-You on an interrogative note), wasn't at all comfortable. In so far as his presence here was the consequence of a small social observance thought up by Hooker it was plainly ridiculous. If there was anything in Hooker's more recently discovered notion of a kind of mediating ministry in the troubled field of Yes or No to nuclear missiles ('guidance' had been Hooker's august word) then they were wasting time in trailing through a series of labs.

There were a lot of labs—all deserted and tidied up as at the close of play—and to George they were incomprehensible and boring. But not so with Father Hooker. To Father Hooker they were as is the renewed scent of battle wafted to the old warhorse from afar. There could be no doubt about that, and it was interesting in its fashion. This hardened theologian (and windbag, in an uncharitable regard) had a soft spot for experimental philosophy, a nostalgic thought for the career he had renounced to become a parson. Put thus, the thing sobered George's impatience at once. To a disenchanted view, Hooker was as absurd as the dogmas he had turned up at Plumley to argue for. But he kept on, as it were, dodging into postures and persuasions one had to respect. George again realized that when Hooker departed he would miss him quite a lot.

'And now,' Scattergood was saying, 'you may care just to take a glance at the hotel. We call it that. And, as far as we can, we try to make it four-star.'

George knew at once what the hotel was. Had things fallen out differently, Bill and Bess might have checked into it. Jeoffry and Old Foss (and, for that matter, Sinbad and Peter) were probably accommodated in it now.

One whole side of the Institute, and a spacious courtyard within it, turned out to be devoted to this residential purpose, comprehensively conceived. It had already become clear that the place was a dogs' home and a cattery: so much had been implicit in the tariff obligingly cited by the man in the glass box. But there were also rats and rabbits, hamsters and (perhaps as the totemic creature of the concern) guinea-pigs as well. Nor was it exclusively a mammalian hostelry. There was an aviary thronged with brightly-plumaged birds. There was an aquarium, chilly and dimly lit, in which were to be observed, through transparent panels conveniently disposed, fish dun and liveried, harlequin-like and monkish, darting, or mysteriously suspended with faintly flickering fins. If the Institute wasn't positively a zoo, this was because there was nothing very large in it. There were several spider monkeys, but elephants and hippopotamuses were not in evidence. There appeared, indeed, to be a premium set on the medium-sized and the small. Very probably—George thought—there was a lavish provision of entities not visible at all, like the micro-organisms and amoebas so skilfully deployed by Len in his discussion with Mrs Archer during that railway journey not very long ago.

But the cats and dogs were—so to speak, and to vary the image—the parlour boarders. The dogs, in particular, were handsomely housed, their quarters having the appearance less of kennels than of cubicles—and indeed less of cubicles than of well-equipped bed-sits. This must have been a concession to sentiment, the Dog being the Friend of Man. In various ways individual tastes appeared to have been consulted in the appointments of these homes from home. But there was one exception to this. Every dog, of whatever breed or size (and the range was great), had been issued with an identical rubber bone—a simple point at which, one could feel, invention need not have failed. But none of the dogs was at present interested in its bone, because all the dogs were asleep—immobile in cushioned ease, save for those occasional twitches and yelps which reveal that dogs, too, may experience disturbing dreams.

The lighting was dim, and it was moments before George distinguished another uniformity than that of the innutritious bones. Each dog must have worn a collar, since from its neck depended a small glittering object which George couldn't very clearly see. He supposed this to be an identity disk. It might, of course, be a long-service medal. All the dogs were beautifully groomed, and this was true, too, of the cats: a fact apparent even although all these creatures could be viewed only through expanses of glass.

The cats (a hundred or so, it seemed to be) were awake, although many of them seemed to spend a good deal of time with luxuriously closed eyes. The cats (equipped with the same obscure objects at the neck) radiated health and contentment. A curious susurration or hum, which George at first took to be the product of a superfluity of static electricity about the place, actually indicated that a quite wholesale purring was going on. Was it Rousseau who, amid the solitude and silence of the Alps, had become conscious of sounds, of reverberations, that proved to issue from a stocking manufactory? The cats were creating an effect rather like that. George attempted to identify from among them the missing Plumley Park couple, but failed to do so. He then reflected that it was all unconscious of their fate that the thronging feline victims uttered their monotonous little hymn of thanksgiving for an easy life.

This thought (the mildly edifying cast of which belonged to the lately discarded phase of George's career) was suddenly banished by a disconcerting discovery. Father Hooker had disappeared, and so had Scattergood. The former (as Hooker himself would say) had bolted from the cats' hotel, and the latter had solicitously followed him.

George hurried into the corridor, and found that the two men had not gone far. Father Hooker was standing only a few yards away: pale, trembling, and apparently on the verge of nervous prostration. Scattergood was studying him with curiosity and a decent element of concern.

'Good God!' George exclaimed. 'Has Hooker been taken ill?'

'Cat phobia, I think. Not an uncommon thing. But quite a severe attack. Interesting, if the sheer number of cats enhances the trouble. Deserves investigating.' Scattergood turned to the sufferer. 'That right?' he said. 'A phobia about cats?' He spoke in a loud and urgent voice, as perhaps one does—George thought—to a person in danger of falling into coma.

'An aversion.' Achieving this less pathological nomenclature seemed to brace Hooker a little; he ceased shaking like a jelly, and something of his dignity returned to him. 'A chair, if possible,' he said. 'And, if not inconvenient, a glass of water.'

These modest requests were complied with. George, who was much distressed, recalled that 'aversion' had manifested itself when the Plumley cats had thought to chum up with Hooker on the evening of his arrival at the Park. But this was much more disturbing. A congeries of scores of cats, suddenly come upon, was no doubt a pretty stiff experience.

'But an aversion, I fear, that is indeed sadly irrational.' The need for formal utterance had returned to Hooker. 'The frailty must be attributed, no doubt, to some forgotten—or, as they say, "repressed"—episode in childhood.'

'Very likely. But there's not the slightest need, you know, to carry it to the grave with you.' Scattergood now permitted himself to speak a shade impatiently. 'Buy a picture-postcard.'

'I beg your pardon?'

'Of a cat. Not a comic cat, but a realistic, if sentimental, one. Have it somewhere unobtrusively around the house. After a couple of weeks, put it on the mantelpiece in your sitting-room. Pause that way for about a month. Then substitute a small china cat—again a realistic one—for the postcard. Another month, and you'll be able to live with a full-scale soft toy. Or—better, perhaps—there's a kind of hollow cat you can keep your pyjamas in. In no time after that, you'll be thinking of having a real live cat to snuggle up with.' Scattergood paused on this, possibly aware of the incongruity, and even impropriety, of the image it conjured into being. 'Good heavens!' he said. 'What's that?'

It was a rhetorical question. About just what it was, there could be no doubt at all. Pandemonium had erupted outside the Institute. The demo had begun. And the Director of the Institute, who had not long before owned so dismissively to expecting 'a spot of bother', was now considerably perturbed. That was reasonable enough. Even at this remove—for the three men were almost at the centre of what was a very large building—it was at once clear that 'spot' was a singularly inapplicable word. What dominated the sudden racket was a loud chanting of a more or less controlled and orchestrated sort: much like that—George thought—which he recalled hearing from around football fields when, as a young man, he had explored for some months those fringes of civilization that lie beyond the Atlantic Ocean. There was even now and then the suggestion of counter-chanting—a rah-rah-rah effect—which enhanced this comparison. Could the police, he wondered, be borrowing from Zulus and Ashantis and fuzzy-wuzzies generally the practice of accompanying with blood-curdling yells their endeavours to maintain the Queen's peace? But the uproar wasn't merely vocal. There appeared to be a brass band, incongruously suggestive of the Salvation Army, which could scarcely have chosen Nether Plumley for a parade-ground that afternoon. There was also a good deal of mechanical noise—a hooting of horns, revving up of engines, screeching of brakes— asserting that the twentieth century was well to the fore.

For a moment Scattergood had been at a loss—but it had been merely about what he was to do with his two visitors. He solved this problem by simply abandoning them, with no more than a hasty intimation that he was 'going to look into it'.

So George and Father Hooker were left to themselves, apparently as the only representatives of *homo sapiens* amid a wilderness of monkeys, dogs, cats, newts and Chinese carp. It was noticeable, however, that this didn't add to Father Hooker's discomposure. He was still a badly shaken man, but nevertheless something of his normal manner was returning to him. This became evident in what he now found to say.

'At least, my dear Naylor, we at length know where we are—and in the most literal acceptation of the term. The purposes of the Institute are clear to us, are they not?'

'I can't say they're clear to me, except that I have a general feeling they're rather sinister.'

'That is certainly the persuasion of the mob outside. But do you seriously mean that, having been afforded a close view of a number of the laboratories here, you are still not cognizant of the activities pursued in them?'

'You forget, Hooker, that I'm no sort of scientist. No doubt I simply don't see what you see.' George had to control a little irritation as he made this obvious point. 'So tell me all about it, like a good fellow.'

'Very simply, then, our friends here are immunologists. And they are concerned to extend the principles of immunology as they may be brought to bear in the field of radiation sickness. Do you follow me?'

'Yes,' George said slowly. 'I rather think I do.'

'I speak, of course, of ionizing radiation.'

'It's all about how the body can dodge the long-term effects of the bomb?'

'Crudely put, yes.'

'It sounds a beneficent activity to me.'

'It may be so. Or it may not.' Hooker paused impassively. 'I'd say the chances are vastly against there being anything in it at all. But popularly—and it may be this that our rulers have in mind—it would come down to the notion that one can dodge the effects of the bomb with a pill. Whether that would be a beneficent fantasy to propagate, I very much doubt.'

'And just where do those animals come in?'

'My dear Naylor, you must have remarked, surely, what the cats and dogs have depending from their necks?'

'Some sort of identity-disks. Names and dates and numbers: that sort of thing.'

'*Sancta simplicitas!*' It appeared to be something like incredulity that drove Father Hooker to this ejaculation. 'And you must be short-sighted—or purblind—as well. Geiger counters, Naylor.'

'Geiger counters?' George was bewildered. 'I'm afraid I don't very well keep up. . .'

'God bless me! Geiger counters were clicking well before you were born. They measure the degree of radiation to which an organism has been exposed.'

'So those dogs and cats. . .'

'Yes, yes—of course.'

'Would the creatures now themselves be a hazard if they—well, found their way out of this horrible place?'

'I don't know. Controlled contacts with the animals here are almost certainly harmless enough. About a roving mob of them,

I can't say. You forget, Naylor, that I'm no sort of scientist either. I just recall a few things from long ago.' Father Hooker stood up—still rather shakily. 'But come, Naylor. We are neglecting our duty.'

George had forgotten about this. Hooker believed that, planted between hundreds of excited demonstrators and what would probably turn out to be the massed constabulary of the county, he could profitably and composingly discourse upon the doctrine of the Just War as it must be interpreted in the nuclear age. Something like that. It was a notion that would have done credit to Don Quixote. You had to give it to Hooker. George saw that he himself must—if only in the simple physical sense—stand by the chap.

'Very well,' he said. 'Scattergood seems to have deserted us. We'll go and see how the land lies.'

But George, although he spoke boldly, was inwardly much disturbed. Distressing though his private plight had recently been, there was a sense in which, at least intermittently, he had been able to savour it in terms of mild social comedy. That was the world to which, in his heart, he thought of his family as belonging; and it was the world in which the interplay of sympathy and incongruity in his relations with Hooker could harmlessly exercise itself. But now it was as if, quite suddenly— perhaps at the moment of that astounding conversation about the price of cats and dogs—the theatre had changed. Here was comedy no longer. Whether or not Scattergood and his colleagues laboured in good faith in their Institute, George didn't know. But if he had understood Hooker rightly, the government, or whatever body funded the place, was eventually going to use them as instruments of thought-control. *Swallow this*—people would be told—*and you needn't even shelter under the stairs*. Comedy couldn't be got out of that. Only a rather savage sort of farce.

They went outside. Beyond the still-vacant compound protected by the perimeter-fence, it was as if a whole city had poured its population out upon the modest environs of Nether Plumley. George and Father Hooker, having found their way with some difficulty into open air, came to an astonished halt before the spectacle. Although from the doorway in which they stood they commanded only a sector of the scene, nearly a dozen motor-coaches were visible: the majority of them already immobile and empty; some still nosing cautiously forward through a milling sea of persons of either sex and every age. There were pensioners brandishing crutches and infants in arms waving rattles. One coach was disgorging a phalanx of citizens of years so tender as only recently to have found their feet, and at their head two agitated women were raising with difficulty a banner saying

TODDLERS NOT TOMBS

Nearby was a perambulator-and-carry-cot brigade, with a similar banner announcing

BABIES AGAINST BALLISTIC MISSILES

Not very perplexingly, there was a man with a placard declaring

DUMB FRIENDS CALL FOR AID

while another placard, rather more aggressively, commanded

HUNT DOWN FOX-HUNTING MAN

But a majority of these waving and flapping scrawls simply enjoined

BAN THE BOMB

There was also in evidence, as was to be expected, a large force of police. Most of them were stationed, no doubt upon the soundest tactical principles, in small gossiping groups here and there around the scene. But at the rear of the crowd there was a whole coach-load of them as yet undeployed; crammed together in their blue uniforms they had much the appearance of cyanosed sardines in a tin; they were certainly enduring much discomfort in the interest of what the next day's newspapers would call an unobtrusive presence or low profile.

But at least it was evident—as, indeed, George had already known—that Simon Prowse and his associates, however dramatically contrived had been their sudden irruption on the field, had failed of really effective surprise. Perhaps Dumb Friends' Lib, which appeared to be an independently conducted

184

concern, had neglected to mask their intentions as they should. And perhaps this explained a certain hostility between these two groups which a penetrating eye could already detect as generating itself within the total mêlée.

Not that much except chanting and singing was happening so far, and doubtless the less spirited among the demonstrators were hoping that 'peaceful' and 'well-conducted' would be among the terms eventually applied to the afternoon's exercise. Indeed, it seemed to George—who, perhaps unlike Father Hooker, had witnessed demos before—that there might be no further very dramatic developments. The perimeter-fence seemed impregnable; those confronting it were not of the desperate sort that arrive armed with wire-cutters and mattresses; the chanting was certainly not increasing in volume, and it was even possible to detect a nascent sense of anticlimax as in the air. Perhaps, having made their point, both wings of the movement (as it might be expressed) would get into their coaches again and drive away.

But this sanguine expectation of a drift into sanity was not fulfilled. Instead, there were fresh arrivals on the scene. Simultaneously and from different points of the compass two television crews had turned up, and were now briskly tumbling their apparatus out of vans, each in evident competition with the other. The helicopter, which was still around, descended, hovered near them, apparently satisfied itself that they were authentic instruments of the media, and respectfully drew away again. The demonstrators, although so numerous and scattered over so large an area, became aware of this gratifying development at once, and took fresh heart from it. The police, similarly apprised, settled their helmets more firmly on their heads, assumed expressions of stolid worth, and prepared to take the air. The demo at Nether Plumley was now a national event, and all were keen to put their best foot forward. The scenario might have been improved, indeed, by the presence of, say, a Cabinet Minister, in the general direction of whom somebody could throw an egg or a bag of flour. But, on the whole, people were pleased, and willing to make do with what they had.

So everything was good-humoured, so far. 'Good-humoured', indeed, was no doubt what several common-or-garden reporters who had now turned up were busy scribbling in their notebooks. But again there was a development—although one, at its inception, not so much alarming as of curious psychological interest. As the camera teams advanced, many of the demonstrators, hitherto standing, sat down in front of them, some offering friendly and familiar waves—even, indeed, inviting and beckoning gestures—as they did so. The police, too, were affected. Moving forwards in twos and fours, they began hauling these sedentary persons away from their chosen site and gently depositing them again a dozen yards off—whereupon others would promptly take their place and be removed in turn. The cameras whirred meanwhile. It wasn't, George knew, in the least an exhibitionistic performance or charade. Rather, it partook of the nature of ritual: perhaps a familiar and slightly jaded ritual, but one seriously undertaken, all the same. Only the television crews had positively theatrical exigencies in mind, in this interest uttering practised injunctions here and there.

So it was all still quite harmless enough. Yet such equivocal situations are always dodgy and productive of awkward turns. It was so now. Before the main gate—at the spot where George and Father Hooker had been informed of the current going rate for cats and dogs—there was for some reason an undisputed and vacant patch of roadway, and upon this suddenly appeared a small band of demonstrators differing in character from the generality. They were, in fact, one and all athletic young men, and at their head was Simon Prowse. It was clear that in some manner they proposed to storm the outer defences of the Institute. The effect upon the police was instantaneous. Constables produced and blew their whistles. Sergeants spoke urgently into walkie-talkies. And the coach in the background, bearing its large strategic reserve, sprang into life. At first nosing cautiously forward, it presently (and surely injudiciously) gathered speed, so that the milling crowd had to dodge hastily from its path. But it was only when it was close to the crisis point that things went badly wrong. Simon and his storm troops were moving at the double on an oblique course in front of the coach, which had to swerve to avoid them. But the swerve wasn't going to be quite enough. The driver, confronted for a split second with the appalling prospect of mass slaughter, boldly accelerated as he swerved. This saved lives, but had the awkward consequence of projecting the vehicle full-tilt against the perimeter-fence, several yards of which were promptly levelled to the ground.

The effect of such a spectacular event upon the demonstrators at large was instant and pervasive. A yell of triumph went up. When the mob before the Bastille believed itself about to free innumerable captives from their dungeons, or when the loyal soldiery of Queen Victoria had satisfied themselves that Sebastopol was down, a not dissimilar effect must have been created. And the yelling was swiftly followed by action. The whole body of demonstrators poured through the breach. The police drew their truncheons. What the papers would call ugly scenes were suddenly the order of the afternoon.

Gazing down on this arena (as it must now be called), Dr Scattergood's two visitors not unnaturally experienced some alarm—the more so as Scattergood himself, who might have directed them to a place of security, remained an absentee. Perhaps, George thought, he was endeavouring to assuage with dog biscuits and cat food any agitation which the fracas was occasioning in the guests at his four-star hotel. Or perhaps he was on the telephone, insisting to the Lord Lieutenant of the county that an occasion had arisen requiring the calling out of the armed forces of the Crown. As it was, George and Father Hooker had to shift for themselves, and they did so to the moderate extent of withdrawing a little, and placing a door—although, as it happened, no more than a plain glass door—between themselves and the disturbing spectacle without.

What George first observed from this more circumspect position was an elderly woman with a placard demanding

AMITY NOT ENMITY

—a praiseworthy injunction which he had just deciphered when the placard was abruptly brandished in air and brought down hard on another elderly woman's head: this to the helpless dismay of a policeman evidently endeavouring to interpose in deprecation of violence and brutality. Thus alerted, George further saw that the whole extensive disorder before him was now definitely threatening to take on an internecine character. There seemed little sense in this, since the interests of the two parties involved, if not wholly coincident, at least substantially overlapped. But if sense was lacking, excitement was in abundant supply. And now George saw something else, alarming in a more intimate fashion. On the fringe of the crowd, but not so far off as to render immediate identification impossible, there had appeared and drawn up his niece's venerable car. And instantly Hilda and both her brothers jumped out of it, together with a second girl whom George recognized as Simon Prowse's devoted follower, June Gale. All four of them were in the sort of haste to be remarked in children who fear to miss the first turn in a circus.

Although the demonstration at Nether Plumley might perhaps be described as of a high-minded order, George didn't at all care to think of his niece as getting involved with it, even as a detached observer of human vagary. But this thought wasn't given leisure to dwell in his mind, since a fresh bizarre spectacle presented itself. Two men appeared in the middle of the crush shouldering a wooden contraption which George at first supposed to be a portable siege-engine of a primitive sort, such as Boadicea or some similarly insurgent Briton might have fondly imagined capable of assaulting the might of Rome. Then he saw that the contraption had been designed for a wholly pacific use; it was, in fact, a library ladder of a superior kind—the property, perhaps, of a nobleman whose great-grandfather had collected books. A Boadicea-like figure was nevertheless at hand, since the ladder, now planted on earth, was being mounted by the female Animal Liberator who had been so forcibly enjoined to turn from Enmity to Amity. She proceeded to deliver from this perch what the historian Gibbon might have called an allocution to the legions. And at once a surprising number of demonstrators desisted from their chanting and prancing to listen. The spectacle of this—George saw at once—profoundly affected Father Hooker. Hooker, indeed, disapproved—but his disapproval was directed at the sex of the orator; he would doubtless have agreed with Dr Johnson that a woman preaching is like a dog walking on his hinder legs. Equally clearly, Hooker was inspired; his ambition himself to harangue the assembly revived in him; he cast upon the library ladder a positively acquisitive eye.

George had only fleetingly become aware of this when something else happened. That Dumb Friends' Lib should thus capture (as it was doing) the preponderant attention of the media was not at all to the taste of the rival organization, which now deployed its ultimate reserve. Just as the police had brought up reinforcements in that near-fatal coach, so did these now bring their juvenile contingents to the fore. In two converging columns, that is to say, there advanced the anti-ballistic babies in their prams and the toddlers (the alternative to tombs) on their uncertain feet. The babies continued to wave their rattles. The toddlers, red-faced and shouting, brandished little sticks on the ends of which had been stuck diminutive cut-out cardboard coffins. This was an enormous success. The cameras whirred again like mad. Even the ranks of Dumb Friends' Lib could scarce forbear to cheer.

George turned to Father Hooker with an exclamation of horror. But Hooker wasn't there to hear him. Hooker, like Scattergood before him, had vanished. Supposing that he had begun a prudent retreat within the recesses of the Institute, George glanced behind him. He saw nothing but an empty corridor, from the far end of which were beginning to sound odd noises that he didn't pause to analyse. He looked outward again, and there Hooker was. The crowd having given way before his Sunday clerical attire precisely as they would have done before a fireman flourishing an axe or ambulancemen with a stretcher, he had just succeeded in reaching the lady on the library ladder. Amazingly—for amazing things kept on happening, and were so to keep on for a little time yet—amazingly with only a few words spoken, the lady descended from her bookish rostrum, and Father Hooker took her place. He made a gesture commanding silence, and quite a number of people did, in fact, stop bellowing. Hooker began to hold forth, presumably on the doctrine of the Just War as it is to be interpreted in a nuclear age. He was speaking fluently. His morning's sermon, after all, must still be fresh in his head.

But now George had to turn round again, since there was uproar behind him. Within seconds he realized that the

Institute of Animal Genetics had somehow been stormed and taken from the rear. There were cheers, whistles, triumphant shouts—amid which the commands 'Let them out!' and 'Let them go!' were prominent. And suddenly George found himself skipping out of the way of the first of the dogs.

And of *all* the dogs. There could be no doubt whatever as to that. Dogs in their endless variety—such, assuredly, as Adam and Eve never had to put a name too—poured through doors and windows now thrown open in the Institute. Not a few clutched between their jaws their regulation issue of rubber bones, as if determined to cherish them as souvenirs of their stay. Even these contrived to growl. The rest barked, yelped, yapped or gave tongue according to their breed. On all the Geiger counters glittered in the sun.

On these liberated creatures the main body of their rescuers advanced with shouts of welcome and waving arms. Unfortunately the dogs didn't care for this. After the decorous routines of the Institute an undisciplined throng of bipeds offended and alarmed them. First one dog, and then a second, and then the whole lot turned tail and slunk back in quest of their familiar bed-sits.

Not so the cats.

The cats were far more numerous than the dogs; there seemed to be a whole army of them. They were also less heterogeneous. Although most were common cats and a few were special cats with Persian or Siamese affiliations, they all seemed much of a muchness, mere coloration apart. All moved with the same menacing softness, so that the Geiger counters scarcely stirred at their necks. One could feel at once that they weren't forgetting; even that their intentions were malign. (The cat is less magnanimous than the dog.) Although most appeared in excellent fettle, a few—perhaps senior residents—looked rather the worse for wear, like obscure persons recently released after helping police with their inquiries. All the cats now massed together before the Institute in what was, for the moment, a fixed and frozen way. Only their tails moved—very gently waving at the tip. Unaccountably (one may think) a certain hush fell upon the confused ranks of the demonstrators.

The cats, too, were ranked, but not in confusion. When they

moved, as they now did, it was to wheel with the precision of a platoon of Guards. It may be asserted, without fear of exaggeration on the chronicler's part, that here were several hundred people suddenly believing themselves under threat. Only Father Hooker, perched up on his ladder, might have felt tolerably secure. Yet Hooker was, of course, more scared than anyone else. His voice had died away. He was staring in horror at the advancing feline army. Above his dark parsonical attire his face was as white as a bleached rag on a line.

But because of his elevated perch, Father Hooker was the first to see what lay directly in the path of these long domesticated but now feral creatures as they raced ahead. It was the toddlers still holding aloft their coffins and the babies with their rattles still rattling hard. Numerous people had begun screaming—a sound disliked by cats, so it didn't help. Father Hooker didn't scream; he acted instead. Father Hooker, in fact, jumped down from his ladder and, waving his arms, made for the cats at the run. It is to be supposed that he had seen some possibility of heading them off. But, having started well out on a flank, he could have made no impact on the situation but for the two Plumley cats, Jeoffry and Old Foss. These creatures—perhaps because such recent arrivals at the Institute—were in the van, and they must have recalled Father Hooker as one to whom they had made friendly advances on a first encounter at Plumley Park. Forgetful or regardless of the fact that these advances had been repulsed with pathological distaste, Jeoffry and Old Foss swerved towards Father Hooker now. So, following them, did several score of their new companions.

It was thus that, within seconds, Father Adrian Hooker disappeared—buried beneath a pyramid of flailing, clawing and abundantly radioactive cats.

At the Park they had waited dinner for Charles. It was Charles who had gone to the hospital with the ambulance. When he came into the drawing-room nobody seemed to want to be the first to ask a question. So Charles himself broke the silence.

'They weren't saying much,' Charles said. 'God! Is there any gin? Or is it just that bloody sherry?'

There was gin. In such matters Edward Naylor was thoughtful and reliable. So Charles poured and drank.

'But I nobbled a young houseman and pumped him,' he said with satisfaction. 'He said he'll pull through so far as the shock goes, although not, perhaps, so as to be a hundred per cent in the top storey. And there may be a spot of trouble a good many years on. Hard luck on the poor bugger. . .I hope there's a decent meal.'

Having thus managed a perfunctory (but perfectly sincere) expression of commiseration, Charles himself led the way to the dining-room. In his heart he was feeling that matters weren't too bad. Since Uncle George was about as crazy as his minder, it might well have been Uncle George—which would have been even more horrible. And that afternoon there had been a marvellous telephone call from Scotland to say that he must certainly stay for the first week with the grouse. So things were looking up.

Uncle George was silent during the meal, and Hilda decided not to try to talk to him till the following morning. They would certainly discuss the strange catastrophe then. So after the ritual coffee-drinking she kissed him on the forehead and went straight up to her room. Her diary lay open on her writing-table, and beside it was her uncovered typewriter: both of them invitations to what had become an utterly pointless activity. The comedy was over, and the doomed puppets had better go back to their box. Hilda closed the diary, put its lid on the machine, and went to bed.